Next-Door Incubus

BECOMING LUST
BOOK ONE

EMILIA ROSE

Copyright © 2020 by Emilia Rose

All rights reserved.

No part of this book may be reproduced or transmitted in any form or by any means, electronic or mechanical, including photocopying, recording, or by any information storage and retrieval system without the written permission from the author, except for the use of brief quotations in a book review. For permission requests, write to the author at emiliarosewriting@gmail.com with the subject line: Attention: Permissions Coordinator.

This book is a work of fiction. Names, characters, places, and incidents either are products of the author's imagination or are used fictitiously. Any resemblance to actual persons, living or dead, events, or locales is entirely coincidental.

Front Cover Image: Covers By Christian

Beta Readers: Abby Gibson, Kayla Lutz, Madi Lozada, Diana Klikova, Lauren Greenwell, MaKenzie Blank, Erin Krakow, Amber Mattingly

Emilia Rose

emiliarosewriting@gmail.com

This book was originally written and released under my other pen name, Destiny Diess. I have since moved it over to my Emilia Rose brand; however, it is the same book. So if you've read it prior to the author name change, everything is the complete same.

Chapter One

I swayed my hips from side to side, humming to music as it played through my AirPods. Mom's necklace, a small rose-gold pendant in the shape of a *v*, glided across my chest and swung to the beat.

The morning sun flooded into my room through my sheer white curtains, and rays of light shined almost too conveniently on the pile of dirty clothes littered on my floor from last night. I stepped out of my shorts and tossed them into the hamper along with the rest of my clothes, then walked down the hall to the laundry room, eyes closed in utter bliss.

My housemate Maria was out with her friends today which meant that I had the whole apartment to myself. What was better than being able to walk around half-naked, stuff my face without being judged, and hold a concert for one in the living room on a Sunday morning? Nothing, absolutely nothing.

"Dani!"

My eyes snapped open. Maria, two of her friends, and three insanely attractive guys sat on our leather couches in the living room. The girls were clinging on to two of the guys, their fingers curling around the guys' biceps, heads resting in the crooks of their necks. When they saw me, everyone stared with wide, shocked eyes. Except one.

He stared at me with a smirk on his lips and sin in his eyes. Brown tousled hair, a grey Henley shirt that hugged his shoulders, and the scent of cinnamon and apples, he looked too perfect to be real.

Over the hum of my music, I heard the girls explode in a fit of laughter. The basket of clothes slipped out of my sweaty palms and tumbled onto the floor. All of my underwear, my latex mini skirt that I wore for Trevon last night, and my dignity laid at their feet. I swallowed hard and pulled down the bottom of my shirt, trying to cover myself.

I quickly backed into the hallway, and once I was out of sight, I sprinted into my room, slammed my door, and leaned my back against it.

Oh, my God.

Maria said she'd be out today. For the whole damn day. Why was she back here with... with whoever they were?!

I pulled out my earbuds, drew Mom's necklace between my fingers, and rested my head against the door. Although ridged at the top, the broken piece of the pendant felt cold and smooth against my thumb.

Breathe, Dani. I'm sure none of them saw anything anyway.

My gaze drifted down to my bare legs and black lacy panties. "Damn-it."

Someone banged on my door. "Dani, it's me. Open up!" Maria said. I tugged on some shorts, opened the door, and narrowed my eyes at Maria. She handed me my now-full laundry basket, a smile tugging at the corner of her lips. Her dirty-blonde hair was pulled back into a messy bun. "Well, that was a very impressive introduction to our new neighbors."

"Neighbors? Those guys are our neighbors?!"

Great, I've embarrassed myself in front of men I would see almost every day. Unless... I don't leave my apartment or room ever again. I could become a hermit and live my days in my room, curled up in my plush white sheets with a vanilla candle flickering deep into the night from my bedside table. Never have to be horrifically embarrassed ever again. Never have to face that man with the tempting green eyes.

"Dani! Hello?" Maria waved a hand in front of my face. "Are you even listening to me?"

No, I'm trying to get myself out of this mess.

She rolled her eyes and grabbed my wrist. "Since you're all dressed now, let's go introduce you to them!" She turned on her heel and started toward the door.

"Maria, are you crazy?" I dug my heels into the hardwood. "I'm not going to go see them. Not after that!"

"Well, you were the one who decided not to wear pants when we had company."

"You told me you would be out all day!"

"Yeah, well, there was a slight change of plans as soon as we saw how hot they were. But, that's besides the point! Come on" —she continued to drag me—"there's one that I think you'll like!"

"No, no, no, no, no, no..." I tried peeling her hand off of me, yet she continued down the hall. "Maria! Stop! I don't want to mee—"

"Hey guys! This is my roommate, Dani."

The guys gave me a half-smile, then turned back to Maria's friends who were desperately vying for their attention, eyes glazed over in a haze, breasts pressed against their chests—not something I'd expect from women who had been going to church religiously since I'd known them. I fingered my necklace, not daring to look over at *him*.

But, when his sweet scent drifted over to me, I couldn't stop myself from looking up. He sat on the loveseat by himself, his arms —covered with black tattoos—stretched across the backrest. Inch by inch, his gaze traveled up my body. The seconds passed so slowly. I shifted. And, when his dark gaze pierced through mine, a sudden rush of pleasure coursed throughout my body.

He stood and stepped closer to me. "Dani..." His name rolled off his lips effortlessly. "I'm Eros."

I stuck out my hand for him to shake, wanting to keep a distance between us. Something was screaming at me to stay away. To run. Now. But, when he grabbed my hand, I froze.

Instead of shaking it, he brought it to his lips. They were soft and lingered for more than a moment. He was more gentleman-like than I ever expected.

After taking a deep breath, he gazed down at me with dark—black—eyes, and I gasped. "You had quite the entrance there," he said, his scent becoming overwhelming. My cheeks flushed, and I looked down. Great, Dani, just great. He grazed his finger against the bottom of my chin and lifted it until my eyes were gazing into his. "Don't be embarrassed." He leaned over slightly, his lips grazing against my ear. "I should be the one embarrassed."

Cinnamon. That's all I smelt.

"What do you mean?" I asked, tingled running down my arms. My breath caught in the back of my throat, and Mom's necklace chilled my skin as soon as Eros dropped his hand and brushed his knuckles against it.

He stared at the pendant with soft eyes, as if it was a relic that had been lost for centuries, as if it was the only thing that ever mattered. But, then, he looked at me. "It's not every day I find a woman like you." And I felt like I was the only one that ever mattered.

He took me in so steadily, gaze shifting from eye to eye, drifting down my face, thumb brushing against my cheek. And I just stood there, staring back, unable to speak, unable to think, unable to get myself to push him away.

"It's not every day a woman in her underwear runs away from me." He stepped back and blessed me a smirk that would destroy me if I wasn't careful. "And it's not every day that I want to follow that woman back into her bedroom and take her right then and there."

My eyes widened and nervously darted around the room to see if anyone else had heard what he just said to me. Maria had her arm around one of the men, her head falling into the crook of his neck, eyes closed, looking like she was in Heaven. The other three girls weren't better off. Even Maria's shyest friend—Hallie—was resting her cheek against one of their shoulders, eyes cloudy and distant.

I parted my lips and pressed them back together. My head felt foggy, like I was in a daze, in a trance, in something, because who in their right mind would say something like that to someone that they just met. And his eyes flashing black? Those couldn't be real. But what if they were? What if I wasn't imagining it?

I needed to get away, yet I couldn't peel my eyes off of him. I wanted to feel his nose running up the side of my neck, his teeth dipping into my flesh, his hands pinning mine against my leather headboard, refusing to let me go. I pushed my knees together.

Sinful words from a sinful man that made me think sinful thoughts. Mom always told me that the devil disguised himself as our deepest desire.

When I looked back at Eros, he chuckled. I tugged on Mom's pendant. "I... uh..."

"You want me," he said. But his lips didn't move, not even a little.

Okay, I was definitely just hearing things. God, I was really going crazy.

He brushed his fingers against my hip and stepped closer. Black specs reappeared in his eyes. His breath warmed my neck. Cinnamon. "Tell me you want me, Dani, and I'll enact all those fantasies running through that dirty little mind of yours. Every. Last. One of them," he murmured.

My tongue ran over my bottom lip. "... erm..."

The tips of his fingers snuck under the hem of my shirt and

grazed against my stomach. I let out a shaky breath, not being able to distinguish the real from the fake. "I... uh... gotta go."

Without hesitating, I stepped away from him, staggered back, and sprinted into my room.

Fuck. Fuck. Fuck. Fuck. Fuck. Fuck. Fuck.

Every time I closed my eyes, I could feel his fingertips gliding against my skin, burning into my flesh. They were tormenting me already in places he hadn't even touched yet.

I cocooned myself in my plush pink throw blanket, trying to put as much space between Eros and me as possible. If this was how I felt after five minutes of meeting him, how would I feel seeing him every single day? How would I feel when Maria brought them over again?

There was only one thing that I could do now.

Let Project Hermit begin.

Chapter Two

"Can you just open the door?" Trevon asked through the phone. "I left my key to your place back at home." I gnawed on the inside of my cheek and walked to my bedroom door, hand on the handle, heart thrashing against my ribcage. "Hello?" he said, a hint of annoyance in his voice.

"Hi... I... uh..." I pressed my ear to my cold door, listening to the light hum of the refrigerator in the kitchen. No talking. No shuffling. Maybe they weren't here. "Give me a second."

After peeking my head out and gazing down the empty hallway, I tiptoed to the kitchen. Shadows from the cabinets loomed over me in the darkness, but at least it wasn't Eros's shadow.

I stood on my toes and checked through the peephole. In the brightly lit hallway, Trevon had his hands stuffed in his pockets and his eyes shielded by the navy baseball cap I had given him for his birthday last year. But still I waited. I didn't need this to be some sort of prank and have Eros appearing out of nowhere.

When Trevon looked straight at the peephole with the most heavenly brown eyes I had ever seen, I pulled open the door, wrapped my hand around his wrist, and yanked him inside.

"What the fu-" He stumbled forward.

I slammed the door. "Sorry," I said, standing on my toes and kissing him.

"Is everything okay, babe?" He tilted his head to the side slightly, like he did when he was thinking, and eyed me. The bitter scent of beer sickened me. I licked my lips nervously, nodded my head, and pulled him into my room.

Another door Eros would have to get through to get to me.

Trevon tossed his hat onto my dresser. "You haven't returned any of my calls or texts since yesterday morning."

"I've just been busy with my psych internship and... um, stuff..." Like trying to hide from Eros. Maria had brought him over all day yesterday and even for breakfast this morning, and I couldn't handle it anymore. If I saw him one more time, I was going to—

Trevon threw his shirt onto the end of my bed and crawled under the comforter, the light from the candle flickered against his brown and brawny abdomen. "I know when you're lying."

The wind whistled lowly, blowing the curtains away from the window and brushing against the side of my bed. Outside, the city night was unusually quiet.

I parted my lips to speak, then closed them. What was I going to say? That an undeniably sexy man moved in next-door and he just so happened to have the hots for me. No. No way I'd do that to Trevon. He had known me since I was five, helped me through Mom's death, was one of the only constant people in my life that I cherished. "I... I just haven't been getting much sleep lately."

It wasn't a lie. For the past few nights, I'd been tossing and turning. Last night was the worst; my mind kept replaying the interaction I had with Eros. Over and over. The thought—his promise—wouldn't leave me alone. And, it was getting too damn frustrating.

Light from my candles glimmered off of my black headboard. Trevon leaned against it, crossing one leg over the other. He grabbed my hand, pulling it away from my necklace. "If you keep doing that, you're going to break it again." He pulled me down next to him.

Like I had done nearly every night for the past five years, I curled into him, resting my head on his bare chest. He laced his fingers into my hair and scratched lightly. I sighed and drew my finger across the only tattoo he had on his body—a tabono symbol —that he got on his chest after winning his first college wrestling match.

"So, when were you going to tell me you got new neighbors?"

"I, uh..." Don't stutter, Dani. It'll make you seem like you're hiding something. "... didn't think you'd care. They seem annoying."

"You met them?"

"Just once. Maria brought them over," I said, brushing my finger across my hand where Eros had kissed, the skin burning lightly. "How'd you know about them?"

"I met one of them out in the hall," he said. God, if he met Eros... "Ian? Or Evan? Nah, that's it, it was Eros. Seems pretty chill."

Oh, my Lord. I licked my lips and sat up, intertwining my fingers with his. "What did he say?"

"Nothing. I told him that you were my girlfriend though." He trailed his hand alongside my forearm, sending goosebumps up it, and smiled. "Just so he won't get the urge to hit on you."

If he only knew that Eros had already made it perfectly clear that he wanted me.

Trevon brushed his lips against my cheek, toying with the ends of my shirt. "I wouldn't be surprised if he still tried though, you're hot as hell."

I pushed him away playfully and blew out the candle. Okay, good, he didn't know anything, and it would stay that way because nothing would happen between us. Nothing.

When Trevon wrapped an arm around my waist and his breath evened out, I listened to the soft sound of his snoring. I tried to fall asleep, but light was now blaring under my door. And, even with Trevon's arms wrapped tightly around me and his breath fanning my neck, I felt unbelievably cold.

Lips brushed against my collarbone, setting it ablaze. "Oh, Dani," Eros murmured against my skin. The room smelled of cinnamon and vanilla—a striking scent. His fingers grazed down the center of my chest and over my breast. "Your skin is so soft... tender...."

A breathy moan escaped my lips, and I sunk into my plush sheets. He dipped his fingers between my legs and gently rubbed my red lacy underwear. "... imagine what I could do to it..."

Moonlight filed through the sheer curtains, illuminating his sharp features. He slipped his fingers inside of me and smirked against my neck. I gripped his shoulders, digging my nails into him. "Eros," I breathed, throwing my head back.

His lips—quickly, hungrily, brutally—travelled down my chest and stomach, up the insides of my thighs, hovered between my panties and teased me with their heat. In one swoop, he clenched my panties in his hand and ripped them off of me, leaving me bare.

He gazed up at me, eyes completely black. So big and bold, so absolutely terrifying yet so damn sexy.

"Is this what you want, Dani?" he mumbled against my aching core. Slowly, he drew his fingers down the insides of my thighs.

Images of him pressing his lips onto me, holding my legs apart until I was trembling around him, of pleasure pumping through my body flooded my mind.

He wrapped his hands around my thighs, pulling me closer to him, and pushed his lips against my clit. His fingers moved in small torturous circles inside of me. I gripped his wrists, trying to pull him away. It already was too damn much to handle. He gripped my wrist with his other hand and pinned it to the side of my body, holding me in place. I clenched myself around him, my core tightening, and moaned. He slowed down his pace.

He gazed back up at me with those big black eyes. "Beg for it."

My lips parted, but no words came out. The pressure. Oh, God, the pressure.

"Beg," he demanded.

"Please."

"More."

"Please, Eros... please."

His tongue moved faster, his fingers thrusting quickly. I dug my nails into the blanket underneath me and moaned out.

My mind was foggy. My body numb. Wave after wave of pleasure rolled through me. Eros sat back up, resting my legs on his shoulders. "I could do this all night," he said. I widened my eyes, staring down at him, my senses finally returning. He smirked. "I told you that I would enact your fantasies, Dani. You just had to tell me that you wanted it."

Chapter Three

I sat up in my bed with sweat rolling down my back.

What the hell.

My curtains swayed, cinnamon lingering faintly in the air. I scanned the room. Trevon's baseball cap was still lying on my dresser. Mom's necklace was still resting around my neck peacefully. There was no sign of Eros.

I rested my head against the headboard and closed my eyes. Of course, he wasn't here. It was just a dream, Dani, just a dream.

A damn sex dream.

About the hot guy next door.

While I was sleeping next to my boyfriend.

Oh, God. I was going to Hell for this, wasn't I? I'd burn in the pits of lava and get eaten alive by flesh-eating demons and—

"Babe?" Trevon groaned. He rubbed a hand across his face and slowly opened his eyes. The faint scent of alcohol still lingered on his breath. "Is everything okay?"

"Everything is fine." No, it wasn't.

After chuckling lightly, he rolled over onto his side and wrapped an arm around my waist. "Good, now come lie back down. We still got a few hours—" He stopped suddenly and rubbed my waist, fingers slipping lower than I wanted them. "Damn, babe, sleeping with no underwear on? If you want to fuck, you just have to ask. Don't need to be teasing me and shit."

I swallowed hard and pushed a hand under the blankets. No underwear? Why wasn't I wearing any underwear? Maybe I slipped them off while I was sleeping. It was hot last night, deathly hot, scorching hot.

Trevon nuzzled his head into my neck. "Come on, let's have some fun. You already got me excited."

"I'm... uh... not in the mood," I said. I scurried out of the bed and rushed toward my bedroom door. "I'm going to the bathroom. I'll be right back."

Dull light filed in from the living room window, illuminating the apartment. I glanced down the hall and into the foyer. Empty. Maria's door was closed, like usual. Nothing was out of place.

When I reached the bathroom, I leaned over the counter and gazed at myself in the mirror. The dream felt so real, so damn real. But I couldn't understand why I was dreaming of Eros. I had a perfectly good man—no, a great man. One that cradled me every time I woke up from a nightmare about the night of Mom's death. One that took me on breakfast dates to Ollie's every Saturday morning. One that I had loved for five whole years.

And, here I was, dreaming about my undeniably sexy neighbor.

I turned on the sink, the soothing sound of water calming me slightly, and splashed some on my face. In the mirror, I watched beads of water run down the sides of my cheek, the dark purple circles under my eyes.

You will not think of Eros, again.

You will not think of Eros, again.

You will not—

eyes widened. There were red fingerprints on my hips, four on each side. I rubbed my fingers against them, trying to make them go away but only making them redder. I swallowed hard—thinking the worst—then shook my head.

Damn, what was I even thinking anymore? These fingerprints were probably just from Trevon holding me. Why was I so paranoid all of a sudden? Next, I'll be thinking Eros was actually in my room last night.

But that would be ridiculous.

Sorry, babe. Work called. I would've woken you up, but you looked too peaceful to bother. I'm taking you out tonight. Be ready at 5. Love, Trevon.

I grasped Trevon's note in my hand, smiled, and walked into Dr. Uriel's office. After getting back to bed last night, I actually had a good sleep and woke up five minutes before my alarm feeling well rested.

"Morning, Dani," Dr. Uriel said from her royal blue sofa. She handed me a file and a cup of tea. "This is my 9:30 client. She had an absent father and is struggling with feelings toward a new lov—" Her dark brown brows furrowed together. "Are you okay?" she asked suddenly as I took a seat across from her. "You're quiet this morning. Anything you want to talk about?"

She crossed one leg over the other and leaned forward, the way she did when listening to all of her clients' problems. I shifted in my seat. If I knew anything from the last five months of interning under Dr. Uriel, it was not to tell her anything that I didn't want her to pester me about.

I made that mistake once when I told her that I still had nightmares about the piercing red eyes of Mom's killer. She was hung up over it for weeks, telling me that I should talk to someone—meaning her—because suppressed feelings were nobody's friend.

"I'm fi—"

"And don't tell me you're fine either. You know I see right through that," she said.

If I closed my eyes and imagined hard enough, I could hear Mom in her voice. When she sat me on her knee at five years old and asked me what happened in pre-school one day, when she waited so patiently for me to tell her that the boy I liked was pushing another girl on the swings, when she gazed down at me with her pretty light blue eyes—so light that they looked like they were glowing—and said that it was okay not to be fine.

Instead of reminiscing, I gazed out the window and sighed.

From Dr. Uriel's office, I had a whole view of the city. The morning sun gleaming off of the river next to us, hundreds of people brushing past each other on the sidewalks, red and blue buses picking up riders. I leaned against the back of the couch. "I just haven't been getting much sleep. A few guys moved in next store and they were over all day Sunday."

"Tell me about these new guys," Dr. Uriel said, clasping her hands together. "Are they loud?"

I moved Mom's pendant between my fingers, listening to it glide against the chain. Dr. Uriel eyed it. "No," I said.

"Are they over a lot?"

"Yes."

"What are their names?"

"Javier and Zane," I said. She sipped her tea, waiting for me to continue. "And Eros."

She paused for a long moment, gazing out of the glass windows. "Eros," she said softly. "Is he the reason that you're not sleeping?"

Damn. Was it that obvious?

When I didn't say anything, she frowned. "Dani, I will tell you what I tell all of my clients. Whatever you're feeling toward him—"

"I feel nothing toward him."

She raised a sharp brow, and I pressed my lips together. "What you feel toward him is nothing compared to your relationship with Trevon, right?"

I closed my eyes when Eros's black one flashed in my mind and nodded. "I know."

Leaning toward me, she readjusted her black blazer and placed a hand on my knee. "Those feelings—those lustful feeling—are nothing compared to feelings of absolute love. They will pass, and so will he."

I drew my finger across my knee. She was right. Lust was nothing compared to love. But love never made me feel like this before.

Chapter Four

Trevon wrapped an arm around my waist, pulling me close, as we walked into Crimson's Nouveau, an upscale dining restaurant in the center of the city. Couples sat at the rustic bar in the center of the room, waiters placed plates of food in front of people in black leather booths, and the hostess who was standing in front of a chalky brick wall gave us a perplexed look when we just walked right by her.

"Aren't we getting a table?" I asked Trevon.

He gazed down at me, leading me through a maze of people. "We're meeting Maria and Eros here," he said.

I stopped, pressed my lips together, and yanked on his sleeve. "What?"

"We're meeting—"

"Why? Why them?" The only plan that I had come up with today after my little chat with Dr. U was to avoid Eros. No, not confront the problem head on like she would want me to do. Just ignore the problem and hope he'd go away.

Trevon shrugged. "I saw him this morning, and he asked if we wanted to go out. I didn't think you'd mind, but we can leave if you want."

"Dani! Trevon!" Maria yelled from a booth from across the bar. She waved her hands in the air, as if I could miss the bright orange cropped shirt she had on. Eros and his roommates were sitting in the booth.

Eros's eyes were on me and only me. I gulped and squeezed Trevon's hand.

Lust was nothing compared to my incredible, amazing, trustworthy, handsome boyfriend.

Trevon pulled me over to the table and immediately dropped my hand. He slid into the booth next to Javier, one of Eros's roommates, and I grumbled to myself, taking the only open seat left which was directly across from the man himself—Eros.

My gaze stayed glued to the menu. Yet, I couldn't help smelling that cinnamon scent, tasting it on my tongue. I didn't have to look up to know that Eros was staring right at me.

Truth was, I was afraid that, if I looked up, Eros would be able to read every one of my thoughts about him last night. It was absurd, but I couldn't risk it. Those thoughts were intimate and so damn embarrassing, especially with Trevon sitting—cluelessly—next to me.

After we ordered, Trevon curled an arm around my waist and leaned close. "Is everything alright? You're tense." His eyes were bright, and a small smile was plastered on his face.

Hoping that it would help me shake my lustful thoughts, I tried remembering all the times I'd seen that small smile on Trevon's face. On the swings in elementary school when he shared his grape juice box with me. Through one of the foggy classroom windows while I sat in fifth grade detention alone because some girls were picking on him for his hair, and I wasn't going to let them hurt my best friend. While we danced together in the rain in his backyard the night of prom because Kellan from his wrestling team never showed up as my date.

I had always loved Trevon, and one annoyingly sexy smirk wasn't going to change my mind.

"Everything is *fine*," I said, sipping my white wine. It was the only thing getting me through tonight.

"We can go if you want," Trevon said to me.

Yes, please, let's go home. Far away from Maria who kept gazing at me, then at Eros, then back at me like something had happened between us. Far away from Eros's smoldering stare. Far away from these feeling that wouldn't leave me alone, no matter how hard I tried.

"No," I said. Trevon was happy, and this was one of his only nights he had off of work during the week. I didn't want to ruin that for him, even if I had to endure the rest of dinner. He gave me a big smile, planting a kiss on my cheek, and turned back to the Javier and Zane, Eros's other roommate.

Under the table, Eros's foot grazed against mine. I pressed my lips together, trying to ignore it, but then it happened again. "Quit it," I whisper-yelled across the table, not daring to look at Eros.

He continued.

"Stop."

Still, his foot brushed against mine.

I raised my gaze and glared at him. He leaned back against the leather booth, swirling his glass of red wine in his hand. The black ring on his left index finger clanked against the glass. He narrowed those piercing green eyes at me as if he was trying to figure me out. And just when I was about to turn away, his eyes darkened.

They reminded me of my dream when his eyes were beautifully black with no whites in them at all, but...

My eyes widened. My dream.

Heat crawled up the sides of my neck, and I rubbed Mom's pendant again. God, he had to remind me of that stupid dream.

"How was your night last night, Dani?" he asked.

Did he know that I dreamt about him last night? How I begged for him? That I couldn't stop thinking about him? The mischievous glint in his eye made me think he knew everything. But he couldn't.

"Good."

"Just good?" He cocked his brow. A strand of his dark hair curled onto his forehead.

"Just good," I repeated, trying to convince myself of it.

He took a long sip of his wine—jaw clenched—and nodded. When he placed his glass down, his fingertips were white. "We'll have to fix that next time."

I narrowed my eyes at him, leaning against the dark wooden table. "What did you just say?"

Without answering me, he gazed back at our friends. A smirk still clear on his face. I leaned closer to Trevon; fingers interlaced with his. "I'm going to the bathroom." I needed to get away from Eros. He was making me absolutely insane. I didn't know what was real and what was fake anymore. Reality and imagination were so closely woven together, I couldn't pick anything apart. Maybe talking with Dr. U would be a good thing.

I hurried to the bathroom, closed the bathroom door, and groaned. "Why? Why? Why? Why? Why? Why?" I leaned my back against the chic brick wall and covered my face with my hands.

This was not how Project Hermit was supposed to go. I should've been back at home with my faced stuffed into the *Games People Play* book that Dr. U gave me to read before I left today, blasting music through my ear buds, locked in my room. Not out with Eros, sitting across from Eros, thinking about Eros, dreaming about Eros. Why wouldn't he leave me alone?

One of the toilets flushed, and a high-heeled woman, who couldn't be any older than me, walked out of a stall. She washed her hands in the sink and gazed over at me. "Is something wrong?" She tossed her toffee brown hair over her shoulder, her amber perfume overwhelming me.

My cheeks tingled, and I looked away. "Nothing." Strangers didn't need to be in my business.

After drying her hands, she pulled out a stick of bright red lipstick from her Versace purse and leaned closer to the mirror.

"Come on. Tell me Sweet Cheeks. I'm not going to spill your secrets to anyone." She applied a coat of lipstick. "Let me guess. Boy trouble?"

I sighed. "Something like that."

"Bad boyfriend?" She narrowed her eyes at me, then shook her head. "No... hmm... love triangle?" I furrowed my brows together. I wouldn't call it that. "Getting closer..." After a moment, she smiled. "In a relationship but attracted to another guy?" When I frowned, her smile widened. "I guess that's the one." She threw her lipstick back into her purse. "Well, if you ever need someone to talk about this with, I'm Kasey."

I smiled awkwardly at her. "Uh, Dani." Was it normal to make friends with people in restaurant bathrooms?

"Here," she said, handing me her phone. "Put your number in."

I rubbed my sweaty palms together, unsure if I should, but I ended up entering my number anyway. I didn't know how much longer I could keep this to myself and I sure didn't want to tell Dr. U about *everything* that had happened, especially the dream. She'd just lecture me about how these lustful thoughts were the devil's doing.

With a smile, she walked out of the bathroom, her heels clacking. I took one last look in the mirror and followed. I just needed to get through the rest of the night, then Trevon and I could go home and act like nothing happened. Because nothing did happen.

When I stepped out of the bathroom, I bumped into someone's chest. Eros. He grabbed my hips, fingers grazed against my skin, to steady me. Then, he pushed me against the door. "Dani, Dani, Dani," he said.

Great. I swallowed hard. Just... great.

"Why have you been ignoring me?" His fingers dug into my skin.

"I... I haven't."

He chuckled and tilted his head, staring down at me with those dark eyes. "Yes, you have."

"I have a boyfriend," I blurted out, pressing myself into the wooden door.

"Why're you getting so defensive?"

"I'm not."

He raised a brow. "Is it because you've been with him, but all you could think about was me?"

I forced a laugh—the cringiest damn laugh I had ever heard. "No! That's ridiculous!"

He stepped closer, and I couldn't get myself to step back into the bathroom and slam the door in his face. Instead, I stared up at him, thinking about how close I was to him and how hard my heart was beating against my chest.

Half of his face was shadowed by the dim light above us, giving him a dark, dangerous, devilish look. "I haven't left you mind since Sunday, have I?" He leaned down slightly, his nose grazing against mine.

This was sin. Pure sin.

"You're acting stupid now, Eros."

"Am I?" he asked, his lips were mere inches away. Heat radiated off of them, hitting me in waves. His fingers curled around my waist the way they did Sunday morning.

All I could smell was cinnamon.

"Yes," I whispered. "You are."

He stepped even closer, one foot between mine, his waist pressing into the side of my hip. "I've been dreaming of all the dirty things I would do to you, how I'd make you beg, how I'd make you scream out as I tormented this pretty little body of yours." His fingers burned on my skin. "Don't tell me you haven't dreamt of the same thing."

I clenched my jaw, my eyes closing so softly, and took a shaky breath.

His fingers trailed up the side of my body until they reached my lips. He brushed his thumb against my bottom lip, making it tingle. "... so soft, tender..."

Those words... those were the same ones he had said in my dream.

He grasped my face gently and gazed down at me. Every sinful thing that I wanted him to do to me flashed into my mind. His lips on mine, his long slender fingers tormenting my body, everything.

Mom's pendant shifted against my chest.

He chuckled. "Even with a boyfriend, you're so responsive to my touch."

Trevon. My eyes widened. I pulled myself out of the damn trance he seemed to put me in every single time I was close to him and glared up at him. "I am not."

"Whatever you say."

I pressed my lips together. "I'm not!"

He dropped his hands and turned away from me with that damn smirk on his stupid face. I crossed my arms over my chest. I couldn't believe him. No—scratch that—I couldn't believe myself.

All those days of Sunday school, all those late Saturday nights at church with Mom listening to a priest preach about a devil that I didn't think existed, thinking about how weak those people who fell into temptation were.

The devil wasn't real, but temptation sure was.

Eros gazed back at me and pushed his hand into his pocket. "Oh, and Dani... I found these this morning." He pulled something out of his pocket. "They looked like yours. Thought I'd return them to you."

He tossed me the panties I had worn last night and walked away.

Chapter Five

I gazed down at the underwear, then at Eros walking toward the table, then back. My fingers curled around the soft material. Where did he get these? When did he get these? *How* did he get these?

After stuffing the underwear into my pocket, I marched after him. Who did he think he was? Offering us to go to dinner with him, flirting with me, stealing my panties while I was sleeping?

"Don't you just walk away from me! We need to talk—"

Eros slid into the booth and picked up his fork to eat. He gazed up at me with the most innocent eyes I had ever seen, a forkful of chicken breast and apple relish in his hand. "What do you want to talk about?" Innocent eyes, but a devilish smirk. That goddamn perfect, sexy, annoying smirk.

He trapped me. He knew I wouldn't be able to confront him here. He knew how much I'd stumble over my words, trying to find an excuse as to why I needed to talk to him in front of Trevon. And I hated it.

I sat next to my loving boyfriend, fingers grazing against his. "Nothing," I said. I dipped a piece of bread into my bean stew. "It's nothing."

Trevon gazed at me briefly, then continued his conversation with Javier.

Eros paused for a moment, twisting his ring around his index finger with his thumb, and leaned back against the white leather. "Oh, come on, *Dani*."

Ignore him.

"Don't be shy."

He's just trying to anger you.

"I bet you're not this shy *elsewhere*."

I snapped my eyes to his.

"You're probably loud, aren't you?"

I kicked my foot into his shin under the table. Did Trevon not hear this man?

When I looked over, Trevon was in a deep conversation with Javier and Zane about the best places to go in the city on the weekends. He didn't even glance in our direction. Big smile, wide eyes. I sighed and gazed back at the man of mystery in front of me.

Once I got home, oh boy, I was going to march straight to his apartment and demand that he tells me how he got my panties. I was having no more of this. He couldn't go around flirting with me and stealing my underwear for no good reason at all.

After enduring another forty minutes of dinner, watching Eros play with his ring and hoping that he wouldn't talk to me ever again, I had decided that going to his apartment was probably the worst idea I ever had. I could barely keep it together when we were out in public. God only knew what would happen if I ended up at his place.

Trevon slapped a hand on my thigh and smiled at me. "You ready?"

I grabbed his hand, yanking him out of the booth. Oh, I was more than ready to get out of here. He pulled the phone out of his back pocket and grabbed my waist, slowing me down. "Babe, what's the rush?"

"You can check your phone when we're in the car. Hurry up," I said.

We walked out of Crimson's Nouveau, the cold breeze biting my exposed legs. The car was parked less than a block away across the street. There wasn't even any traffic. I was so close to freedom. So damn close.

Trevon stopped. "Shit," he said. The light from his phone illuminated his dark skin. "Something happened at work. I need to go. I'll give you a ride back home, but we'll have to make it quick."

"I can take her back," Eros said from beside him. Appearing from absolutely nowhere.

"No, that's not happen—"

Trevon nodded. "That would be great, man. Thanks."

My eyes widened. I snatched his arm, pulling him to the side. A bus rumbled down the street toward us. "Trevon, I'm not going with him!" I whispered.

"Come on, Dani. I really have to go."

"No! I—"

His phone started to buzz again. He tapped the screen and lifted it to his ear. After pecking me on the lips, he told me he'd make it up to me.

I crossed my arms over my chest, watching him jog across the street to his car, nearly getting hit by the now-angry bus driver.

Eros walked up beside me, arm grazing against mine. "Looks like it's just me and you."

"So, what does Trevon do for work?" Eros asked, one hand on the steering wheel, the other dangerously close to my thigh. His car was strikingly clean, the sleek bronze and black leather seats had no scuffs, the silver accents were glimmering in the moonlight, and the small screen on the dashboard had no fingerprints on it.

I gazed at the city lights through the windshield, jaw clenched. I couldn't believe I was here. "He owns a bar on Sixth."

He tapped his ring against the wheel, turning onto a four-lane freeway. "You must get lonely."

"Excuse me?"

"You spend your nights alone when he's in the bar." Eros slowed to a stop at a red light. The car screen lit up with *Incoming Call: Luci*, and Eros hit the decline button.

I narrowed my eyes at the screen, then at him. "And that makes you think I'm lonely?"

The corner of his lip curled up. "No. I think that you're lonely because of the way you act."

"And how do I act?" I asked, voice rising with each word. Why does he have to get under my skin every time I talk to him? Why was I even here? I should be in Trevon's car with him, not with Mr. I'm-So-Hot-And-I-Know-It.

"Needy... Wanting..." That infamous smirk stretched across his face. "Horny."

My eyes widened. "What!" I dug my nails into the leather seat. "You're the one who's been acting like that. You're the one who stole my underwear! Who does that?"

He pressed down on the gas, and we drove forward slowly. Calm. He was so calm. "I didn't steal them. I found them and thought I'd return them to you."

I crossed my arms over my chest, glaring out at the trees that lined the street. Fiery red and orange leaves hung off of them. "Pfft, yeah okay. You just magically found the same panties that I was wearing last night."

"You're hot when you're angry."

"Well, you're not hot at all, so stop talking to me." I lied, and he knew it. He was so damn hot, but if he didn't stop talking to me, I wasn't sure what was going to happen. I just wanted to be home and be alone—where I'd be able to stay in control of this unexplainable urge that I had to rip Eros's clothes off and let him do what he wanted to me.

"Why are you lying, Dani?"

"Why are you so full of yourself, Eros?" I clenched my jaw. "You act like you're this oh-so-powerful sex-god, but I bet you're not even good in bed. You probably suc—"

Eros hit the brakes, and I flew forward in the car, my seatbelt digging into my collarbone. He tangled a hand into my hair, grabbed a fistful of it, and forced me to look at him. I could see my wide-eyed reflection in the black pits of his eyes.

"You have no idea what I'm capable of," he said. Despite the harsh grip he had on my hair, he gently grazed his thumb against my cheek. "I can leave you trembling under my fingers, Dani." He roughly grasped my jaw. "... under my lips..." His hand traveled down the column of my neck, sending a wave of heat through me. "When I'm finished with you, you'll be begging for more." His fingers grazed against the hem of my dress, dipping along my cleavage. "Craving more," he whispered.

I pushed my knees together, my core throbbing. Oh, God. Oh, God. This wasn't good.

"Until you can't handle it any longer." His fingertips grazed against my nipples through my dress. I shut my eyes.

Stop him, Dani.

My fingers dug into the leather, my head resting back on the seat.

I needed to stop him.

He drew his fingers across them again, and I pulled my knees together even more.

It felt too good.

Someone hit their horn behind us, the sound vibrating through the car. Bright headlights flashed in the rearview mirror. Eros released me and stuck his hand through the window to apologize to the car. He pressed onto the gas.

I stared down at my knees—wide eyed as realization shot

through me. Please let that be a dream. Please let that be a dream. I couldn't begin to comprehend every thought running through my mind. Why did I let Eros touch me? It felt so good. But it shouldn't. I hadn't felt that good—ever.

Not even with Trevon.

Chapter Six

I laid in my bed, staring up at my plain, boring ceiling and thinking about one person: Trevon. The sleepy smile he gave me every morning, him drawing patterns on my skin with his fingers and brushing his hands through my hair so soft and soothing. The morning sun filing into the room, hitting his brown eyes and making them a sea of honey.

Five years. Five whole years of memories with him, and I had to blow it all.

After cocooning myself in my blanket, I curled into a ball. The music in my earbuds stopped playing twenty minutes ago, but I didn't have the energy to get my phone from the dresser. Too much shame was weighing me down.

My fingers grazed against my necklace. Even if Eros made me feel better than Trevon, the feelings I had toward him were purely physical. It was infatuation. They'd go away. They always did.

But I couldn't keep this from Trevon. I needed to tell him.

I lugged myself out of bed, picked up my phone, and dialed his number. Voicemail. I hung up and tried again. After calling for the fourth time, he picked up.

"Hello?"

"Hey," I said. "Sorry for calling you at work, but I need to tell you something."

"Dani, did you get in alright? Thank Eros again for me."

"Actually, I wanted to talk to you about hi—"

I heard a woman say something through the phone, voice muffled. Trevon said something back. People started yelling. "Dani, I got to go. Some guys are fighting in the middle of the bar. Tell me about this later."

Before I had the chance to respond to him, the line went dead. I sighed and threw the phone next to me.

Damnit. Damnit. Damnit. Every time I tried to tell him about Eros, something always interrupted us.

My phone buzzed beside me. I picked it up—hoping Trevon was calling back already.

From: Unknown

Message: Breakfast tomorrow? ;)

My eyes widened. I swear, if this was Eros, I was going to—

Another buzz.

From: Unknown

Message: This is Kasey btw (restaurant bathroom girl)

I sighed in relief and added her number to my contacts. The candle beside my bedside crackled in the dark. It probably wasn't the smartest idea to go have breakfast with someone I just met in a public bathroom but I needed to talk to someone about my problem. Maria was too nosey, Trevon was too busy, and Dr. U would only talk sense to me. I rested my head against the pillow and texted her back.

Getting out of this apartment would do me good—anything to take my mind off of Eros would help me at this point.

"Dani," Eros murmured against my ear. I was lying on my stomach with the side of my face pressing against my pillow, the sweet scent of cinnamon and vanilla filling me. He trailed his nose up the back of

my neck and pressed himself against my backside. "I can't wait to make you mine."

My toes curled. He felt so good.

He sucked on the skin just below my ear, teeth pressing against my flesh ever so lightly, making me moan. His fingers curled around my chin. "Do you like the way I touch you?"

I nodded, his stubble against my neck making me shiver.

"What should I do to you tonight?"

Anything. I just wanted more and more. I never wanted him to stop. I pushed my hips back against his.

"Tell me what you want," he said, steadying my hips with his.

"I... uh..."

He slipped his fingers under the waistband of my shorts, rubbing me roughly through my thin panties. I squirmed under his touch, the pressure already building inside of me.

"Tell me," he said, harsher this time.

"I want... oh, God..."

He removed his hand from my shorts and pushed me onto my back. Lying on his side, he propped himself up on one of his elbows. The moonlight streamed in through the sheer curtains, bouncing off of his bare abdomen. I ran my fingers down his abs, down his v-line, and let them linger at his waistband. I gulped, gazing at the bulge in his pants.

After tucking his finger under my chin, he made me gaze into his eyes. They were black again. Completely and utterly black. No hint of white, no piercing green. Endless black pits.

They should've scared me.

He moved his lips closer until they were hovering above mine and grabbed my hand, placing it firmly on his bulge. "Is this what you want, Dani?" he asked, lips grazing against mine.

"Yes."

. . .

I rubbed a hand over my face and pulled my blanket over my half-naked body. Another stupid dream about Eros.

From my bed, I gazed out the window. My curtains were pulled back, and I could see the morning's pink and purple clouds over the city skyline. Why couldn't I have a normal night for once? Why was he haunting my every dream?

My phone lit up on my side table. One unread message from Kasey asking me about breakfast. No messages from Trevon.

After sending him a good morning text—and not receiving one back—I rolled out of bed, dressed for my internship, and walked out of the room, following the scent of bacon and eggs. When I reached the kitchen, I paused and gazed at the Eros who was sitting at the counter with Maria and his roommates.

"Dani!" Maria said, hopping off of a stool. Strands of her blonde hair hung around her face. "Come eat with us. We made extra!" She walked over to the skillet. "I'll make a plate for you."

"I have plans. Maybe next time," I said. I grabbed my jacket from the coat hanger.

"Is Trevon coming with you or is he staying here until you come back? Because if he is, he should come eat." She stuck her head down the hall. "Trevon!"

"Trevon isn't here."

She placed a hand on her hip. "Mhm, sure. That's why you have that big bruise under your ear. You must've given it to yourself last night, if he wasn't here."

"Bruise?" My fingers grazed against the skin below my ear. It was tender, but there wasn't a bruise there. There couldn't be. I opened the camera on my phone, staring at the screen in disbelief.

A text from Trevon popped up, but I ignored it. My skin was dark purple and red. It looked like a hick—wait a second.

My gaze lifted to Eros. He was tossing an apple into the air, staring at me with the greenest eyes I had ever seen. I shoved my phone in my jacket pocket. "Eros, can I speak to you?"

I didn't wait for his reply. I just walked out the front door and waited for him to follow. He shut the door behind him, leaning against the doorframe. The hallway was empty—thank God. Eros threw the granny smith apple from hand to hand. "You and Trevon must've had some fun last night."

"Stop it." I dug my nails into my palms. "I don't know what you're doing, but I know that you're up to something and it needs to stop."

"What do you mean?"

I placed my hands on my hips. "First, you steal my panties. Second, I have this huge hickey on my neck!"

"What makes you think I gave you that hickey?"

"Because you gave it to me in my dre—" I stopped. I sounded so stupid. I had no proof that he did this to me. And, besides, I locked all the doors and even pushed a chair in front of my door so, if someone came in, I would know. Nothing was out of place this morning.

He tilted his head, still tossing that apple.

"Were you in my room last night?" I asked.

"Do you think I was?"

If I was wrong about this, I'd make a fool out of myself. But I already made a fool out of myself the first day I met him when I was dancing around in that damn underwear. So, I swallowed my pride. "Yes."

He cocked a brow, eyes flickering down my body for a moment, and kicked himself off of the doorframe. "If you're getting breakfast with Trevon, I suggest you cover that up." And, with that, he opened the door and walked back inside.

Chapter Seven

"What the Heaven happened to you?" Kasey asked, staring at my neck with wide eyes. Coffee was brewing behind the counter, filing the room with the bitter scent of mocha. I was just glad that it wasn't cinnamon.

I fiddled with Mom's necklace and scooted into the leather booth across from Kasey at Ollie's. Her lipstick was almost as bright as the blood red cushion covers. "Just-uh..."

I tried to think of a quick excuse, but what would explain this big, disgusting bruise? Burning myself with the straightening iron? My hair wasn't even straight, just a big frizzy mess. No one was that stupid.

"I don't know." I slumped against the table and gazed out of the windows. People in suits were rushing down the sidewalks, coffees in hand. A woman who looked as if she just walked out of Hell itself—with zombie-like eyes and knotty hair—stumbled down the side of the street. She gazed in my direction, and I sucked in a breath. Her eyes—for a split moment, I swear—were yellow. I blinked once, and the color was gone.

Was I going crazy now? Seeing yellow eyes. Thinking Eros actually gave me a hickey. I needed sleep.

Kasey cocked a sharp brow. "Yes, you do."

"No, I really don't. I just woke up with it."

"You have a suspicion though, don't you?"

The whole thing was stupid. Eros. My dream. Him actually being in my room. But there was no other explanation for it. "There's this guy..." And, so I told her about my next-door neighbor—about him stealing my panties, about him constantly flirting with me, about me—possibly—enjoying his attention.

She placed her fingers at the edge of the table, plump lips wrapping around the straw in her smoothie. "You think he's doing more than just creepily staring at you while you sleep?" She wiggled her eyebrows.

"It's not like that," I said. But who knew? I wasn't awake while —if—he was in my room.

The light in the mason jar above us swayed slightly. She leaned back in her seat, inhaling deeply through her nose, and giggled. "I bet he's just waiting to dig his claws into you."

"Claws? Jeez, Kasey, he's not a cat. And, besides, I have a boyfriend anyway."

Trevon had been my excuse for a few days now, and even that wasn't doing it for me anymore. If I didn't get my shit together before I saw Eros again, the past five years would be for nothing. I would hurt a man who had loved me even in my awkward middle school stage that I never seemed to grow out of; I would hurt a man who had helped me through every night that I woke up sobbing while thinking about Mom. I'd be a sinner, and Mom would be looking down on me with so much disappointment.

A waitress approached our table, and Kasey looked over. Her dark, natural curls rested around her glowing brown face. She pulled her pen from her pocket, cheeks flushing. "What can I get you ladies?"

"Eggs and bacon, please," I said.

Kasey smiled at the waitress, fingers grazing against her forearm. "Can I have a strudel?" She leaned forward, her breasts pressing into the table, and brushed her fingers against the waitress's nametag on her pink uniform top. "And, *Mycah*, make sure it's extra creamy inside."

The waitress blushed harder, her dimples appearing on her round cheeks. "I'll put it right in." Kasey's gaze followed her until she disappeared behind the kitchen door. When she looked back at me, she pushed my hair away from the bruise, examining it further. "Speaking of your boyfriend, has he seen what your boy-toy did to you?"

"No." And he wasn't going to because it might've never even happened. I could be one of those people that gets unexplainable bruises on their body. Anything was possible... right?

The bell on the diner's door chimed, and Kasey gazed behind me. "Is your boyfriend a bit muscular, dark eyes, has a blue baseball cap?"

Oh, God. He was here, wasn't he? He would see my neck. He would ask about last night. He would find out—everything.

My heart thumped against my chest, but I took a deep breath. Damn it, Dani, you have done nothing wrong, you have nothing to worry about.

Kasey leaned across the table and pulled my hair in front of my neck. "Don't move and you should be fine," she said lowly.

"Dani!" Trevon called from across the diner.

I gripped the edge of the table harder. I could just imagine him walking down the aisle toward us, arms swaying front to back, with a huge grin on his face. After moments of waiting in pure agony, he finally approached the table. "Where have you been?" He placed his baseball cap on the table between us. "I've been looking for you all morning." He turned to Kasey. "And who is..."

Kasey wrinkled her nose and pulled her hands away from my hair. "I'm Kasey."

"You haven't told me about her, Babe." He sat next to me.

Of course, I hadn't. He hadn't given me much of a chance to tell him anything since Sunday.

Grabbing my hand above the table, he interlocked our fingers. "I wanted to ask what time you'll be at the Halloween party on Friday."

"Halloween Party?" Kasey asked.

"My bar holds a Halloween Party every year," Trevon said. "It's the biggest one in the city."

I tensed and pulled my hand away from his. "Don't you remember what happened last time?" I asked. "I can't do that aga—"

He pushed some stray strands of my hair behind my ear. "You promi—"

"We'll both be there," Kasey said, grabbing my hand from his. "But we're having a girls' day right now, so you have to leave."

Trevon placed a kiss on my cheek. "I have to work tonight, so I'll see you tomorrow."

When he left the diner, I gave him a half-smile through the window.

Kasey glared at him. "What an asshole." She gripped her smoothie in her hand tightly, bringing the straw between her red-painted lips.

"Why is he an asshole?"

"I don't like him."

"Any particular reason?"

She shook her head, jaw clenched. "No."

A few moments later, Mycah appeared with a plate of eggs and bacon in one hand and Kasey's strudel which was oozing cream in the other. I grabbed my fork. "Well, I'm not going to the Halloween Party."

"If I'm going, so are you." She smiled, eyes lighting up. "And I know the perfect costume for you."

Chapter Eight

"Dani!" Maria yelled from the living room. I groaned and rolled onto my side, gazing at the city lights glowing in the darkness. It was Thursday night, and all I wanted to do was figure out an excuse for missing Trevon's Halloween party tomorrow night. There was no way that I was going. There was also no way that Kasey would let me stay at home. So, my excuse needed to be believable.

So far, I had come up with running late with Dr. U's clients, catching the measles, and getting possessed by a demon.

"What?" I shouted back. When she didn't answer, I got up and stuck my head out the door. The bathroom light was on. "What, Maria?"

"Do you wanna get dinner with the guys next door?" she asked.

"No."

"Awh, come on, Eros will be there!"

"Maria, I have a boyfriend." For the fiftieth time. What didn't she get about that? It's not like I had ever been single for the past three years we've lived together.

She walked out of the bathroom, blue mascara stick in her hand. "There's no harm in some innocent flirting, is there?"

None of the flirting that we've done was innocent. It was sinful.

"I'm not going." I shut my door.

"Your loss! I guess I get to toy with him for the night."

I pressed my lips together, peeled off my striped blouse, and hurled it into the hamper. She got to flirt with him? Is that what she did when I wasn't around? I inhaled the scent of my candle and rubbed Mom's necklace. It didn't matter what they did. I didn't care.

A few moments later, the front door closed, and I dug my fingernails into my palms.

Damn her.

An hour later—after I had *calmly* paced around the house just thinking about what Maria had said—I was lying in bed, about to fall into a peaceful sleep without worrying about Eros for once.

Someone knocked on my bedroom door, and my eyes snapped open. I gripped the white sheets in my hand, pulling them over my bare legs. If this was another one of Eros's little games, I swear to God I would—

The door opened, and Trevon walked in juggling a pizza from Giorgino's in one hand and a bottle of white wine with two glasses in the other. "Delivery for a sexy, little lady." He planted a kiss on my lips and dropped the pizza on my bed.

A smile crept onto my face, and I sat up. "What are you doing here? I thought you had to work tonight," I said, grabbing the bottle of wine.

He took off his baseball cap and tossed it onto the dresser. "I took the night off, wanted to see you." He wrapped his arms around me and pulled me tight into his chest, fingers lightly scratching the top of my head just where I liked. "I miss you. I feel like we haven't spent any real time together in a while."

His arms relaxed, and he sat back against the headboard. I poured two glasses of wine for us and snuggled up against him. We stared at the city lights through my window, watching the lights turned off in the buildings downtown every few minutes.

At 8 o'clock sharp, I watched Dr. U's office go dark and silently thanked her for that little talk she had with me.

Eros was nothing compared to Trevon. I knew that. And I was so glad that I hadn't gone out with them. I would've had a bad time, sitting next to Eros at dinner, having him flirt endlessly with me, gazing at that stupid damn smirk. So confusing, overwhelming, unnerving.

Trevon gripped my waist, pulling me closer, and tugged on one strap of my tank top. "What're you dressing as tomorrow?" He brushed his nose up the side of my neck. "Something sexy?"

"I'm not going."

"Oh, come on, Babe. What happened last year is over. Nobody remembers anything."

"I do." I couldn't go through that kind of embarrassment again.

He grabbed my glass of wine and placed it on my dresser, then crawled on top of me, pressing his lips against mine. "What do I have to do to get you to go?" He dipped his fingers into my underwear and pressed them against me. "This?"

"Trevon," I said, smiling. I grabbed his hand. "No."

"No?" He placed kisses down the middle of my chest to my naval and smirked up at me. "What about this?" He kissed me through my underwear, hooked his fingers under the string, and pulled them down.

I giggled softly at him and shook my head, pulling him back up to me. "I just want to spend time with you." I brushed my fingers across the side of his head, where the kinky texture of his hair faded out. "I don't want to go out."

"Will you at least think about it? For me?"

I sighed. "Fine, but no promises."

At 12am, I walked Trevon to the door. He told me he had to be at the bar at 6am for delivery, so he wouldn't be able to stay the night. Again.

The apartment was deathly silent since Maria still wasn't home yet, and it was making me anxious. I leaned against the doorway, bouncing my foot up and down, and watched him walk toward the elevators. "See you tomorrow night, Babe!" he said as the elevator doors closed.

I groaned and rubbed my hand over my face. The sacrifices I made for that man. I was stuck going now.

"That bad, huh?" someone said from behind me.

Damn it.

Eros was leaning against his door frame, arms crossed over one another. The sleeves of his grey crew-neck sweater were pulled up his forearms, and he was giving me those eyes again.

"What?"

"That's the first time I heard you groan all night." He smirked. "I think it's safe to say he didn't please you like he should have."

I narrowed my eyes at him. "I don't think you'd understand, but you don't have to fuck in order to enjoy the time you spend with someone you like."

He raised his brow. "Like? You don't love Trevon?"

I crossed my arms over my chest. "That's not what I meant. Of course, I love him."

"Maybe, you wouldn't have to pretend to love him if he could actually please you."

My nostrils flared, and I stepped into the hallway. "Well, maybe, you wouldn't have to flirt with a girl who's already taken if you could actually get someone to like you."

He took a step toward me. "Maybe if you didn't like it so much, you wouldn't flirt back."

I marched right up to him and stared into those deep, dark eyes. "You think I like your constant, uninvited flirting?"

"Oh, I do, Dani." He brushed his fingers against my hips and pushed me against the wall. "I think you love every... single... second of it." He posted his hands on the wall next to me, trapping me.

Push him away, Dani.

I swallowed hard.

He was close. So damn close.

His stubble brushed against my neck, making me shiver. His fingers felt rough against my skin. I inhaled his cinnamon, eyes fluttering closed. Don't fall under his spell, Dani. Don't do it.

"Aren't you supposed to be out with Maria?" I whispered. I didn't know why I was still standing here this close to him. Maybe it was because I couldn't move—my arms felt heavy, my legs wouldn't budge, my head felt muddled—or maybe I just didn't want to.

He chuckled lowly, and my heart raced at the sound. I didn't know how far gone I was until now. How could I ache for something so immoral? Why did I want to sin with him? Mom had to be cursing me out up in Heaven for thinking such devilish thoughts, but I couldn't stop.

When he gazed into my eyes, all I wanted him to do was to push his lips against mine, tug on my hair, thrust me against the wall over and over until I was gasping for breath, until my nails were digging into his back, until I was screaming out his name.

He trailed one finger up the column of my neck to my chin, his gaze following, then gently wrapped his hand around the front of my throat and drew me close to him until his lips were against my ear. "You can try to fight it, Dani, but you won't win."

I placed my hands on his taut chest, wanting to push him away.

"Go ahead," he said, fingers stroking my jaw. "Tell me that you never want me to touch you again."

I dug my nails into him softly and parted my lips. Say it, Dani. "Do it."

Cinnamon. Sweet cinnamon. Drifting through the air, coiling around me, consuming me.

When I didn't answer him, he pushed himself away from me and sneered in victory. "I'll see you at the party tomorrow then, Dani." He turned around and walked to his apartment. "Oh, and, if it makes you feel any better"—he stopped and looked back—"I didn't go out with Maria tonight."

Then the door closed.

I parted my lips, staring at the gold label *56C* on his stupid door. "Yeah... well..." I said to myself. "I don't care."

Chapter Nine

Kasey banged on the bathroom door. "Come out!"

I gripped onto the latex costume that she had given me and tried to pull it up again, but the damn thing wouldn't even go past my hips.

"Just give it a little tug!"

After a few more pulls, I released the material from my fists. "It's too small. I guess I won't be able to go tonight. Oh, darn, maybe next year," I said. I couldn't go to a Halloween party without a Halloween costume. It was the perfect excuse to get out of tonight and it wasn't even an excuse which made me feel that much better about it.

She wiggled the handle and pushed open the door. I covered my chest with my hands. "Kasey!"

She leaned down and grabbed the one-piece. "It's gonna fit!" Then, she pulled, prodded, yanked, and yelled for ten minutes. When she had finally got it up over my curves, she took a deep breath, wiping a bead of sweat off her forehead. "Almost done." She reached for the straps of my bra and tugged on them. "Just take this off and pull it up."

"My boobs don't just stay perky without a bra," I said, pulling the straps back up.

"That's why this costume has a built-in push-up bra, Sweet Cheeks." She pouted her red lips, unclipped my bra, and pulled up the costume. When she stepped back and looked at me, she grinned wider than I had ever seen her grin before. "You're so hot. It looks so good on you." She dragged me to the toilet seat and forced me to sit. "Now I just have to add the final touch. Close your eyes."

I sighed and closed my eyes, letting her do whatever she wanted to do to me. She tugged on strands of my hair and clipped something heavy to my hair on each side of my head. Then, she squealed. "Oh, my gosh. He's gonna love it!"

When I opened my eyes, she was holding a mirror in front of me. I gazed at myself, my eyes widening. She put horns on my head —horns. My fingers grazed against the black matte curves on my head. "You think Trevon will like *this*?"

She toyed with the curls in my hair. "Oh-uh, yeah, Trevon. He'll like it, I guess."

I gazed at my reflection in the bathroom mirror. The black latex suit showed every single curve of my body—my hips, my waist, my breasts—leaving no room for the imagination. She had painted my lips a maroon color and eyelids a smoky black.

"You're going to be the hottest demon there." She wiggled her brows at me and applied another coat of red lipstick. I'd probably be the only demon there.

I grabbed Maria's lilac perfume off the counter near the sink. If I was going to go all out, I might as well finish the look. But before I could spray it, Kasey grabbed it from me. "Don't use that. You smell too good already. He won't be able to resist you."

And, after giving myself one more lingering look in the mirror, I took a deep breath. I sure hoped that *he* was going to like it.

. . .

Trevon's bar, Elysium Taproom, was crowded when we arrived. People were hanging around the wrap-around bar in the back which was lit with dim white lights. Others were crowded around in a tight circle in the middle of the room, dancing on each other. And the stench of alcohol was overwhelming me with bad memories of last year.

All I wanted to do was walk right back out.

But Kasey had intertwined my fingers with hers and was pulling me toward the group dancing. I pulled away, shaking my head and telling her I was going to find Trevon first. Maybe I'd dance later, when everyone was too drunk to remember me from last year.

I shuffled through the crowd, careful not to get too close to any guys that might actually be Eros dressed in a costume. Someone grabbed my hips, but I pushed him away and continued towards Trevon's office in the back of the bar.

"Hey Dani!" Samantha, the bartender, called from behind the bar. She pushed a drink toward someone, collected money from a woman that looked like she had already had one too many, and smiled at me. "Didn't think you'd come back after last time."

God, everyone *did* remember.

"Yeah, me either." I rubbed Mom's necklace.

"Can I get you anything? White sangria? I know you like those." She tossed her chocolate-colored hair over her shoulder and smiled.

"Water," I said. "Please."

After she poured me a glass, she slid it toward me. "Have fun tonight."

This was going to be a long night. I could already feel it. I sipped my water and looked at her. "Do you know where Trevon is?"

She leaned against the edge of the bar, gaze lingering on my lips. "I think I saw him walk back through the crowd."

I scanned the room for Trevon, wanting to show him that, yes,

I did show up. But my gaze fell on the one man that I didn't want to see tonight. Eros was pushing his way through the throng of people, walking in my direction. Some girl dressed in a sexy nun costume trailed her black manicured fingers across his chest, but he continued walking. Not sparing her a single glance.

Go find Trevon, Dani. Don't just wait for Eros to get here.

Yet, I didn't move. Even in a crowd of a hundred people who reeked of sweat, bad perfume, and spilt drinks, I could smell his sweet scent of cinnamon.

He shoved through the last group, and when finally he saw me, he stood still. His eyes grew wide, and he stared at me like I was the only person in the entire room.

Large, white wings hung off his back, a silver chest plate covered half of his bare chest. An angel. A seductive, sexy, sinning angel.

Moments passed, and I still didn't move. My heart was racing in my chest at the way he was staring at me.

A woman brushed her hand against the back of his neck, whispered something in his ear, and grabbed his bicep, trying to pull him to the dance floor. But he didn't budge. Instead, he started walking forward again—each step dreadfully slow—until he was mere inches from me. I gripped the glass in my hand.

I should've been terrified that Trevon would appear at any moment and see me this close to Eros, but all I could think about was how I had never seen his eyes this soft. They were always fixed on me with such intent, always so intense. Never so gentle.

"Wow," he finally said. His gaze traveled across every inch of my face. "You look... amazing."

My breath caught in my throat. I didn't expect a compliment from him. I expected one of his flirtatious remarks. Mom's pendant rested in the center of my chest—its usual cool feel now burning my skin—and I had the urge to tug on it.

His fingers trailed up my jawline and grazed against the horns in my hair. "I've never seen someone look so good in these."

"I-uh..." What do I say to something like that? "I'm a demon," I said.

My cheeks burned. What the hell was that? Way to state the obvious.

He chuckled, lips curling into a tender smile. "I know. Me too."

I took a deep breath, trying to brush off my embarrassment. "You look more like an angel to me." He had the whole costume—except a halo on his head. My gazed traveled down his bronze abdomen to the white-skirt-like material that hung loosely off of his hips. It was so small and thin.

Don't think about it, Dani.

But it was too late.

"Dani!" Trevon yelled from somewhere in the crowd. I snapped my head in his direction, stepped away from Eros, and sipped my water—hoping to cool off the parts of my body that were burning.

Trevon curled an arm around my waist, pulled me to him, and pecked me on the lips. "You actually came." He smelt of booze, and his tie was off-centered.

"For you," I said.

He took my hand, stepped back and looked me up and down. "I'm glad. You're the sexiest witch here."

I furrowed my brows together. "I'm not a witch."

"She's a demon," Eros said, clenching his jaw.

Trevon grinned. "Well, you're the best-looking demon here."

Neither Eros nor I said a word. For some odd reason, I felt offended. Did I look like a witch? Was Trevon just too drunk to even realize what I was? I smiled tensely at him and readjusted his tie. And what was with his—

"Trevon!" Samantha shouted from the bar. "Can you come here? I need your help with something?"

After quickly kissing my cheek, he disappeared through the crowd and reappeared a few moments later at the bar. Chatting with Samantha for longer than I wanted. I hoped that it wouldn't be like this the whole night.

Eros grasped my elbow. "Come sit with me and the guys."

"I'm here with a friend," I said, looking for Kasey. If I spent one more minute with him, I would rip off that tiny costume and—

"It looks like you're alone," he said. "Come on." He nodded to the corner of the bar where I saw his roommates and Maria sitting in a booth. And—only because Kasey had disappeared and left me by myself—I followed him.

Chapter Ten

Eros took my hand and lead me to Javier, Zane, and Maria. I scooted onto the very end of the booth, next to Maria who was smirking at me.

She was wearing a sexy mermaid costume—a skintight green sequin skirt with two colorful seashells covering her breasts and a lilac-colored starfish pinned in her hair. "Girl, you look so sexy," she said.

I adjusted the horns on my head and sipped my water.

Zane leaned against the table—his green elf hat nearly falling off—and raised a brow. "Is that water? How are you supposed to have any fun with that?"

Heat crawled up my neck. Truth was that I wasn't planning to have any fun tonight. Not after last year—especially if people remembered.

Maria wrapped an arm around my shoulders and pulled me closer. "Dani's going to have the time of her life tonight—with or without alcohol." Her breath smelled like beer, but I was grateful for her. At least she didn't tell them what had happened.

Throughout the night, I watched Maria flirt with Javier and Zane who each had a girl that I had never met before tucked under

55

their arms and were whispering to them. The two girls and Maria were giggling at Zane's vaguely pointed elf ears and trying on Javier's plastic golden cross that was a part of his priest costume.

Eros, on the other hand, didn't pay attention to any of them. He didn't even try to flirt. Instead, he was gently tightening and relaxing one of his hands into a fist on top of the table. His ring glistened under the dim light, giving it a slight pink tint against his tan skin.

His gaze was fixed on me. But when I looked at him—even if it was for a moment—those green eyes would darken, and he'd look away.

I gazed around, trying to find Trevon or even Kasey, but they both seemed to have disappeared. Samantha was still behind the bar, pushing drinks to customers who were too drunk to stand straight. Bouncers were walking through the crowd every now and then. At one point, Maria even tried to drag me onto the dance floor with the rest of the group, but I declined.

Eros and I stayed at the table alone.

The girls were grinding against Javier and Zane, eyes closed slightly. Their skirts riding up their legs, hips moving so sensually. *Partition* played through the speakers, and a part of me wanted to get out there and forget about my worries. Let my body move with ease. Let loose with Eros behind me. His hands on my hips, pulling me closer. His lips against my ear, whispering something sinful to me.

I gnawed on my lip and glanced over at him. He was staring right at me and didn't look away this time. His fingers grazed against the stubble on his face. "Are you thinking about me, Dani?"

My cheeks flushed, and I looked down. I wished I had the liquid courage to admit that I was thinking about him—had been thinking about him—and couldn't stop, but I was a coward and I was taken by a man who would rather spend his night drinking in his office than see me dressed up for him.

I grabbed Mom's pendant and glanced around the room, not being able to hold his stare. Trevon was leaning over the bar, chatting with Samantha, a half-empty glass in his hand. I sighed.

"No," I said.

Eros leaned his forearms onto the table, biceps flexing. He picked up his drink and swirled it around, still staring intensely at me. "I hope you know that liars are sent to hell."

I'd been sinning since the day I met him. I doubted that I'd be sent anywhere else.

"It's good I'm not a liar then."

He chuckled lowly and shook his head, pieces of his dark hair falling onto his face. "Dani, there's a special place in hell for you."

I shuffled up in the seat, dropped Mom's pendant from my fingers, and leaned close to the table, breasts pressing into it. "And I bet it's filled with demons that'll eat me alive, right?"

His gaze traveled down my chest, then back up it. "They'll tear you apart."

My eyes lingered on his plump lips, hanging off of each word that he said.

"They'll leave you trembling."

I pressed my knees together.

He brushed his fingers against my cheek, his ring warming my skin, and lightly grasped my chin. "They'll bite into your soft flesh."

"They'll make me scream, won't they?" I asked.

He took a deep breath, jaw tensing. "Damn it Dani, they'll make you do more than that."

My God, I wanted him closer.

"Hell doesn't seem that bad," I whispered.

A stabbing pain split through my stomach. I placed a hand over it, hoping that it wouldn't ruin this moment because I was about to do something so sinful and Hell looked way too appealing for me to pass up now. I was sure that Mom would've thought Eros was pure evil, but all I could think about was the growing ache between my legs and how he was the only one who could stop it.

His gazed dropped to my lips. He smelled so good.

Another pain pierced through the other side of my stomach. "Fuck," I whispered, leaning back. I squeezed my eyes shut. This couldn't be happening. Not again.

"Are you okay?" Eros asked, brows furrowed together. That lustful look in his eyes had disappeared. "You look pale."

No. No. No. No. No. Not here. Not now.

He brushed his hand against my cheek, but I pushed it away. My stomach tightened, and I gripped the table, pulling myself to the edge of the booth. Everything suddenly felt weak. "I need to get to the bathroom." I used all of my energy to stand, and then I doubled over onto the ground. My stomach churned. Bile burned the back of my throat. And it happened.

I placed my hand on the filthy bar floor, my arms shaking. Everything I had eaten earlier was now lying in a thick puddle in front of me.

A girl screamed when she stepped in it with her shiny silver stilettos. People scurried away from our booth, wide eyes fixed on me.

All I felt was a heap of shame and embarrassment. I stumbled to my feet and rushed to the bathroom before it happened again. Sweat was dripping down my back in this latex suit. My fingers were trembling. Tears were streaming down my cheeks.

I slammed the bathroom door and locked it. I grasped onto the sink, using all of my strength to hold myself up. And, again, I puked.

Why was this happening again? What was wrong with me?

Tears welled up in my eyes. Not only did I just embarrass myself in front of everyone here, but Eros too. One moment I was thinking about sinning with him, the next I was on the ground, puke spewing from my mouth. Why was I such an embarrassment?

My mascara was rolling down my cheeks, leaving black splotchy lines. My hair was disheveled. Someone knocked on the door. "Dani?" Maria said. "Can I come in?"

I wrapped my arms around myself and leaned against the wall. I didn't want anyone to see me like this. I just wanted to go home —where I should've been.

"Please open the door," Kasey said a few moments later. I didn't respond to her either.

Another pain gnawed at the inside of my stomach. I squeezed my eyes shut, hoping that it would go away this time, and thankfully it did. Tears raced down my cheeks. How could I go back out there tonight? I couldn't. Maybe Trevon would let me hide in his office until the night was over. No way was I going to face all of those people—even for just a moment.

After talking myself out of jumping through the window and disappearing for the night that way, I opened the door, expecting to see either Maria or Kasey.

Eros was leaning against the wall with his jaw clenched, eyes focused intensely me. He gripped my glass of water in his hand. "Did you leave your drink alone?"

"Can-can you just leave me alone, Eros?" I whispered and wrapped my arms around my body. I tried to squeeze by him and sneak into the hallway to Trevon's office, but he grabbed my arm.

"No, I can't. Someone spiked your drink." He pulled me closer to him. "Now, did you place your glass down anywhere?"

I shook my head. "No..." Tears pricked at the corners of my eyes again. "I never set it down." Not once.

My gaze shifted behind him to Trevon who was storming toward us, lips in a tight line, tie loose around his neck. He had a dirty mop in one hand. "Dani, I need to speak with you in my office. Now." He hurried down the hallway to his office and held the door open for me.

After giving Eros my weakest grimace, I walked into Trevon's office. There was an open bottle of Brandy on his desk, and a pile of costumes and accessories that people must had left or lost tonight on the plush green chair across from his desk. He slammed the door and placed the mop against the wall. "What was that?"

"I—I'm sorry."

"Sorry, Dani? That's all you have to say? This is the second time you've puked everywhere in my bar. And each time I have to clean up your mess."

I parted my lips, keeping my eyes trained on the floor. "Eros said that my drink was spiked."

He gave me a hollow laugh. "You think your drink was spiked? Really? You think someone would spike your drink two fucking parties in a row? Do you know the probability of that?" he asked, his breath reeking of alcohol. He walked to his desk and shook his head.

"I'm sorry," I said. "I don't... know what you want me to say."

"How much did you have to drink tonight?"

"I didn't have anything."

"Don't bullshit me," he said, jaw twitching. The raging look he was giving me was absolutely terrifying—I had never seen him look so wrathful before.

"I didn't! Why would I lie to you?" I clenched my teeth together. "Why are you acting like this?"

Guilt flashed across his face but disappeared almost immediately. After a few moments of complete silence, he shook his head again and snatched a gold chain off his desk, throwing it into the pile of clothes on the green chair. "How much?"

"What don't you understand about the word 'none'? I had nothing! Maybe if you actually saw me tonight, you would know that. But you were out having such a merry fucking time with everyone else. Couldn't be seen with the girlfriend that you begged to come."

"Dani—"

"No!" I stepped forward. "Don't Dani me. I came here for you. Not to dress up and dance and have a good time. I came here because you wanted me to. You told me you wanted to show me off. And what do you do? Ignore me all fucking night?"

"Is that why you puked everywhere?" His voice was oddly calm. "You wanted to get my attention?"

I dug my nails into my palms. "Are you serious right now? Are you really fucking serious?" I stormed to the door. I wished he never opened this stupid damn bar. "I'm not taking this anymore."

"Less I have to clean up later on," Trevon said under his breath.

I slammed the door. Fuck him. Fuck this whole damn thing. He wasn't going to ever have to clean up my mess again because I would never come back to this place. This bar was far more important to him than I ever was.

<h1 style="text-align:center">Chapter Eleven</h1>

I didn't know where Kasey was, Maria wasn't at the booth, and I had $2.75 of spare change in my wallet. So, I walked to the bus stop at the corner of Sixth and Liberty bounced up and down on my toes, trying to keep myself warm.

Sharp pains continued to pulse in my stomach. I feared that as soon as I stepped onto the bus, I'd throw up again. But it was my only way home.

A familiar black car pulled up to the curb with its window rolled down. With one hand resting against the top of the wheel, the other on the gearstick, Eros leaned over the passenger seat and gazed out the window. "Get in."

I clenched my fists by my side. "No." I didn't need him cleaning up my mess either.

"Get in, Dani, or I'll put you in myself."

My bus approached a red light down the street. I pulled out my wallet.

Eros sighed and parked the car. "Why do you have to make this hard?" He got out of the car.

"I'm not going with you. I'll just puke all over your car."

"I don't care what you do in my car."

"Well, I do."

He opened the passenger door and waited patiently for me. "Just get in, Dani. It's cold out." After a couple of moments, he took my hand and pulled me toward the car.

I frowned at him, feeling torn, and sat. I just wanted to get home as soon as possible, so I could curl up into my blankets and forget about this whole night.

The ride was silent. I stared out the window, watching beads of rain race alongside the glass. Did Trevon really think of me as work? Was that what I was to him—just a mess that needed to be cleaned up? Tears welled up in my eyes. Why didn't he believe me when I told him my drink was spiked? It was like he didn't even care about it or about me.

I took a shaky breath and gripped the handle on the car door tightly in my hand. Don't cry, Dani. Not in front of Eros. You've embarrassed yourself enough tonight.

A tear slipped down my cheek. I quickly wiped it away with the back of my hand.

"Dani," Eros said quietly, looking at me from the driver's seat. "It wasn't your fault."

My chin trembled.

It was my fault. I was the one who couldn't hold it in. I was the one who made a mess. And I was the one who couldn't even clean it up.

"Look at me."

Another sharp pain pierced through me. I clutched my stomach, eyes widening. "Pull over."

"Dani—"

"Now."

As soon as the car stopped on the side of the road, I stumbled out and fell to my knees on the concrete. My throat burned, and I hurled but nothing came out. My stomach was turning over and over, not stopping. My arms were posted on the ground, trembling.

More tears were falling.

I wanted to go home.

Eros got out of the car, and the next thing I knew I was in his lap, his arms curling around my body. He laced his fingers into my hair and gently rubbed the top of my head.

"I—I wasn't faking it," I said, choking on my words. I wasn't even trying to hold back the tears anymore.

"I know," Eros whispered.

I squeezed my eyes shut, letting the rain drench me. At least he didn't think I was just looking for attention. I grasped onto him, hoping that he'd never let me go.

He gently held the sides of my face. "Dani, can you look at me?" His eyes were a soft green and his hair was plastered against his forehead. Drops of water were rolling down his cheeks and falling off of his jaw.

"I didn't even want to go tonight."

"Don't sacrifice your happiness for someone else, especially for someone who treats you like that."

Ollie's Diner sign blinked above his perfect fucking face, and I paused. I wasn't sacrificing my happiness, was I? I just wanted to make Trevon happy. When he was happy, I was happy. It was just a bad night. We would get over this.

He picked me up in his arms and placed me back in the car, adjusting the vents so the hot air would warm me.

As soon as we got home, I brushed my teeth and rinsed my mouth with mouthwash, getting the vile taste of tonight out of my mouth. Eros was in the kitchen, pouring me some medicine. Needing desperately to also take a warm shower, I locked the door and peeled off the top half of my costume.

I hooked my thumbs under the material and tried pulling it down. After five minutes of struggling, I let out a scream. Tonight just kept getting worse and worse, didn't it? All I wanted was to take this off and forget about everything. Just one simple wish.

Eros knocked on the door. "Are you okay?"

"I can't get this damn thing off." I wiggled my hips again, pushing and pulling it in different directions. It should be so simple, so goddamn simple.

"Do you need help?"

"No."

Yes, I did. Someone helped me get it on, someone probably needed to help me get it off. But that someone couldn't be Eros. I didn't have the energy to deal with his flirting right now.

I jerked up my knee, hoping that it'd help loosen something—anything—but I banged it against the closet door. "My God."

"Let me help you," Eros said.

I glared at the door, debating whether or not to actually open it for him and let him see me so bare. "If I unlock this door and you try something, I'll suffocate you with this damn suit," I said.

"I'm not going to try anything, Dani."

I covered my breasts with my arm and opened the door. He stood in the doorway, medicine cup in one hand. He had changed his angel costume out for a tight blue crewneck that hugged his body perfectly.

After placing the cup on the sink, he took a deep breath and knelt down in front of me. His fingers grazed against the sides of my hips. He loops them inside of my waistband, balled his hands into fists, and flexed his biceps. When he pulled down, the veins in his arms grew slightly more pronounced.

The costume slid over my hips almost effortlessly for him. Very slowly, he pulled it down my legs. Inch by inch by inch. His gaze followed. Once the costume was at my feet and I was standing in nothing but my underwear in front of him, he looked up at me. "You're sure you couldn't do that by yourself?"

"Yes."

For a mere moment, his gaze flickered to my hips.

"Don't look at me like that," I said.

"How am I looking at you?" he asked.

"Like... like..."

He stood up and turned away. The muscles in his back were flexed. "If you don't want me to look at you, I won't," he said. His words didn't calm me down like they should have. He tossed me a towel that hung off of the doorknob and gestured to the toilet. "Sit."

I wrapped the towel around my body. He searched through the bathroom closet, pulled out Maria's makeup wipes, and knelt next to me. "Close your eyes."

He grasped my chin in his hand and gently wiped the wet cloth against my skin. My shoulders slumped forward, and I sighed. Maybe Eros was right. I shouldn't sacrifice my happiness for someone else.

After wiping off my mascara, he softly brushed the cloth against my lips. I opened my eyes and watched his gaze travel across them. So slowly, taking in every inch. He trailed his thumb over my bottom lip, making it tingle.

The faint scent of cinnamon drifted through the air. He blinked a few times, drew my face into his hands, and leaned in. My heart raced, yet I leaned in too. Closer and closer until he brushed his nose against mine.

Our lips were so close that I could almost feel them on me. Pressing against mine. Moving down my neck. Running up the inside of my thigh. God, I was so hungry for him.

Starved. Famished. Ravenous.

And it terrified me because I had never felt this strongly about Trevon, I had never felt this way period about Trevon.

Unsure of myself, I closed my eyes and reluctantly pulled away. Eros's head fell for a moment, then he sighed. "I should go," he said quietly and walked out of the bathroom.

Regretting my hesitation, I jumped up, held the towel to my chest, and said, "Wait."

He stopped in the middle of the living room but didn't turn around. All I wanted was to see those lovely greens that always saw right through me, the ones that knew my every thought before I even did.

"Why were you so nice to me tonight?" I asked.

He turned, and for the briefest moment I saw pain in his eyes. "Because I know how you feel. I've felt that way before."

How'd he feel? Embarrassed? Ashamed? Betrayed?

"Wha—"

"Good night, Dani," he said before I could finish. Then he walked right out the door, leaving me in this lonesome apartment with daunting thoughts about *us*.

Chapter Twelve

My phone rang for the fifth time in the past hour. I gazed at it vibrating on my plush blanket. Kasey lit the vanilla candle on my dresser, then pointed the lighter at me. "Don't even think about it." She pursed her red lips and crossed her arms over her chest. "He's not worth your time."

The ringing stopped. "I can't ignore him forever."

"Yes, you can, and you should. Trust me." She snatched the phone and leapt onto the bed. "You know what, I'm just going to delete his number."

I tugged my phone away. "Don't be ridiculous. He's probably just calling to apologize."

Trevon's name glowed on the phone again. Another text message from him. The twenty-seventh one today.

Kasey inhaled in annoyance and leaned back on the bed. "And you're going to accept this apology?"

"Once we talk it through."

"Why?"

"Because that's what you do when you're in a committed relationship." Dr. U's words echoed through my mind. "You fight, talk, try to work things out..."

She frowned and leaned against the headboard. "Not to hurt your feelings, but by the way he acted at the party, it didn't even seem like you two were together." She toyed with the tag on the blanket and gazed out the window.

I sighed and followed her gaze. Well, I couldn't argue with that. He didn't even care that I was sick. He just yelled at me until I left.

Eros cared. He even left the party to bring me home. Held me in my arms when I was sick. Took off my make-up. Almost kissed me.

God, what was I even thinking? Comparing Eros to Trevon? Eros wasn't even someone that I'd ever consider dating. He flirted way too much. Probably had girls on speed dial. Like that chick *Luci* that had called him the other night when he drove me home from the restaurant.

Pfft. Definitely wouldn't date him.

I was just vulnerable and lonely last night.

Kasey flipped onto her stomach and kicked her legs back and forth in the air, humming to herself.

Even if I considered it, I wasn't sure how he felt after I pulled away from our almost-kiss—which definitely only happened because we were in the heat of the moment. I hadn't seen him since.

"When was the last time you and Trevon went out on a date?" Kasey asked, pulling me out of my daydream about Eros.

"Um, last week we went out to dinner with a few people."

She tilted her head, red lips in a frown. "I mean just you two."

I sighed and rubbed my palms across my face. "I... don't know. A month ago? Maybe, longer."

She grabbed my hand and pulled me down on the bed with her. "He says that he wants to show you off, but never takes you out, Sweet Cheeks." She gazed at Mom's pendant on my chest and grasped it between her fingers. Immediately she released it, as if it burned her, and pulled her hand away. "I know that he tells you he loves you—and he might—but make sure he's actually showing you he does."

I sighed softly to myself and sunk into the bed. I would make sure he did. I'd give him a chance to clean up *his* mess. One chance. Then I'd be done.

My heart clenched at the thought of breaking up with Trevon. The past five years would have been for nothing, but I couldn't dwell on the past. I needed to make sure I was happy. I deserved that much.

"Are you going to be okay?" Kasey asked. I nodded. Yes, I would be okay, hopefully. She raised a brow. "Don't lie to me."

"Yes, Kase, I'll be fine. Thank you."

She hopped off of the bed and looked in the mirror. "Okay, well, if you need me, call me. I have a hot date to get to." She adjusted her bra in the mirror, pushing up her breasts, then winked at me.

After Kasey had left, I put the phone on my dresser and leaned against the headboard, knees drawn to my chest. It had continued to ring, but I couldn't bring myself to answer it. I didn't know if it was because I didn't want to talk to him or if I didn't want to keep lying to myself about what I really wanted.

Maria barged in, snatched the phone from my dresser, and turned it off. "Come on. I'm tired of you just sitting in your room and listening to this phone buzz." She blew out my candle, letting the room darken, and tugged on my arm.

Light from the hallway filed into the room. "I can't go out there. I'm so embarrassed."

"It's just Eros and Javier. They probably don't even remember what happened. They were both so drunk at the party."

I swallowed. Had Eros been drunk last night? He definitely *was* acting strange. Complimenting me. Taking me home. Caring for me. It wasn't like him to do that, even if he was just empathizing with me.

"Dani, it'll be fine. It's just a movie."

Nothing was ever just anything when Eros was there.

The scent of popcorn drifted into my room. I gazed past her, listening to Eros and Javier talk in the living room. There was no harm in watching a movie with them, right? Maybe it was just what I needed—to get out of my own head for a while. Then I'd answer Trevon's calls and everything would be back to normal.

I followed her down the hall to the living room. Javier stared at me with his lip half-curled when I walked in.

My cheeks flamed, and I took a deep breath. He definitely remembered. No doubt. Probably thought about it all night. Wanted to come over and torment me about it. Why did I even agree to this again?

Maria leaned closer to me. "Stop thinking the worst." She gazed at Javier. "He's just being friendly." Then she nudged me. "Who knows, maybe he wants you too." She released my hand and curled into Javier on the loveseat.

My gaze drifted back and forth between the two, and I suddenly had an urge to lock myself in my room and never come back out.

"Well, are you going to sit down?" Eros asked.

I fiddled with my fingers. I was afraid that if I looked at him, I would forget about the one chance I promised myself that I would give Trevon.

His head was tilted slightly, those eyes dark. He sat on the other couch alone. I scurried to the single-cushioned chair—on the opposite side of the room—and sat. Even after last night, I couldn't trust myself around him.

We gazed at each other for a few moments until the movie started. I kept my eyes trained on the screen, but my mind was too foggy too actually pay attention. My thoughts were ping-ponging back and forth between Eros and Trevon.

About halfway through the movie, I finally gazed over at him. I had the sudden urge to ask him about last night, to have all of my questions answered about what he had meant, to really talk to him for once—instead of some not-so-innocent flirting.

Maria made a soft noise from the couch. I gazed over at her and Javier and wrinkled my nose, trying to ignore whatever was happening under their blanket.

Eros cleared his throat. She stopped and giggled awkwardly, her cheeks tinting pink. "I'm going to go get some more popcorn in the kitchen."

Javier wrapped his arm around her shoulder and leaned in closer to her. "Babe, stay here." His hand slipped under the blanket, and she giggled again.

Oh, God. They were actually doing this right here, weren't they?

I jumped out of my seat and grabbed the empty popcorn bowl. "I'll go get it." I needed to get out of here because, if I wasn't careful, I would be next. Sitting in Eros's lap, his fingers slipping into my pants, touching me in all the places I'd only ever dreamed of, the sweet scent of cinnamon keeping me in a complete daze.

When I reached the kitchen, I placed the bowl on the counter and took a deep breath. I couldn't wait until this movie was over. I'd sneak back into my room and take a nice long nap—away from all of my problems with Trevon, away from all the nasty things Javier and Maria were doing, away from Eros.

Unless he haunted my dreams again. Then I'd be fucked.

My cheeks warmed. Figuratively and literally—in my dreams, of course.

"Let me help you," Eros said from behind me. I sucked in a slight breath and fumbled with the bag of popcorn, listening to his footsteps. Closer and closer. Each step he took was dreadfully slow. It always was.

Calm, Dani. Stay calm.

One more step, and I felt the heat from his body against my

backside. His fingers pushing my hair to the side. His breath on my neck.

Damn it.

I gulped and opened the microwave a little too forcefully, making the bowl slip off the side of the counter. Eros grabbed it before it fell and chuckled lowly. "Do I make you nervous, Dani?"

Trevon, Dani. Think of Trevon. The man you're going to give another chance to. The man who was holding you in his arms, just a couple nights ago—before the big fight. The man you spent five years of your life on.

"No." I lied. "You don't." I turned around to face him, chest against his, back against the counter. "You make me angry."

Angry that I couldn't control myself around him.

He tilted his head, inching closer to me. "And?"

"Frustrated."

His lips twitched, and he moved even closer. His fingers curled around my waist. "And?"

"Anxious."

His nose grazed against mine, breath on my lips. I wanted him closer. "How else?" he asked.

I gazed into his eyes, searching those deep greens. They were endless orbs that I never wanted to stop staring into. I could look at them for days, weeks, months, even years and never get tired.

"And, content," I whispered.

He gently grasped the sides of my face, his thumbs grazing against my lips. "I want to kiss you."

And I would've been lying if I said that I didn't want him to.

Chapter Thirteen

For the second time in the past twenty-four hours, my lips were inches from his. I could practically feel them against mine—moving so slowly at first until we both couldn't handle it anymore and were devouring each other.

I curled my fingers into his chest and shut my eyes, wanting nothing more than to close the distance between us. He pulled me an inch closer, his cinnamon breath making my lips tingle. God, I had never wanted anyone more than him.

Someone knocked on the door. "Dani," Trevon said. "It's me."

I dropped my head, resting my forehead against Eros's. For a moment, I enjoyed being this close to him. His fingers tickling my skin. The light hum of his breathing.

Trevon knocked again. I sighed and walked to the door. Tell him what you need to tell him and send him on his way. Don't take his bullshit, Dani. I grasped the handle and opened the door.

He stood there in his blue baseball cap, hands stuffed into his pockets. "I didn't think you'd answer."

"I shouldn't have," I said.

After he stepped into the apartment, Maria and Javier glanced over. Maria wrinkled her nose at him and turned back to the TV, muttering something under her breath to Javier. Javier chuckled lowly.

Trevon looked at them, then at Eros who was now leaning against the counter with his arms crossed over his chest. "Can we talk in private?" Trevon asked.

I nodded, gesturing for him to walk ahead of me to my room. When I passed Eros, he grabbed me by the wrist. "Remember what I told you the other night, Dani."

Be happy.

"I know." I was about to turn to follow Trevon, but I stopped myself. I didn't know how long I was going to be with Trevon, and a part of me wanted—needed—to have my questions about what Eros said last night answered before I had the conversation with Trevon. So, I took a deep breath and asked, "What did you mean when you said you knew how I felt the other night?"

He was quiet for a moment. "Dani, that's not something that we should get into now. Maybe another day."

I didn't like the sound of that, but I'd take it. That meant that maybe—just maybe—he'd let me in on his life someday. He'd show me a different side of him.

Trevon was sitting on my bed, forearms resting on his knees, running his hands over his hair. When I opened the door, he stood up. "Are you feeling better?"

The candle was burning on the drawer, white smoke emitting from it. "You should've asked me that the other night, not now."

"I know, and I'm sorry I didn't."

"You should be."

He sighed. "I don't want to fight with you."

"Well, you should've thought about that before you accused me of faking it. I couldn't help that I puked everywhere. I didn't know that someone spiked my drink. And you thought I just—what? I just drank too much to get your attention?"

"I was just angry. I know how stupid it was to say that. Nothing was going right that night." He closed his eyes. "Shit just kept happening. That's why I couldn't spend time with you."

I crossed my arms over my chest. "You sure had time to talk to Samantha."

"Yes, I did. I'm her boss. I have to make sure she does her job," he said. I heard his phone buzz in his pocket, but he didn't pull it out to check for once. Instead, he reached for my fingers. "Are you jealous of her, Dani?"

The candle crackled. "Should I be?"

He raised his brows like he was surprised that I would even ask, but he's the one who brought it up. "No. Why would you even think that? I... I don't understand." He paused. "In the past five years have I ever given you the—"

"You know what I don't understand? Why you even asked me to go to that damn party. You know I don't enjoy going out, and you weren't even there to see me."

"I didn't plan on ignoring you all night. I had work to do," he said, voice laced with annoyance.

"Yeah, but—"

"Yeah, but, nothing." He raised his voice. "I wanted you to have a good time with your friends for once. I wanted to show you off to everyone and—"

I pressed a hand onto his chest, pushing him away. "Stop treating me like an object. I'm not a car. I'm not your arm-candy." My heart was racing. "And even if you wanted to show me off to everyone, you never ask me out anymore. We haven't been out by ourselves in months."

His brown eyes widened in anger. "That's because you don't want to go out!" He groaned and rubbed his hand across his face. "Look, I'm sorry about being a jerk, but I can't be the only one willing to negotiate in our relationship."

I could only imagine Dr. U smiling so freakishly wide at our argument, telling us both that disagreements were healthy, that negotiation was healthy, that trying new things was healthy.

"Can you try to be more willing to do things with me, Dani? And I'll work on myself for you," Trevon asked, sitting on the bed and grabbing both of my hands.

I took a deep breath. If Trevon worked on himself, he could make me happy. He really could. But I didn't know if this was what I wanted anymore.

"I need some time to think," I said.

Trevon furrowed his brows and squeezed my hands tighter. My heart was breaking for us. "Are-are you breaking up with me?" he asked quietly.

I squeezed his hands back. "Trevon... I just need some time."

After a few moments of silence, he nodded his head. "Okay," he said, grabbing his baseball cap off of the dresser and clutching it to his chest like it was the only part of me he had left. He walked to the door and turned around. "Dani, I love you. I really do."

I leaned against my black leather headboard, clutching my sheets to my chest, eyes wide. My gaze was fixed on the figure at the end of my bed. A man—if I could even call him that—sat with his back facing me. Two deep scars laid parallel to each other, nearly running the length of his spine. Every little muscle in his back was flexed. His head was tilted toward the ground.

"Dani," he said. I swallowed hard, recognizing Eros's voice. But he didn't turn around, and I didn't know why.

I found myself crawling toward him. My fingers grazed against his shoulders, and I wrapped my arms around his torso, my barely covered breasts pressing against his back. His cinnamon scent was overwhelmingly stronger than it usually was. I placed a kiss on his spine, between the scars.

"Think through your decision with Trevon," he said.

"I don't want Trevon. I want you."

He took a deep breath. "You don't know what you're getting yourself into with me."

"I think I do."

"No, I don't think you do." He turned to me. His eyes were black —completely black. I'd never seen them so dark.

My gaze travelled up his face, admiring every sharpened feature of it, and that's when I saw it. The horns. The same ones I wore on Halloween night were sitting on his head.

At first, I had the urge to laugh. He really stole them from my closet and put them on his head, but then I realized how damn sexy they looked on him.

They protruded from his head a few good inches, curvy and rigid. I pressed my knees together. He looked so naturally demonic— and I was oddly attracted to him.

I reached out, unable to stop myself from touching their curves.

"Don't tease me," he said breathlessly.

I grabbed the horn firmly in my hand, fingers barely able to wrap all the way around it, and pressed my lips to his neck.

He pushed me back onto the bed, hovering over me. His hips were pressing onto mine. "You don't know what you've done," he whispered in my ear. He gently wrapped a hand around the front of my neck.

Pure darkness stared down at me, and I couldn't get myself to look away. I was fascinated by him. He slipped his other hand into my panties. "You don't even know what you do to me." He wasted no time plunging his fingers inside.

They moved fast and hard, thrusting into me with all of their might over and over again. I clenched around him, heat rushing to my core.

"Oh, God." I squeezed my eyes shut. This was what I wanted. I knew exactly what I was getting myself into.

His teeth were on my neck, nibbling softly. "Tell me what you want, Dani."

"I've told you already..." I threw my head back. "... please don't stop..."

"Say it again," he murmured. "I love the way you say my name."

I moaned, toes curling. "You, Eros. I want you."

His fingers quickened, and soon my legs were trembling as wave after wave of ecstasy rolled through me.

<h1 style="text-align:center">Chapter Fourteen</h1>

I woke up lying on my stomach, my cheek plastered in sweat against the pillow—mouth half-opened, drool dripping from my lip. The window was cracked half an inch, letting a crisp November morning breeze chill my room. I rolled onto my back and rubbed my hands over my eyes, groaning.

These dreams needed to stop. I couldn't handle another sex dream about Eros. But, damn, did I love them. He looked so sexy with those sharp horns and piercing black eyes. I pressed my knees together. If only it were real.

"You're moaning an awful lot in there," Maria yelled from the hall. A few moments later, my door opened, and she peaked her head in—the wide grin on her face immediately disappearing. "Oh, you're in here alone."

I sat up and pulled the blankets over my bare chest. "Maria! You can't just walk in. What if Trevon was over?"

She tossed her blonde hair over her shoulder and twirled a mascara stick in her hand. "I knew he wasn't here. He came over an hour ago to see you, but you were sleeping."

"Then why'd you think someone was here?"

"I thought maybe Eros paid you a visit this morning." She

shrugged like Eros being in my room with me while I had a boyfriend was nothing, then she walked to my mirror and continued to apply her make-up.

Heat crawled up my cheeks. Oh, Eros was here last night—just not the way that she thought. But if she found out I was having hot dreams about Eros, she'd make a huge deal out of it and probably would even tell him.

Her blue eyes widened in the mirror. "Oh my gosh. He did, didn't he?"

"No, no, no. Maria, he didn't."

She turned on her heel. "Then why are you blushing?"

"I'm not blushing!" I was definitely blushing.

"Yes, you are!"

"Maria!"

"Did you have a wet dream about him?"

"MARIA!"

"You did!" She squealed and hopped onto the bed with me, grabbing my wrist. "Tell me how good he was! I have wet dreams about Javier and Zane all the time and let me tell you, girl, they drive me crazy, especially Javier! He's so good with his—"

I tugged on the t-shirt I had on last night before bed and rolled out of bed. "I don't have time to talk about this right now. I have to get ready for work." And I really didn't want to know what Javier did to her, especially after the movie last night.

Dr. U stood in front of the wall-length windows in her office and sifted through some papers. The sunlight was reflecting off of her glasses. "Morning Dani." She took a sip from her Ollie's coffee mug and quickly glanced at me. "You look refreshed."

I had rushed to put myself together this morning—wanting to get out of the house before Maria had the chance to ask me question after question about Eros.

She placed her coffee on her desk and leaned against it. "I suspect you figured out your dilemma with Trevon?"

"Oh, um, yeah." Sure.

She raised a sharp brown brow and nodded to the couch. "What happened?"

My fingers brushed against the plush cushion, and I sat down. "Nothing." It was bad to think this, but, after last night, I didn't want her to talk any sort of sense into me.

She tilted her head and smiled softly, waiting for me. I sat there in the awkward silence, kicking my feet back and forth, and gazed out of the window. God, this woman would not let this go. "He wanted me to go to this stupid party he was throwing at his bar, and we got into a fight."

"Have you talked to him since?"

"Yes."

"What did he say?"

I didn't want to tell her because she had always liked Trevon. We matched on so many levels. It was absolute love, she had said. Rare these days.

I gazed out the window. Bright beams of sunlight were shining through a pocket of plush white clouds. It reminded me of the time Mom took me to the park for my birthday. When we were lying on the ground, grass tickling my arms and legs, she pointed up at the sky and told me stories of angels rising up to Heaven. That morning, we watched the crepuscular rays for hours. That was the last morning I saw her alive.

I grasped her pendant and took a deep breath. Whenever I saw those rays, I knew she was with me.

"He said that he'd work on himself for me," I said.

Dr. U gazed out the window and paused for a moment. "When you've had arguments, before has he followed through with his promises?"

"Yes."

"And your relationship improved, didn't it?"

My heart clenched. "Yes."

"So, what's bothering you?" she asked. When I didn't answer, she leaned closer to me and placed a hand on my knee. "Dani, you know I won't judge you for your answer. I'll just provide you with as much help and guidance as I can." Her voice was soft, yet I knew she'd push me toward Trevon, toward a heavenly good.

I parted my lips and took a shaky breath. "I... I..."

Moving around the desk, she sat next to me and wrapped an arm around my shoulder. "I want you to make the best decision for yourself, and I know that you have loved Trevon for years. From what you tell me, your relationship is strong. I don't want you to lose something like that for a lustful fling."

She paused for a moment, and I saw Mom in her eyes.

And I knew one thing: I couldn't disappoint Mom.

Chapter Fifteen

I stepped into the Elysium Taproom and immediately wanted to step right back out. The room was buzzing with people who had just gotten off of work, dressed in suits and sipping on beer. Couples sat across from each other in the maroon booths, smiling and laughing and I wished that I had never gotten myself into this mess with Trevon.

Kasey and Maria were telling me to break up with him. Dr. U and Mom were telling me not to. And Eros... I didn't know what he was telling me to do or what he really wanted. Hell, I didn't know what I wanted.

All I knew for sure was that I needed a drink. Something—anything—to give me the courage to talk to Trevon, but I just didn't want it to be spiked again. Trevon would get angry, and this whole vicious cycle would repeat.

I walked to the bar, searching for a place to sit and hoping that Trevon was still in his office and not on the main floor. My mouth was far too dry to talk to him right now.

Eros leaned against the bar top with a drink in his hand, talking to Zane. His back was turned toward me, and his sleeves were pulled all the way up his forearms, giving me a clear view of all his dark tattoos. I sucked in a breath. Well, this was what I got. Try to avoid Trevon, run into Eros.

Zane nodded his head in my direction, and Eros looked my way. His dark hair was tousled, strands falling onto his forehead. Sultry green eyes looking so much softer than they did last night in my room. "What's a sexy little thing like you doing here on a weeknight?" he asked, smirking.

"I'm here to see Trevon."

His soft features faded.

"I haven't seen him," Zane said.

Eros sipped his drink, knuckles white. "He's probably in the back."

"Probably," I said, drawing my fingers along the strap of my purse.

His gaze flickered from the offices to me to Zane. When I didn't move, he raised a brow. "I thought you were here to see him?"

"I am, but I have time." To talk to you.

Eros leaned closer, gaze wandering down my body and lingering on my hips, brow arched. "I bet you do."

Zane placed his beer down on the counter. "I'm gonna head out. It was nice seeing you again, Dani."

Eros placed his glass on the bar. "Do a favor for me and take Javier on your way out. I don't want to deal with him tonight." Eros gazed back over at me, taking me in.

"Javier came with you?" I asked. I expected him to be doing Maria somewhere in the apartment.

"Yeah, he's probably drunk off his ass in the bathroom," Zane said, rolling his eyes and heading toward the back.

Eros brushed his finger against my blazer, dangerously close to my abdomen, and pulled me closer to him. "Sit down, Dani. Have a drink with me." He lifted two fingers to the bartender, asking for two shots, then turned back to me.

I sat on the stool, knees touching his. "You remember what happened the last time I had a drink at this place, don't you?"

"Your drink won't be spiked again."

The bartender placed down glasses and carefully poured two shots of Vodka. He was *new*. I wondered why they hired him. Usually Samantha worked the bar Monday nights.

When he was finished, he slid them across the counter. I gazed down at the drink, feeling paranoid. "How do you know it's not spiked?"

"Dani, you just watched him pour it in front of you," Eros said.

So many bad memories have come from this place, I was afraid to try anything.

Eros took the glass from me. "If you really want me to make sure..." He brought the drink to his lips like he was going to drink it and sniffed. "All good."

"What was that?"

His foot brushed against mine. "I was making sure your drink wasn't spiked."

"You can do that by smelling it?"

He clacked his glass against mine and threw the shot back. "I can do a lot of things you don't know about." There was a dark glint in his eyes.

I stared at him for a few moments and smiled. He was something else. I sat back in the stool and relaxed, my fingers curling around the glass. I placed it on my lips and threw it back. The alcohol burned the back of my throat, but it was just what I needed.

Eros ordered two more, and I wasted no time drinking it down again.

My head started to feel light. I felt better, good even. So damn good. For the first time—in a long time—I could just relax.

I was working on my third drink. My cheeks were warm. He brushed his foot against mine again, eyes dark in this light. Every time I looked at him, all I could picture were horns on his head and alluring black eyes. So sexy.

My gaze lingered on top of his head, and I pressed my knees together. Fuck, Dani. Get yourself together.

But I couldn't stop staring. My heart was racing.

"Is there something on my head?" Eros asked, eyes studying mine.

I licked my lips, trying to moisten them.

After wedging one of his knee between mine, he smiled. I watched his soft lips move so effortlessly. "What are you thinking about, Dani?" He rested his forearm against the bar and leaned closer, fingers trailing down my shoulder.

"Nothing." I shook my head. "Nothing—It's stupid."

He chuckled. "I think we're past the point of looking stupid in front of each other, don't you think?"

My cheeks flushed even more. I looked down at my glass, then back at him. "It's—uh..." I shook my head. Fuck it. "You were in my dream last night."

His lips curled into a smirk. "And?"

"And..." I smiled, looking back down. "You were wearing those horns I wore at the Halloween party." I gazed back at the top of his head, gnawing on the inside of my lip. The dream was torturing me. Visions, sensations, feelings of last night replayed over and over in my mind. Not letting me think straight once today. It wasn't even real and here I was frustrated just by the thought of it. "I just thought you looked really, really good in them."

He raised a sharp brow. "You liked them?"

"Yes."

"You've been thinking about me with horns?"

"Yes. And..." My head swayed slightly.

"And?"

"Your eyes." I brushed my fingers against his cheek bone, heart pounding in my chest. "They were so black."

He smirked. "What'd you think of that?"

I thought *a lot* about it, but all of those thoughts would get me sent straight to Hell. So, instead of telling him what I really thought of them, I giggled softly to myself. "They were... nice."

"Nice?"

"Yes. Very, very nice," I said. I closed my eyes, listening to him chuckle, and smiled. "Crazy dream, huh?"

He sipped the rest of his drink and gazed at the table, looking like he was contemplating something. After a few moments, he gazed back at me. "No, not really."

"What do you mean?" I asked, my head feeling light.

His fingertips paled around the glass. "It's not something that we should discuss right now."

"When?"

"I don't know..." He sighed. "Why don't you go find Trevon?"

"But—"

"Dani, please." His voice was quiet. "When I tell you—really tell you—there isn't any going back. I'd prefer us to stay like this for now."

<h1 style="text-align:center">Chapter Sixteen</h1>

After downing the rest of my shot—because I needed all the liquid courage I could get—I staggered down the hallway, fingers gliding against the wall to guide me toward Trevon's office. I still didn't know what I was going to say to him. Hell, maybe he wouldn't even want to talk to me since I reeked of alcohol and was a tiny bit tipsy.

By the time I made it to his office, I was rubbing Mom's pendant between my sweaty palms and breathing heavy. Scenario after scenario was playing out in my head of how this could all go. Some were bad: Trevon yells at me for being immature by drinking before we talk. Most were really, really bad: I tell him I was going to give him another chance and spend the rest of my life feeling like shit.

So much for drinking to calm my nerves. That plan went right out the window.

I took a deep breath and knocked against the cold door. No answer. I knocked again. Nothing.

I jingled the doorknob and walked into an empty office. I had done it a million times before but barging into Trevon's office never felt so wrong.

His black peacoat was draped over the arm of the couch and his baseball cap was sitting on his desk. I shut the door behind me and wandered over to sit in his big comfy chair. He was probably in the bathroom.

My head still felt light, and I swayed in the chair, knees bouncing.

A manila folder was sitting on top of a bunch of legal documents on the desk. *Termination of Employee: Samantha Bernard.* My eyes widened, and I picked up the folder.

Trevon fired Samantha? Why would he do that? I mean, sure, she was a bit rude to me. Okay... she was very rude to me. But he wouldn't fire her because of that, would he?

I played with the edge of the folder, debating on finding out why. I didn't want him to yell at me again—this time for being too nosy—but I couldn't help it. He was acting suspicious.

Just as I was about to open the file, the doorknob rattled. I quickly placed it back down and stood. If he caught me snooping, he would think I didn't trust him. And he definitely wouldn't trust me.

Someone banged on the door, and then it was pushed open. Trevon stumbled in backwards, a pair of hands squeezing his ass.

What the fuck?

Javier pushed him into the room, lips pressed against Trevon's. Trevon was fumbling with his belt, groping Javier through his pants, grinding himself against him like Javier was the only damn thing that he ever wanted. And he was so desperately craving him right now.

My eyes widened.

Holy hell.

What was he doing? Was this really happening?

I blinked a few times. Maybe I was just seeing things. Maybe I was drunker than I thought. I should've just had one, not three.

Javier pushed Trevon's hand into his jeans, and Trevon

groaned softly against his lips. "Fuck," he said under his breath. "I've been waiting for this all day."

Oh, God. This was actually happening.

"What the hell are you doing?" I shouted.

Trevon jumped back and pushed Javier away. He wiped his lips with the back of his hand. "Dani..." he said breathlessly. His eyes were a hazy and intoxicated brown like I had never seen before. I parted my lips, gazing wildly between the two. I didn't even know what else to say. "Dani, I-I can explain! It's not what it looks like!" He pulled up his pants and buckled his belt.

"Really, Trevon? How is seeing you kiss Javier supposed to look?" I dug my nails into my palms. I couldn't believe this. How could he do this to me? And with Javier?

A wall of heat crashed into me, followed by the strong scent of licorice. Javier stepped toward me, eyes low and viciously dark. Trying to intimidate me. I glared at him—not backing down. All I felt was pure rage for the man who was ruining my life.

My life and Maria's life. I thought he had a thing with her, but I guess I was wrong. He seemed to fuck anything and anyone he could get his goddamn hands on.

Trevon rushed over to me, gently placing his hands on my shoulders. "Dani, I... I-we... we weren't—" So much regret in his eyes. It was all a damn put-on.

"How long has this been going on?" I asked. Trevon just stood there, brows furrowed together, not even attempting to speak a single word. "I can't believe you." I pulled myself out of his grip. "Damn it, Trevon. Did you ever even care?"

He parted his lips, but I cut him off. I didn't want to listen to another one of his lies. I didn't want to be played again.

"You know what—I can't take this anymore. We're done! Done!" I stormed out of the office, not sparing Javier another look, and slammed the door behind me.

Don't cry, Dani. Don't do it.

I hurried down the hallway and through the bar. My heart

raced. An angry tear rolled down my cheek. Fuck Trevon. Another tear. I hated him. I hated him so much.

All those memories—lying in bed late at night, fingers brushing softly against my chin, holding me against his chest and letting me listen to his steady heartbeat. Every early morning, I spent with him as he desperately tried to get his bar up and running. Every late night I waited at home for him with his favorite kettle corn and cheesy Hallmark movie.

So fucking stupid.

How many people has he cheated on me with? How many times? How long has this been going on? And... I drew my brows together, teary gaze fixed on the ground... why?

I had done everything for him, tried to be the perfect girlfriend, tried to give him everything he wanted, sacrificed my happiness for his. And all I got was a front-row seat to Trevon's raunchy escapades.

God, I wanted to march right back into his office and make sure he knew how badly he hurt me. I wanted an explanation. I wanted an apology for wasting five years of my life on him. But something in my gut told me to keep walking and to never turn back. Not even when he knocked on my door with teary eyes and a sappy apology.

And I wasn't going to.

He didn't make me happy anymore. I knew that now.

Chapter Seventeen

"What a dick. Honestly, who the Heaven does he think he is? Does he really think he could just do that to you?!" Kasey paced back and forth in her apartment with her arms crossed and a sinister look in her eye.

I curled into the side of her plush white sofa and clutched a pillow to my chest as closely as I used to with Trevon. When I walked out of the bar three hours ago, I didn't feel this bad. But when I made it to Kasey's, it hit me. Hard.

Trevon would never visit me after work with a bottle of white wine and a pepperoni pizza again. He would never hold me when I woke up at night from a nightmare of Mom's death again. He would never love me—really, truly love me—again. At least, I wouldn't let him. I couldn't.

There was no way in Hell that I'd go back to him now, no way that I'd forgive him for this. I dug my fingers into the pillow. I wanted to rip it apart. I wanted to scream and cry—both at the same time.

Five years. I wasted five years of my life on him. Five years of laughing at his stupid jokes and smiling at his stupid faces and loving his stupid ass. And I never wanted it to end.

If he wanted to see other people, he should've just broken up with me. It would've saved us both a bit of hardship.

"You know what? Screw him. I didn't like him, anyway." Kasey pursed her red lips. "He's a no-good cheater. He's going to Hell. I'll make sure he has the worst time down there."

I loosened my grip on the pillows and laughed lifelessly. I guess I'd see him there. With all the lying and denying my lustful thoughts and dreams of Eros, I wouldn't make it to Heaven, that's for sure.

Someone knocked on the door, and my heart leapt. A part of me wanted Trevon to be standing there, clothes soaked from the rain, a sorrowful expression on his face. Not that I would accept his apology. I just wanted to see that he cared, even if it was just a little.

Kasey stormed to the over and yanked it open. A female dressed in a soft pink dress stood in the doorway—the waitress from Ollie's diner that Kasey had flirted with when we were out. Her natural curls were parted down the middle and a cute maroon bow was clipped in her hair. "Hey Baby," she said, holding out a bottle of wine.

"Mycah," Kasey whispered, immediately relaxing. She took a deep breath and leaned closer to her. "Now's not really a good time."

Mycah gazed over her shoulder at me and frowned.

I stood and dropped the pillow. "I was just leaving. It's okay." It was late anyway.

"No," Kasey said. "You're staying the night."

After shrugging off her coat, Mycah placed the bottle of wine on the counter. "Man trouble?"

"*Boy* trouble," Kasey said. "That bastard cheated on her."

Mycah poured three glasses of wine. "That guy you used to always come into Ollie's with?"

"Yes," I said.

She handed me a glass of wine. "Well, here's a little something to rid him from your mind." Then, she sat on the couch next to me and gently rubbed my knee. "Who needs cheaters anyway?" Kasey lightly grabbed her chin and placed a kiss on her cheek.

For the next few hours, we talked about anything and everything other than Trevon. From Ollie's to Dr. U to my sexy neighbor that wouldn't leave me alone. And when Kasey brought him up, Mycah stood and raised her eyebrows at me. "Do I hear a rebound?" she asked.

My cheeks tingled, and I gazed out at the city through her floor-length windows. "No."

Kasey pursed her red lips. "We'll see about that."

Mycah placed her hand on Kasey's knee and kissed her. "Well, I'm going to bed. I look forward to hearing more about this mystery man."

Kasey watched her disappear down the hallway and grabbed our empty wine glasses.

"So, are you two a thing?" I asked, following her to the kitchen.

"Yeah." She smiled.

"How long?"

Her eyes widened with excitement, and she leaned against the counter. "A few weeks. I'll have to tell you more about her in the morning. If I tell you now, you won't be able to shut me up and I don't want to keep her waiting." She brought me to a spare bedroom and pulled out a few blankets. "Are you alright?"

I smiled weakly. "I will be." Hopefully.

When I laid down and shut my eyes and was finally alone with my thoughts for the first time tonight, I clenched the blankets in my fists. I wasn't alright. My heart hurt. I felt like I was suffocating. The tears wouldn't stop rolling down my cheeks.

Did I drive him to cheat on me? Did I not go out with him as much as he wanted me to? Was I not fun and spontaneous anymore? Was it because I said that I needed time to think?

I wiped the tears. No. This wasn't my fault. I refused to blame myself for this. Cheating on me was his choice, and it was a bad one.

I was lying in a bed and staring up at a plain white ceiling. Gusts of wind blew in through a cracked window. All I wanted was to pull the blankets over my body, but everything felt too heavy to move. My head. My heart. My muscles.

"Dani, it's not your fault," someone whispered.

Eros laid next to me, fingers grazing against my cheek. I turned onto my side, tucking my hand under my pillow, and gazed into his black eyes. He was wearing those horns again.

I waited for him to say something to take my mind off of this, but he just wrapped his arms around me and pulled me into his chest. I inhaled his cinnamon aroma and relaxed in his arms. They were so warm.

We laid like that for hours. My fingers digging into his bare back, me holding him closer than I ever held Trevon, clutching him like he was the only thing I had ever wanted. I didn't know how much I needed this.

"I'm going to make this right for you," he said.

When I woke up the next morning, I swore I could smell Eros on the bed sheets. It felt as if he had been there with me the whole night, but that was an even stupider than the idea of me giving Trevon a second chance.

After Kasey dropped me off at home, I stood in the elevator with my phone pressed to my ear. "I'm so sorry again, Dr. U., but I... I won't be able to come in today."

"Is everything okay, Dani? You never call off," she said, worry clear in her voice.

"Yes." It was. At least, I was feeling a bit better than yesterday.

She paused for a long moment. "Dani, it's not good to deny

your feelings. Don't let them build up. Remember how that unfolded in the past for you."

"I know," I said softly, stepping out of the elevator. Denying Mom's murder made me so hateful of everything until Trevon. Now I had to deal with Trevon and his cheating.

"Take as much time as you need," she said. "And promise me you'll talk to someone about this, even if it's not me."

"I promise."

I hung up the phone and walked down the hall. Trevon was the only good in my life after I lost Mom and now he was gone too —willingly. What did I have left? Who did I have left to talk to about this? Kasey. Maria, maybe.

Everything was eerily quiet as I pushed my key into my apartment door, lost in my thoughts. Then, suddenly, I heard yelling from next door. I was going to ignore it until I heard Javier's voice.

"I can't fucking believe you!" Eros said.

"Come on. You know how I live, Eros," Javier said. I gripped the doorknob, fingers turning white.

"I told you to stay away from her!"

"You told me not to fuck her, and I didn't." Javier's voice was laced with annoyance.

"So, you fuck her boyfriend instead?" Eros paused. "I can't believe that I actually fell for this shit. I should've known. You're just like your father."

Javier chuckled lowly. I could only imagine he had the same sinister look on his face that he gave me when I caught him with Trevon. "You should be used to it by now."

"This is why I left."

"Who are you kidding, Eros? You were banished! You didn't leave. Mother didn't want a son like you. She never did."

Silence.

"Why didn't you tell me that she's—" Javier started, but I heard sudden footsteps and saw the door swing open, so I slipped into my apartment and shut the door behind me. That didn't sound good.

I inhaled deeply, breathing in the scent of eggs and bacon, and closed my eyes. Eros and Javier were half-brothers? Where did their mother banish him from—and, on second thought, who even used that word anymore? Why did Eros warn Javier to stay away from me?

The last question interested me more than the others. Maybe I was hoping that it was because he *possibly* liked me too. After last night's dream, I was starting to think anything was possible.

He probably told Javier that so he could be the one to fuck me. He had made that clear from the moment that he met me that *that* was what he wanted.

The bacon on the skillet was sizzling in a heap of grease. Maria hurried out of the hallway, running a hand through her hair, phone pressed to her ear. "I don't know where she is. She didn't come home last night, and I'm so worried about her, Zane. And this breakfast is burning and—" She looked at me with wide teary eyes and clicked off the phone without saying goodbye. She rushed over to me and pulled me into a hug. "Dani! Where have you been?"

"At a friend's place," I said, awkwardly patting her on the back.

She wiped a tear from her cheek, trying not to mess up her mascara. "I was so worried about you. I heard what happened. Are you okay?"

"I'm fine."

"You are?"

"Yes," I said. "I think so."

Honestly, I was still hurting, but I felt so much better. Last night, my world felt like it was shattering. I didn't think I'd ever spend another day without disgusting wet tears rolling down my cheeks and puffy red eyes.

"Are you okay?" I asked. "You and Javier—"

She frowned. "Javier is an asshole who likes to lead people on, apparently. What we had was nothing compared to you and Trevon."

I gazed over at the burning bacon. "Has Trevon come over?"

"No." She turned off the stove and placed the bacon on a glass plate. "But Eros did."

Eros came looking for me?

"You should go see him. He seemed worried."

"I will," I said. "Later."

All I wanted to do now was sink into my sheets, fall asleep, and dream of Eros. I knew that the Eros in my dreams wasn't the same as the Eros in real life, but dream-Eros had comforted me last night. And I hoped that it would happen again.

Chapter Eighteen

After work, I drove myself to Kasey's hour and knocked on her door. I hadn't seen her or Trevon or even Eros in a few days, and I wanted someone to talk to. There was no answer. I was about to turn away when a shirtless guy opened the door.

His thick brown hair stuck up in all different directions, and he furrowed his dark brows at me. "Hello?"

"Hi, is—uh—Kasey here?"

Who was this guy? He couldn't be her boyfriend; she just introduced me to Mycah a couple days ago. Maybe it was her brother?

He smiled, leaned against the doorframe, and crossed his arms. There was a small scar in the center of his chest. "You must be Dani. Kasey talks a lot about you."

"Oh, um... good. What's your name?" I asked awkwardly.

"I'm Aarav, Kasey's boyfriend."

My eyes widened. Oh, he was her lover. Had she broken up with Mycah already?

Kasey walked behind Aarav, tying a black silk robe around her small waist. "Dani! Come in." She slapped Aarav lightly on the chest. "Hun, go put on a shirt. You're making her uncomfortable."

Aarav jogged to the bedroom, and I walked into the apartment. Heart racing. Maybe Kasey was cheating on Mycah. She hadn't told me they broke up. I thought she would have. Would I be able to look at her the same if she was, especially after what Trevon did?

"What's on your mind?" She puckered her red hips and curled her arm around mine, dragging me to the kitchen.

"Aarav is your boyfriend?"

"Yep."

"When did you break up with Mycah?"

"I didn't. We're still dating."

My eyes widened. "Oh." Wow. Okay. Out of everyone, I didn't think Kasey would ever cheat. She was so angry when she found out that Trevon was cheating on me.

I gnawed on the inside of my cheek. Maybe I should tell Mycah. I would've wanted someone to tell me that Trevon was cheating. It would have saved me from blindly believing that he was still in love with me.

Kasey giggled at my expression, her nose scrunching. "Dani, I'm in a relationship with both of them."

Yeah, that was clear.

"No, no, no. I mean they both know about each other. We're in a polyamorous relationship."

Oh.

"Really?" I asked, curiously.

She sucked her bottom lip between his teeth, brows furrowed. "You don't think that's weird, do you?"

"No, of course not."

I had never met anyone in that kind of relationship before. And while it was different, it wasn't weird. It was intriguing more than anything. Two partners to care about. Two partners who cared about her.

She hopped onto a stool at the counter and tugged me along with her. Aarav walked into the kitchen, a loose white shirt hanging off his body. "Would you ladies like some dinner?"

"Just something light, hun."

Aarav threw some burgers on the skillet and leaned against the counter. "I heard what happened with Trevon," he said. Kasey narrowed her eyes at him. He raised his arms in defense. "What? I just wanted to tell her how well she took it. Not everyone can get over a breakup in a few days, and she's already going on another date."

My brows furrowed together. "I don't have a date."

Kasey grabbed my hand, a guilty look on her face. "Actually, I kind of told someone that you'd go on a date with them tonight."

"What? Why would you do that?"

"Because you need to get back out there, and I know the perfect guy for you!"

"Kase, I'm not ready to go out on a date. I just got off work, have had no time to freshen up, and I'm not meeting a guy for the first time looking like this." And I didn't want to go so soon after the breakup. It was still so fresh, and I was so scared that I would fall for another guy that would break my heart just like Trevon did.

Another pretty face. Another book of lies. Another problem.

A wicked grin stretched across her face. "Well, I'm going to help you get ready. You're going to look hot as Wrat—Hell. Hot as hell."

"No," I said. "I'm not going. I probably won't even like the guy." There was only one guy that I'd consider seeing, and he had disappeared from my life a few days ago.

"Oh, you'll like him. Don't you think so, Aarav?" she asked.

He flipped the burgers and nodded.

"See! Nothing to worry about!"

"There's everything to worry about! What if he turns out to be a pervert? What if I get awkward and do something stupid— like have a heart attack?"

Kasey burst out laughing. She rested her forehead on my shoulder, shaking from laughter. "Dani, calm down."

But I couldn't. I was still getting over Trevon and didn't know if I was ready to date again. I hadn't flirted with another guy in years, except Eros but he didn't count. And, anyway, I couldn't go. I needed time for myself, time to make sure that this was going to make me happy.

"He's not a pervert." She wiped tears from her cheeks, still giggling. "And, I assure you that he doesn't care if you do something stupid. I can't promise you about the heart attack thing because if you two..." She wiggled her brows at me. "... you know, have sex, then you might."

I wrinkled my nose. "There will be no sex on the first date, and..." I raised my brow at her. "How do you know the sex will be that good? Is he one of your ex-boyfriends?"

She made a face. "Oh, Heavens, no."

The burgers sizzled on the skillet, and Aarav chuckled as he shook spices over them.

"Well, who is he?"

"I can't tell you that. It's a blind date."

"Then, I'm not going."

"Please, just this once, and if you hate him, then I'll never make you go on another date again."

I sighed and pushed a hand through my hair. It was a win-win situation for me. If I had a good time, then I might go out with this guy again. I'd be able to get my mind off of Trevon *and* Eros for a few hours. If I had a bad time, then I didn't have to go out on another date again. I could pick up Project Hermit right where I left off, and I was completely fine with that.

"Just this once, and then never again," I said, giving her the hardest eyes I could.

Kasey pulled me off of the stool. "Deal, let's get you ready."

"Oh, come on," Aarav said. He turned around with two

burgers on a plate, each with a smiley face drawn in ketchup on it. "You're not going to eat?"

Kasey placed a kiss on his cheek, leaving a red stain. "I'll eat it later, hun." She winked back at him and dragged me to her room.

Crimson's Nouveau was buzzing with people when I arrived for the date. The last time I was here was with Trevon, Eros, and Maria. Trevon was chatting up Javier so much that night, I should've realized that something was going on.

Men, dressed in suits, were sitting around the bar with beers in their hands. Some watched me walk by in the plunging navy-blue sweater dress that Kasey had forced me to wear. I found an open seat and scooted onto the stool. "A white sangria please," I said to the petite woman behind the counter.

One man gazed at me from the opposite side of the bar, eyebrow cocked ever so slightly. His eyes were a dark brown—black, even, but maybe it was just this dim light. I gazed down at the table, cheeks flaming. God, I hope this wasn't the guy Kasey set me up with. I was hoping for someone less attractive, someone I'd be able to say goodbye to at the end of the night and not feel bad when I didn't call him back.

When I looked back up, he was suddenly next to me—standing a bit too close. He brushed his fingers against my slim wrist. "What's a pretty, little angel like you doing in a bar like this?" His voice was deep and melodic, and his eyes... I swear they really were black.

That same easy feeling I got with Eros filled me, and I found myself leaning closer to him. He smelt so good, like the beach, a salty aroma of shore and sea. Even his hair was a sandy brown.

"I'm... uh..." I moved my lips, failing to form words. "Waiting for someone."

He was so mesmerizing that I almost missed a woman storming straight toward us with a bitter look on her face. She grabbed the man's wrists and pulled it away from me. "I leave you alone for one minute and you're already flirting with—" She looked me up and down in pure disgust, green eyes glistening. "—someone like *her*."

She pointed a slender finger at me. "Don't you ever look at him like that again, or I'll take you right to Satan's kingdom and watch you burn." And, without another word, she dragged the handsome man right to one of the dark back doorways.

I sat there, staring at the almost glistening door that they disappeared behind and raised my brows. The bartender placed a drink on the bar in front of me, and I looked away. "White sangria."

Well, that guy was definitely not the man Kasey set me up with. I drew my finger across the wooden bar, thinking about how my first date I had after Trevon was already going to shit. A handsome, taken guy flirting with me. His girlfriend threatening to take me to Hell herself. The night was bound to get worse.

I was going to stumble over my words, spill my drink on myself. Maybe even spill it on whoever my lucky date was. He'd say it was alright, but it wouldn't really be alright. Then he'd tell me that he was going to wipe it off in the bathroom and would just never come back out.

I fiddled with my necklace as the heat crawled up my neck. Calm down, Dani. It's just a date.

Why did I agree to this again? Why was I even here?

"Kasey, this is the last time I'm doing this for you. I told you last time I didn't want to go on anymore dates," someone said.

My eyes widened, and I stared down at my sangria. He was here.

Someone leaned over the bar next to me, shirt sleeves rolled up with forearms. "Apple cider with Fireball," he said to the bartender. He sounded familiar, but I didn't dare look over. "I told you that I'm done dating dem—"

Oh, God. He didn't even want to be here.

"Kase, I have to go." He shut off his phone and paused for too long. "Dani."

My heart nearly stopped. Just by the way he said my name—so slow and sensual—I knew who he was. And when I lifted my gaze to meet Eros's dark one, I was more nervous than I was a few minutes ago.

He stared down at me, brows creased. "What're you doing here?"

I didn't know what to say, so I just stared at him, wide-eyed. "Um..." I took another sip of my drink. Kasey set me up with *Eros*. My hot next-door neighbor Eros.

But Eros didn't even want to be here. That's why he was probably avoiding me these past few days, didn't want any kind of relationship right now. I shook my head. This was a huge mistake. I shouldn't have come. "Just... drinking some sangria."

The bartender gave him his drink. He rested a forearm on the bar and gave me a light smile. "You only drink when you're nervous about something." He sat on the stool next to me, and all I could remember was sitting at Trevon's bar with him, our knees grazing against each other, him taking in every inch of me, his breath on my face. "Did Kasey send you here on a date?" he asked.

I pressed my lips together and stood. "Uhm, yes." I grabbed my coat from the back of the stool. "But I was just doing it to make her happy, not because I actually wanted to go out on a date." My palms were sweating; I could feel my heart pounding in my chest.

This was the only guy that I wanted to go on a date with but having him sit next to me with that sultry look in his eye terrified me. So, I continued to fumble with the zipper of my coat, hands shaking.

I didn't know why I was letting this rush right by me. This was what I wanted. He was what I wanted. He just didn't want to be here. It wasn't the right time. This—

He grabbed my wrist, stopping me. "You're not going to have a drink with me?"

When I gazed up at him in this dim light, I felt like I couldn't breathe. "Eros…" I said. There was no point in lying. "I heard your conversation with Kasey. We don't have to do this. I don't mind."

"I want to have a drink with you. I just didn't want to date another one of Kasey's friends."

"I am one of her friends."

"Yeah, but…" He gazed down at his drink, lips softening into a smile. "You're you." His fingers grazed against my palm and curled around it. "Now, unzip your coat, sit back down, and have a drink with me."

When I sat, he tapped his finger with his ring against his glass. "I'm sorry about Trevon."

"It's okay."

"No, it's not. You don't deserve to be treated like that."

"I know."

He gave me a boyish smile. His lips were set in a soft curve, and there was a lightness in his eyes. "Good." He grabbed my hand on top of the bar. "Zane and I kicked Javier out."

"You didn't need to do that. It was Trevon's decision to cheat on me, not Javier's."

Eros's jaw clenched for a split second, like he knew something that I didn't. "It doesn't matter. He's not coming back."

I didn't want to talk about Trevon or Javier. This wasn't the time or place to wallow in misery over him. I was on a date with Eros. A rush of heat warmed my body at the thought, and my cheeks tingled.

"Thinking about me in those horns again?" He placed his elbow on the bar top and leaned closer to me, finger curling around my hair.

My face flushed. "Oh, God." I couldn't believe that I told him about that. Liquor really did give me the courage to tell my deepest, darkest secrets. "I-no. I wasn't." But I was now.

Eros smirked and brushed his thumb against my cheek. "You know, I never got that kiss." His breath smelt like a mix of cinnamon and apple.

"What kiss?" I smiled, my gaze flickering to his lips. Of course, I remembered that night in the kitchen when he was so close, when our lips were hovering next to each other, when he told me that all he wanted was to kiss me. "I never said that I wanted you to kiss me."

He raised his brows and pulled his hand away, leaning back in his seat. "Dani, I really don't think you want to tease me."

I tilted my head, feeling confident in myself for the first time tonight. "I'm not trying to tease you."

His eyes darkened. "If you want to play this little game, then I'll play it with you. But just know that you're not going to win." He grasped my chin in his hand, thumb brushing against my lips. "You won't be able to resist me."

When he leaned back in his seat, he crossed his arms over his chest, making his biceps bulge. I already knew that I wouldn't be able to resist him, but it'd be fun to try. Maybe I'd even get him to break before I did.

The thought of it excited me, and this was the first thing that I was looking forward to in the past week.

A game with Eros.

Who'd succumb to the other first?

Chapter Nineteen

After our date, Eros stood next to me in the elevator, leaning against a shiny—almost shimmering—silver wall and stared at me. His eyes were dark, hooded, and oh-so-sultry. This was going to be harder than I thought. I didn't know how the hell I was going to win this, but I knew damn well that I was going to try. And, if I didn't, what would be the worst that could happen? We have sex and I do, in fact, have a heart attack.

I shifted from foot to foot, feeling the warmth pool between my legs, and hoped that the doors to our floor would finally open. "So, how do you know Kasey?"

"She's my sister."

My eyes widened. "Your sister?" Why didn't she tell me? God, I'd been telling her everything about Eros. And by everything, I meant everything. From the first day that I met him to the bar incident. She knew every single intimate detail.

"That would explain a lot," I said.

He chuckled, his shirt tightening against his chest when he did. "Are we that much alike?"

"Yes." They both seemed... turned on—all the time.

The doors to the elevator opened, and I stepped out as quickly as possible. It was getting hot in there. Eros walked me to my door, hand dangerously close to mine. "I had a good time," he said, posting a hand against the door frame, the muscles in his arm flexing.

My eyes fell upon his lips for a moment. "Me too."

Keep your cool, Dani. Remember: You will not break first.

He smirked, leaned down, and grazed his nose against mine. "We'll have to do it again sometime," he mumbled against me.

His lips were so close to mine. So damn close. His breath was sending me into a daze, the way it did the first time I met him. I didn't even know how he was doing it. All I knew was that I wanted more. More of him. More of this.

I'd been craving the feeling of his lips against mine since the day I met him. And I had the chance to close the distance. I stood on my toes, bringing my lips closer to his—waiting for him to close the distance. My fingers traveled up his torso.

"I thought you didn't want me to kiss you." He smirked against my neck.

Don't do it, Dani.

I stopped myself from falling into his little trance and mirrored his smirk. "I don't."

He trailed his nose down my jaw, and I suppressed the urge to shiver at his touch. He brushed his lips against my ear. "You do, Dani," he said. I dug my fingernails into his chest. "But if you want to break me, you're going to have to try harder than this."

Then, he stepped away from me with that stupid smirk on his face like he had total control of me. And, for a moment, I swore he did.

I took a deep breath and smoothed out my jacket. I needed to find a way to get under his skin. I needed to find his weakness. But, most importantly, I needed to step up my game. It was time to show him that he wasn't the only one who could play. And I knew just the way to get the upper hand.

———

As soon as Dr. U let me off of work, I hurried to Kasey's apartment—determined to get all of my answers. She hopped onto her couch and curled into Aarav's arm. "How was the date?"

I raised a brow and threw a pillow at her. "Why didn't you tell me that you were setting me up with Eros?"

"So..." She smirked. "Last night was good?"

"That's not the point!" The point was that, even after our date, my mind was buzzing with thoughts of him. I couldn't get him out of my head. Every time I closed my eyes, I felt his fingers brushing against my cheek, down my hips, up the insides of my thighs. And it was getting awfully tempting to just crumble beneath his fingers.

"Why didn't you at least tell me that he was your brother?"

She grinned. "That wasn't important at the time."

The only thing I thought was weird about this whole situation was that she knew Eros would like me dressed as a demon for Halloween. She surely didn't dress me as one for Trevon. But what was even more bizarre was that I literally dreamt of him as a demon with those horns.

Kasey grabbed my hand. "Tell us about it!"

"We just... talked," I said. I scratched the back of my head, wanting to tell her about the game we were playing. I needed her to help me get the upper hand, but knowing that she was his sister made it a bit awkward.

"That's it?" She sat on her knees. "Come on, you can tell me! I know that you're dying to. And, besides, Eros and I tell each other everything."

I took a deep breath. "We're playing this game."

Aarav raised an eyebrow. "A game?" he asked. So, I explained the game—from how it started to the lack of rules to how I nearly lost already. And, when I was done, Aarav shook his head. "Good luck with that."

"What do you mean?"

"I'd give it a couple days before you break," he said.

Kasey slapped his arm. "What he means is that Eros will be... well... he's good at this type of thing."

My brows furrowed, and my heart clenched. Was this something he did all the time? With other girls? Maybe he's played this game a million times before, and I was just someone else that he could play with.

"Does he do this often? With other people, I mean?"

Her eyes widened. "Oh, no. I can't even remember the last time he even liked someone enough to play with them."

"I can't remember the last time he *liked* anyone," Aarav said.

Kasey turned to him, brows furrowed together. "He liked one of my friends. They were dating for a couple of months last year."

Was that who Luci was? The woman who kept calling him when I was with him?

Aarav snorted. "He didn't like her. She was a pet to him."

"She was not."

"Yes, she was."

"No, she wa—"

"A pet?" I asked.

"Like... uh..." Kasey said, gazing at Aarav for support.

"Like a friend with benefits," Aarav said.

I nodded my head, not wanting to know any more about Eros's past lovers and what he did with them. I was still trying to figure out his true intentions with me. All I hoped was that I wasn't a pastime for him like everyone else had been.

Right now, it was mostly physical between us. But I wanted more, craved more, desired *more*.

Kasey crawled over to me and wrapped her arm around my shoulder. "I think you have what it takes to break him."

Aarav raised his brows. "You think."

Kasey stood and pulled me up with her. "Yes! Look at how sexy she is." She stood back, eyes raking down my body. I didn't miss the way Aarav's did too. "Eros won't be able to resist you, especially after I give you all the tricks." She lightly bumped her hip into mine. "I'll show you everything tomorrow. We have a date with Mycah tonight."

Chapter Twenty

I peeked out the elevator doors, glancing down the hallways to make sure Eros wasn't in the hall. Kasey told me to keep my distance from him until she showed me all the tricks. Twenty-four hours Eros-free should be easy, right?

When I knew that the coast was clear, I hurried to my apartment, gaze remaining on his door. If it opened and he walked out, I'd be done for. I needed to win this game against him. I wanted to get him back for frustrating me all the damn time. I wanted sweet and sinful revenge.

After fumbling with my key, I finally pushed my door opened and rushed in. I made it. No flirting with me tonight, Eros. Too late for—

Eros, Zane, and Maria were sitting at the kitchen table, each with a plate of pizza in front of them.

Damn it.

"Dani!" Maria said, grease on the corner of her lip. She placed the open pizza box on top of a closed one, making room for me. "Come eat with us."

Eros leaned back in his seat, tattooed arms resting on the table, biceps flexing. I gulped. His forest green sweater was clinging to his chest, his lips were set in a soft smirk, and his eyes were fixed on me.

"I can't," I said quickly, peeling my gaze away from Eros.

"Why not?" Eros said, brow cocked.

"Because…" I fiddled with the zipper on my coat. "I need to go take a nap."

Wow, Dani. That was the best you could come up with?

Eros pulled out a chair next to him. "Oh, come on. It's just a slice of pizza."

"Maybe later."

Maria stood and snatched my wrist, her blonde flyaways falling into her face. "Dani, I need to talk to you for a minute." She pulled me into the farthest corner of the living room. "You're not leaving."

"I'm not staying," I said.

"Eros is here. Why don't you just get to know him? It'd be good for you."

Little did she know that he was exactly who I was trying to avoid. "No, Maria." I gazed at Eros who was turned away from me.

"Don't you ever want to have some real fun, instead of just dreaming about all the things he could do to you?"

"No." But, oh, I did.

"Don't you want him to touch you like he does in your dreams?"

"No."

"Kiss you?"

"Maria."

"Fuck yo—" I slapped my hand over her mouth.

Sure, Eros knew that I dreamt of him. But I didn't need him knowing that I had dreams of him doing dirty things to me. That'd be beyond embarrassing.

Maria removed my hand. "Girl, he's right there—wanting to actually do those things to you. Stop hiding from him."

My eyes widened, and I glanced over at him again. He was

talking to Zane, but his gaze was on me. I could only imagine that he heard every single word of our conversation, knew that I, in fact, had dreamt of him many times.

"I'm going to take a nap, Maria."

She crossed her arms over her chest. "Then I'm going to tell him."

"Tell him what?"

"That you've been dreaming of him."

"He already knows."

She smirked. "Well, I guess you won't mind then." She turned on her heel.

Damn it, Maria. I snatched her arm and yanked her back. "You're an asshole," I whisper-yelled at her.

"I'm just trying to get you back on your feet by making sure you get a guy that you deserve." She grabbed my hand and brought me back to the table, pushing me down in the chair next to Eros. "Great news. Dani is going to eat with us!"

Eros grinned, a hint of triumph in his eyes. I pulled out the chair and sat, stewing. She was so annoying. All I wanted was to continue Project Hermit for one more night. Just one. But everyone had other plans for me.

As soon as Maria sat, she fell into an easy conversation with Zane. I grabbed a piece of pizza, picking the pepperoni off of it and stacking it up on the edge of the plate. I chewed on the inside of my lip, watching the shiny small bubbles of grease roll down the side of the slice as I picked it up.

"Why're you ignoring me?" Eros asked.

I took a big bite of cheese and wiped my fingers on a napkin. "I'm not."

"Afraid that you'll lose?"

I scoffed and put the pizza down. "No." Yes. 100% yes.

"I think you are."

"Well"—I narrowed my eyes at him—"I think you're going to be the one to break first."

He leaned one forearm against the back of his chair, the other on the table. A few strands of his dark hair fell into his face. "And what makes you think that?"

"You can't seem to stay away from me." I pressed my lips together and sat up tall. "You're everywhere I go. You flirt with me every chance you get."

"You're right," he said, eyeing me. I raised my brows, not expecting him to agree so blatantly with me. "I can't stay away from you." He leaned closer. "I think about you more than I should admit."

My breath nearly caught in my throat. Eros thought about me?

He placed a hand on my knee, fingers grazing against the insides of my thigh. "But I know that you think about me too."

I parted my lips. He's just trying to break me. "I-I do not."

He chuckled, his hand moving higher up my thigh. "You're a terrible liar, Dani."

Breathe, Dani. Breathe.

His hand slipped under my skirt.

Oh, my God.

Maria and Zane were too busy flirting with each other to notice what was happening on this side of the table, and I silently cursed them for that.

"You love this, don't you?" His fingers brushed across the hem of my underwear. I pressed my knees together. I did love it. I loved every single second of it. He leaned closer, breath fanning my ear. "Answer me and I'll give you what you want."

Don't let him break you. Don't let him win.

"It's... okay."

He raised his brows, and I took this as a chance to regain my composure. I sat up and brushed out my skirt. My core was throbbing, aching, begging me to take back what I said. He was more than okay. I wanted more of him.

But I also wanted to win.

"I can't love something I'm not impressed with," I said.

His eyes darkened, so dark that I thought that I was in another one of my dreams. "Fair enough." He sat back and removed his hand from my leg.

Fuck, I didn't want him to stop. I just wanted to tease him a little, just wanted to break him first.

His jaw was clenched tightly, his gaze fixed on me. Oh, God. Maybe "not impressed" was a bit too harsh.

I glanced at Zane and Maria, trying to ignore his intense stare. They were laughing with each other, then suddenly Maria looked at me. "We're going to the bar. Do you wanna come?"

"Uh—"

"No, we're going to stay here," Eros said, voice tight. My eyes widened, and I found myself nodding along with him.

Maria raised her brows at me. I, on the other hand, tried to give her my best don't-leave-me-I-don't-know-what-I-just-got-myself-into look, but she just brushed it off with a smile.

I wanted to follow them because I was stricken in absolute fear that Eros would break me, but I didn't move. Not even when Maria flipped her blonde hair over her shoulder and gazed back at me.

The door closed behind them, and I finally found the strength to stand up. "Well, uh... I'm going to go to my room."

Eros stood and stared down at me. "Unimpressed by my company now?" He stepped closer to me, and I stepped back, bumping into the table.

"No, Eros... that's not what I meant." My heart raced. "I-uh—"

He took another step toward me, and I placed my palms on the table behind me, leaning against it. He pressed his fingers against the front of my skirt, rubbing gently. "What did you mean, Dani?"

I parted my lips and wrapped my fingers under the edge of the table, trying to hold myself steady. "I—"

Oh, God. Oh, God. Oh, God.

"Hmm?" he asked.

The way he grasped my chin in his hand, stared down at me with irises so black that I could've sworn that this was a dream, pressed his fingers into me like he owned me. It was an enthralling kind of dominance. The kind that struck fear right into me.

"I meant that—"

He slipped his fingers under my skirt and dragged them lightly against my panties. I clenched and gripped his wrist, but he didn't stop. Instead, he began to rub them against my clit—harder and faster than before.

I squeezed my eyes shut, trying to keep my breath steady. "Eros," I breathed. He continued. I dug my nails into his wrist, knees shaking. "Okay. Okay."

"What was that?"

I didn't want him to stop. The pressure was building in my core, and I was so close. Yet he slowed his pace, and I groaned.

"Tell me what you meant," he said. He was staring intently at me, gaze traveling from my eyes to my lips to my legs and watching them shake. When he started to move his fingers faster again, the heat between my legs returned.

Oh, God.

I furrowed my brows. Desperately trying to hold myself together.

Wave after wave of heat hit my core, making it throb. I whimpered. I needed a release so damn badly, and I needed one from him.

Just as I was about to come, he slowed back down. I couldn't take this torture anymore. It was too damn much.

When I calmed down just enough, he started back up. Repeating this vicious cycle and driving my wild.

"What did you mean, Dani?"

"I—" I could feel him about to slow down again, but I wasn't going to let him stop. "I'm impressed. I'm impressed."

The corners of his lips curled into a smirk. I dropped my hand from his wrist—letting him take all of me—and rested my forehead against his tense shoulder. My pussy clenched. "Don't stop, Eros."

And, just like that, Eros pulled his hand away from me and stepped back, a smirk stretching across that damn stunning face of his.

I squeezed my eyes shut and leaned onto the table for support before my knees buckled. "I was so close," I whispered, trying to steady my breathing.

"I know."

"Why'd you stop?"

"If I let you cum, I wouldn't have broken you. I would've just given you what you wanted." He stepped between my legs, pressed his hardness into me, and lightly grasped my chin. "When I break you, you're going to be begging for me."

"You're frustrating." I pushed myself off of the table and walked into the hallway, leaving him in the kitchen.

"Maybe I'll let you finish after our date," he called after me.

I stopped and turned around. "Date?"

"Tomorrow night. Dinner."

"Fine," I said.

Tomorrow morning Kasey would show me the tricks, and tomorrow night I would finally get a chance to use them against the master himself.

Chapter Twenty-One

"I almost lost the game yesterday!" I said, hurrying into Kasey's apartment and clutching the strap of my purse. Even if I didn't technically lose, the feel of Eros's fingers on my body were still tormenting me in the most frustrating way possible. "I need your help now!"

She placed her hands on my shoulders and pursed her red lips. "Calm down, Dani. I'm sure it's not that bad."

My eyes widened. "Oh no, no, no. You have no idea. I haven't flirted like this for five years. I think I've lost it."

"Called it," Aarav said from the couch. Kasey shushed him and led me to the living room. Mycah was curled into the crook of Aarav's arm, resting her head on his shoulder. "What happened?"

After lying right down on her red living room rug and letting out a scream of frustration, I sat back up and furrowed my brows. "Okay, well. Things happened last night, and they might happen again tonight."

Mycah sat up, grinning from ear to ear. "Did you sleep with him?"

"No." Sex with Eros, though. That was something to think

about. If he could make me crazy with just his fingers, how would I react to all of him? I probably *would* have a heart attack.

"Did you kiss him?" Kasey asked.

"No."

"Did you beg for him?" Aarav said.

"Um, not really."

Kasey cocked a brow. "What's that supposed to mean?"

"Well..." I rubbed my palms together, trying to keep myself calm, but the thoughts of last night were plaguing my mind. Tingles spread to every part of my body just thinking about Eros.

Aarav inhaled deeply and looked over at Kasey with hazy eyes. Kasey smiled at him, then turned back to me. "Well, you didn't lose then." She pulled Aarav from the couch and whispered something to him, giving him a pointed look. Aarav smiled sheepishly at her.

Then Kasey clapped her hands together and ushered me to the couch to where Aarav had been sitting. "It's time to teach you the tricks."

"Step one: eye contact," she said. She gazed into Aarav's eyes. "Direct and confident."

Okay, not too bad. I could handle staring into those piercing green eyes. Maybe not confidently because his stare was intense, but I could at least try.

Aarav gazed into Kasey's eyes, a slight smirk on his face.

"Step two: tease him." Her hand moved down Aarav's torso, barely grazing against his abdomen. She moved closer, her lips hovering over his. She mumbled something inaudible, and Aarav took a deep breath. "A light touch of your fingers, your lips—anything will drive him crazy."

I gazed back and forth between Kasey and Aarav. The tension between them was undeniable, and I sat there watching with my heart racing—wondering what was coming next.

"And when he's into it," Kasey said, mumbling against Aarav's lips. "Pull away." When she pulled away from him, he looked like he was high—eyes foggy and distant, lips parted ever so slightly.

I gulped, unsure if I could pull something like that off so well.

"Step three: be direct." She grabbed Aarav's hand. "Knowing what you want and how you want it, not only will help Eros pleasure you but it'll turn him on. He wants to please you."

I gulped. I could barely speak coherently in front of him sometimes, and she wanted me to tell him exactly what I wanted. I was bound to screw that one up.

She turned to me, a smile on her face. "So, how are you feeling about it?"

"Okay..." I said. She cocked a brow, and I sighed. "It's so hard with him. He's so good at this all. It's like it comes naturally to him."

Aarav chuckled. "It does."

Kasey elbowed him and snatched his wrist. "We'll be right back." She pulled him toward the kitchen.

Mycah placed a hand on my shoulder. "I get your struggle. Sometimes Kasey and Aarav flirt and I just feel so lost, you know?" She pursed her plump brown lips. "But from what I've heard Kasey say, it seems like he's really into you. You could definitely break him."

"You think so?"

She nodded, her tight curls bouncing around her face. "Definitely! You just have to find something that he likes. Kasey and Aarav—they both love it when I run my hands through their hair. It drives them crazy."

I'd have to keep that in mind. Maybe Eros had a similar thing that drove him wild.

When Kasey and Aarav walked back over, Kasey was grinning ear to ear and Aarav looked a bit less... *high*. "We're going to join your date tonight. Mycah, do you want to come?"

"You are?" I asked, a sudden relief washing over me. "Why?"

"To help you out," she said.

"It can be intimidating when you're dating a—" Aarav started.

"A guy like Eros," Kasey finished.

And it definitely was.

Eros knocked on my front door, and I glanced in the mirror one last time to make sure everything was perfect. Kasey told me to wear something that accentuated my features, but not too much. *Give him something to stare at but leave something to his imagination.*

I wasn't sure if this black wrap-dress fit that description, but it was too late to turn back now. I hurried to the front door and took a deep breath. Remember the tricks, Dani.

Eye contact. Tease him. Be direct.

When I opened the door, Eros was leaning against the doorframe, dressed in a navy-blue suit jacket. One hand was stuffed into his pocket. The other was playing with the ring on his finger.

He whistled lowly as his eyes roamed down my body and lingered on my hips. They were intense, dark, and confident.

Keep eye contact, Dani.

"You look... amazing," he said.

I refused to succumb to the urge to look away and stepped toward him, fingers grazing against his abdomen. "Are you ready?"

He smiled, held out his hand, and led me to the car. "Always."

During the entire ride to downtown, I repeated the three steps to myself so I wouldn't forget. Eye contact, tease, be direct. Eye contact, tease, be direct. Reiterating it like a hymn.

Once we parked, Eros grabbed my hand and wrapped an arm around my waist to shield me from the biting cold. The walk to Crimson's Nouveau would be short, but I didn't mind the extra body heat.

His jacket hung, unzipped, off his shoulders. I slipped my hand under it, fingers grazing against his chest—making him tense—while we walked.

This was my chance.

I moved my fingers down his torso, slowly tracing his abs, and dipped it down his hip bone until I reached the waistband of his pants. They lingered for a few moments, then I pulled them away.

"What was that?" he asked.

I gulped, trying to think of something sexy to say. "I just wanted to know what I'll be enjoying after dinner."

His gaze flickered to my lips, eyes darkening. "You'll be enjoying more than just that if you keep that up."

"Oh, yeah?" I asked. "Like what?"

"There you are!" Kasey shouted. She, Mycah, and Aarav were huddled next to the entrance of the restaurant on the other side of the street. Mycah waved to me, a big smile on her face.

Eros hurried with me across the street, a look of ambush on his face. "What are you doing here?" he said.

Kasey looked at me. "You didn't tell him?"

My eyes widened. I didn't have any time to tell him anything. The whole day I was focusing on one thing, and that was preparing to seduce Eros.

Kasey pouted her red lips. "We're joining you."

"You can't just invite yourself to a date," Eros said.

"Dani invited us."

"Uh—yeah." Sure, I did.

Mycah bounced up and down on her toes. "Okay, can we take this arguing inside? It's freezing!"

Eros clenched his jaw, fingers curling tighter around my waist. We walked into Crimson's Nouveau, and my night of seducing Eros began.

Chapter Twenty-Two

"And here are your Fervor Crisps to-go." The waitress placed two brown bags with a black heart-shaped logo on our table. I gently closed my eyes, breathing in the sweet—almost sinful—aroma.

From across the table, Kasey smiled at me with her freshly painted lips. "Have you ever tried Fervor Crisps?" When I shook my head, she slapped Eros on the shoulder and furrowed her brows at him. "You haven't made her any?"

Eros clenched his jaw for the hundredth time tonight. "Kase-" he started. My fingers lightly dug into his thigh, hoping that it'd calm him down. It was as far as I had gotten with flirting with him. He and Kasey had been bickering the whole night.

Kasey took my hand. "Eros makes the most delicious ones that you'll ever taste."

I raised a brow at him. "You bake?" He gave Kasey one more hard look, then smiled sheepishly at me. My eyes widened. "That's so cute!"

All I could picture was Eros in a tiny white apron with flour in his hair, rolling dough—if that's even what they were made of.

His cheeks tinted pink, and he took my hand from Kasey. I

drew my finger over his ring, feeling it's the warmth from within it. Eros held my hand to his chest, and I gazed at him. The dim light from above accentuated his sharp features, yet they looked inviting somehow. "I'll make them for you sometime," he said softly.

Kasey pointed a manicured finger at him. "And take her to The Lounge. They have some good Fervor Crisps too."

"What's The Lounge?"

Eros narrowed his eyes at Kasey and pulled me out of the booth. "It's a bar," he said slowly. "We'll be going now." After snatching one bag, he tugged me through the crowded restaurant, leaving Kasey, Aarav, and Mycah all smirking wickedly at me from the table.

Alone time—finally.

As soon as we reached the car, Eros gazed at me from the driver's seat. The moon gleamed through the windshield, lightening his dark eyes. He placed a hand on the back of my black leather seat, leaned forward, and said, "I've been waiting all night for this," with that husky voice of his.

My heart thumped against my chest. Here goes nothing. I crossed one leg over the other, my black dress riding up my leg. I turned toward him and fingered the collar on his shirt. "For what?" I asked, holding eye contact.

He drew his nose against mine and smirked. "For this." He leaned in, snatched the warm bag of Fervor Crisps from my lap, tore it open, and pulled out two pastries, grinning like a maniac.

Heat crawled up my cheeks, and I shifted awkwardly in my seat when he handed me one. Great, Dani, you try to act sexy when all he wanted was some damn Fervor Crisps.

In one bite, Eros stuffed one into his mouth and groaned. "Mmmmm, it's so good."

Doughy like an éclair with a thin layer of sugar and powder

coating the outside, the Fervor Crisps were only about a finger length long, but they looked delicious.

He relaxed against the back of his seat in pure delight, eyes shutting softly. There was a bit of white powder on his bottom lip. I wanted to wipe it off, but he looked too peaceful. I just wanted to savor the moment.

Once he swallowed, he nudged my Fervor Crisp closer to me. "Go on," he said. "You'll like it."

When I bit into mine, my mouth filled with intense creamy goodness and thick rich dough. Sweet with a pinch of salt. I moaned softly. "How haven't I eaten one of these before?"

Eros grabbed another one and broke it apart, letting the milky cream ooze from the middle. "They're not popular around here."

"Oh. Are they popular where you used to live?"

He tensed and slowly chewed his food. "What do you mean?"

"Like your home?"

"You mean where my family is from?"

I furrowed my brows at him. "Uh... yeah..."

After gazing out of the foggy windshield for a few moments, he clenched and unclenched his jaw. "Yeah, they're popular in Hell."

"Eros, I'm being serious," I said. Was his family that bad that he didn't even want to tell me about them?

The dashboard lit up with the name *Luci*, and I clenched my jaw. Why did she keep calling? Nearly every time that I drove with him, I'd see her name. *Missed call from Luci. Incoming call from Luci. Voicemail from Luci.*

Breathe, Dani.

Eros and I weren't a thing yet. I couldn't get jealous over such a stupid girl's name. So, I gazed over at him and brushed a stray piece of hair from his face. "I won't judge you. You can tell me."

He looked so chillingly distant. Nothing like that boyish grin he had a few moments ago. "I told you that you don't know what you're getting yourself into with me. I need to be sure that you're going to be okay when you find out." He played with his ring, making it spin around his finger.

I wasn't sure what he was waiting for. I was ready for any family-related problem that he could throw at me. From growing up without parents to my experience listening to Dr. U's patients talk about all the family problems that they had, I had a decent grasp on how to handle wild family drama.

"Okay," I said quietly. "I can wait for whenever you're ready."

The dashboard lit up again with Luci's name, and Eros forwarded the call to voicemail and started the car.

After the dreadfully silent ride home, Eros walked me to my door. He placed his hand on the doorframe and grabbed my hand with the other. "Sorry for being so pissed tonight. Kasey sometimes just..." He took a deep breath. "Gets on my nerves."

"It's okay."

"I wanted it to just be the two of us." His voice was soft, vulnerable almost, and that boyish smile was back. "I hope you had a good time even though it didn't turn out how I wanted."

I handed him the bag of pastries and smiled. "I did."

He opened it and pulled out the last one. "Share it with me." He pushed it in my direction, but I pushed it back.

"You first."

His green eyes sparkled, and he bit into it. White cream oozed out of the center, nearly dripping onto the ground, but he caught it on his finger before it ruined the carpet.

I gazed up at him, smirking. Think sexy, Dani.

I grasped his wrist and pulled his hand to me. My lips wrapped around the tip of his finger, and I slowly sucked off all the sweet creamy goodness. He swallowed the rest of his food, eyes widening. With a light pop, I pulled his finger out of my mouth and licked my lips.

"Fuck," he said under his breath, lips parted just slightly. His eyes were a hazy green.

My fingers trailed down his chest, just like I had seen Kasey do with Aarav, and I wrapped them around his belt loops and pulled him closer to me. I brushed my lips against his ear. "I bet yours tastes better."

His breath hitched. And, for a moment, I celebrated the slight advantage I had over him.

He regained his composure and pushed me against the door. "I bet you'd love to find out," he said. When he grinded his hardness into my hip, I let out a small moan, my eyes fluttering closed.

Calm, Dani, calm.

"I love the sounds you make," he murmured against my ear. Heat rushed to my core.

Stop it, you're stronger than this.

My fingers relaxed under his belt loops, totally mesmerized by his scent. I moved them to the front side of his pants and grasped his hardness through them. He was so big.

"It's all yours, Dani. All you have to do is beg."

My hand moved down his length, and I felt him tense under my touch. He was confident, but I had an effect on him. I continued, knowing it was driving him crazy.

"I'm not going to beg for you," I said against his ear. "I don't need you to please me."

He tensed, harder this time, then pressed his fingers against the front of my dress, wasting rubbing them in small circles. He slipped them under my dress and into my underwear, playing with my folds. "Do you think anyone else could please you the way I can?"

I pressed my knees together, smirking, and pushed him away. "No, and I don't plan on trying to find anyone else." His eyes were dark, and after weeks of waiting I just wanted him to thrust me against the wall and fuck me senseless.

But I wasn't going to beg.

"I'm perfectly capable of pleasuring myself."

His eyes darkened, and he smirked. "You're going to touch yourself?"

I paused for the briefest moment, trying to gather my thoughts. He was always so blunt. I opened my door, gave him a once over, and smirked. "I'd ask you to come in, but I'm going to be busy for the rest of the night."

Chapter Twenty-Three

"Oh, my gosh!" Kasey screamed over the phone. "I bet he was drooling when you shut the door on him. He was probably thinking about you all night."

I shrugged on my coat, giggling. "I don't know about that, Kasey," I said. But I was definitely thinking about him lying in bed with me, hand around my throat, fingers trailing down the center of my chest, touching me in places that I had only ever dreamt.

After I shut the door on Eros last night, I laid on my bed—candle crackling softly in the corner, fingers gliding into my underwear—and thought about the night. Oddly enough, most of my thoughts weren't occupied with the incident in the hallway, but by the one in the car. When Eros said he didn't want to tell me about his past until *I* was ready.

I rested my forehead against the cold living room window and sighed. *"I told you that you don't know what you're getting into with me."* He had said it like he had told me those exact words before, but he hadn't. I only remember him saying that in my dream, and that wasn't even really him.

Maybe I was just remembering wrong, because the more

dreams I had of Eros, the more they seemed real. Dream-Eros and Real-Eros were starting to blur.

"Come over later! You need to give Mycah and I all the gossip," Kasey said.

"I'll be over after work." I smiled and hung up the phone.

Outside the window, the city was covered in a thin layer of snow that I would have to trudge through on my way to Dr. U's office. But, honestly, I'd rather just be curled up next to Eros, watching the snow fall from the warmth of my apartment today.

I wrapped a scarf around my neck and opened the front door. But when I heard Javier and Eros arguing out in the hall, I shut it softly—still inside my apartment. For a moment, I debated whether or not to listen. I could almost hear Mom scolding me for eavesdropping on their conversation, but I was already going to Hell. So, I pressed my ear to the door, anyway.

"Your father says to bring her to our family dinner," Javier said.

"No," Eros said, voice stern. I had never heard him so irritated before.

"He says that you don't have a choice if you want your banishment to be lifted." Javier's voice rose with each word.

"I don't care what he says. I'm not getting her involved in this."

"They know about her. She's already involved, Eros."

There was a loud bang against the hallway wall, and I jumped back. I hoped that Javier wasn't getting physical with Eros.

"Did you tell them about her?" Eros shouted. My eyes widened. Oh, God, he was angry.

Another loud bang. "She can be your key back to the fucking family!" Javier said. I frowned at the door. What was going on? What kind of family were they from? And how was I the key back to it?

Eros paused. "No."

Javier growled. "Why are you so stubborn? I fucked her boyfriend, so you could finally take her, but you refuse."

"I never asked you to do that," Eros said, distaste so clear in his voice. "You didn't even do that for me. You did it to hurt her, you wrathful bastard."

"But you're glad I did, aren't you?"

I waited for Eros to answer—my heart hammering against my chest—but was met with silence. After a long pause, he finally said, "Why do you want me back so bad? Mother and father don't."

His words sounded so empty, like this had been going on for quite some time now and he was numb to the pain. I grazed my fingers against Mom's pendant. I couldn't imagine what Eros was going through. His parents were still alive and well, yet he didn't want to see them. My mom was dead, but I'd trek through Hell to see her one last time.

For the next week, I didn't see Eros once—not even in my dreams. Maria mentioned that he came over a few times, but I was always *conveniently* not home. I hoped that he wasn't ignoring me.

Maria had been busy with Zane, and Kasey was distracted by Aarav and Mycah. I tried to stay occupied by volunteering at the food pantry downtown during my lunch break and at the ice-skating rink after work—desperate to take my mind off of the loneliness that came during this time of the year. But, each night, I sat in my room alone wondering how I was going to get through the holidays with no one.

Since Dr. U was the only person who I saw consistently this past week, I had asked her to go with me to the Harmony Grove Nursing Home to deliver holiday joy to the residents—like Mom and I used to every winter. Trevon and I had planned to go together again this December but those plans obviously fell through.

When we arrived, a nurse led us to a recreation room where people in wheelchairs were watching TV. While the room was a bare white color, there seemed to be an almost divine aura in the air. Dr. U handed me a candy cane and nodded to an elderly man sitting near the window in a maroon recliner, grinning at me like Mom would.

As I approached the man, he smiled. "What an angel," he said in a soft, fragile voice. He reached for my hand with his wrinkled one and squeezed.

I knelt by his side, placing a hand on his. "What's your name?"

There was a twinkle in his eye. "All dressed in white and that halo on top of your head," he said. My smile tightened, and I gazed down at my ugly Christmas sweater and black leggings. Definitely not dressed in white and definitely hadn't been acting as an angel would lately. He cupped my face and tilted his head. "Beth! Beth!" he said.

A nurse appeared at our side.

He raised a shaky hand and pointed to me. "He sent me an angel!"

She placed a hand on my shoulder and whispered into my ear. "This is Mr. Bennett. He's been hallucinating lately. Don't worry about it." Then she beamed at him. "Her name is Dani!" she said loud enough for him to hear. "She has come to wish you happy holidays!"

Mr. Bennett gave me a crooked grin and rested his head against the back of his recliner. "I can finally have a peaceful sleep." He paused for a few moments, squeezed my hand tighter, and turned back to me. "Thank you."

I nodded my head. "You're welcome..."

He closed his eyes, hand slowly falling from mine.

"Mr. Bennett, why don't we get you to your room?" Beth said.

He didn't respond.

She nudged his arm gently. "Mr. Bennett?" When he didn't respond again, her eyes widened. "Oh, my goodness." She retrieved another nurse from the next room, and together they shuffled out all the other residents.

I just stood there, staring down at Mr. Bennet with wide eyes. Did—did he just die in front of me?

Dr. U placed a hand on my shoulder. "Dani?"

I nudged his arm, but he didn't move.

Holy Hell.

He was really dead.

Beth ushered us out of the room, telling me that he was an elderly man and that I had nothing to worry about. It was bound to happen sooner or later.

Dr. U brought the car around front—deciding it would be best to leave early and come back next week. I scooted in and stared at the windshield with teary eyes. I didn't know what to think. Everything was going from bad to worse. Trevon cheated on me. Eros was ignoring me. Now, someone just died right in front of me. What would happen next?

Everyone was leaving me.

When she pulled up to my apartment building, I still sat there. "Dani," she said. "Are you okay?"

My lips trembled. "No, I—I..." A tear slid down my cheek. "My boyfriend cheated on me, my friend is ignoring me, a man just died in front of me, and Mom is dead." I wrapped my arms around myself. "No, I am not okay."

It was probably just the stress of the holidays or the pure shock that I was in, but it seemed like everything hit me at once. The pain of Trevon's heartbreak. The distance Eros was suddenly keeping. And the hurt in my heart since Mom's murder.

Dr. U was right. I should've talked about this with someone.

She curled an arm around me, pulled me closer to her, and just held me like Mom used to when I was younger. I remembered her fingers gently stroking my hair after story time each night. I'd beg her to tell me every tale she had about all of the monsters in this world. Four-year-old me was obsessed with them at the time. I'd sit in her lap and listen to the passion in her voice. I'd tuck my face into her side and let my tears soak her shirt, overwhelmed with a sense of sadness when she always ended with: "*And there may be monsters who haunt your dreams or lie under your bed, but the scariest monsters are the ones that hide behind the faces of good people.*"

And, right then, I didn't know who in my life was one of the good monsters or the bad. Everything was getting harder and weirder and too confusing to understand anymore. I didn't even know where I stood. Was I the heavenly angel like the old man had said or the hellish sinner that Eros had made me? Maybe I was both.

Chapter Twenty-Four

When I walked into the apartment, Maria was standing in the kitchen—dripping wet—holding a bath towel around herself. "There you are." She placed her phone down on the counter.

I peeled off my coat, tossed it over the side of one of the kitchen chairs, and gave her my strongest smile. "Here I am."

On the counter, there was a brown paper bag with my name written across the side of it. She looked down at it and smiled. "Looks like you whipped Eros into shape real quick. He's baking for you and everything."

"Baking for me?" I asked, grabbing the bag. Inside, there were six freshly baked Fervor Crisps. "Eros brought these over?"

"A few hours ago, said he'd be back later to see if you got them." She winked and walked toward the bathroom. "So, you better be ready for when he does!"

I pulled one out of the bag, sunk my teeth into it, and sighed. My heart felt fuzzy just thinking about him making these for me. It was definitely needed after watching someone die right in front of me.

Someone knocked on the door, and I immediately jumped up.

Eros. He was here already, and I looked like I walked straight out of Hell with my puffy eyes and smudged mascara. I ran my fingers through my hair, hoping that I would look somewhat presentable, and hurried to the door.

I couldn't wait to finally see that damn sexy smirk after a week of being ignored; I couldn't wait to tell him about today either, to get it off my chest.

When I pulled the door open, my eyes widened. Not Eros. Definitely not Eros.

Trevon was standing awkwardly in the hallway, his hands stuffed into his pockets. "Dani," he said. "Can we talk?"

All I wanted was to slam the door in his face and give him what he deserved, but I also wanted to know why he was here. Why now? Why more than two weeks after cheating show up to his ex-girlfriend's front door?

"We're not getting back together," I said, grinding my teeth together.

He took off the baseball cap that I bought him, and I noticed the dark circles under his eyes. "I know."

For a good minute, I just stared at him. Trying to figure out why he was here. Wondering if I should really let him in or just let him wallow in his own misery.

"Zane, is that you?" Maria asked, walking out of the bathroom with a mascara stick in her hand. When she saw Trevon, she dropped it, eyes widening. "What are you doing here?"

"I'm just here to talk," he said, fiddling with the hat.

Maria picked up the mascara and pointed at me. "Don't let him fool you into thinking he wants to get back together. He's still screwing Javier."

There was no way in hell that I'd ever go back to Trevon.

"Maria, I'm sorry," Trevon said. When she walked back into the bathroom and slammed the door, he sighed. "I really screwed up, didn't I?"

I stood there, nostrils flaring. "Yeah, you did."

He sat on a stool and rested his elbows on the counter, then pushed his head into his hands and took a deep and shaky breath. For some stupid reason, I had the urge to comfort him, but I kept my distance. He wouldn't fool me again.

"Dani, I'm sorry. I never meant to hurt you." His gaze remained on the counter. I walked around it, so I was standing across from him. "It never should've happened. I should've broken up with you when it first started happening."

I pressed my lips together. So, it had happened more than once. "Trevon, if you're going to apologize to me, look at me when you do. At least give me that much respect."

He picked up his head, and I noticed that his eyes were darker than they usually were.

"Are—are you okay?" I asked.

"I need to tell you something. I need to let you know all of it. I need to get it off my *fucking* chest."

"Okay," I said quietly.

"It started when we went out with Eros, Javier, and Zane for dinner. I didn't have to work that night. I was going to meet him at my place," he said. Tears pricked at the corners of my eyes. It had been going on since they met?

"I don't know why I did it. I just couldn't help myself. In my heart, it felt wrong—so wrong. But I couldn't resist him." His chin trembled. "I never had that type of experience before—man on man—and I didn't even think I was going to like it."

"But you did," I said.

"Yes, with him."

"Have you tried with others?"

He looked away from me. "After you found out... but... I didn't enjoy it as much. Maybe not at all."

I paused. "How many times did you cheat on me?"

"A few."

My heart ached. Did that mean three, ten, twenty times? I didn't know. And that was just with Javier. Who knew if there were other women. A tear slid down my cheek, but I wiped it away with the back of my hand. "Who else?"

Trevon lifted his gaze and looked me right in the eye. "No one."

I stared at him. "No one?"

"Samantha had flirted with me and tried to get with me, but I would never do anything with her." He said it with so much honesty that I actually believed him.

He hadn't been this open with me since the weeks before we met my new next-door neighbors.

"If you didn't do anything, why'd you fire her?"

"Eros told me that he thought she spiked your drink during the party, so I reviewed our surveillance cameras and found that she did."

What a damn bitch. That's the only word I had for her. She deserved to be fired. She deserved to be put in jail for the rest of her life. She deserved to rot in Hell. I couldn't believe that she did it, and her end goal was to get with Trevon—a guy who didn't even want her.

So many emotions were rushing through me. I was angry at Trevon and at Samantha and at Javier, but all I could think about was that Eros believed me that night. He had cared for me when I was puking up my stomach on the side of the road and in the pouring rain.

Trevon fiddled with his fingers. His nails had grown longer since we had split. And as much as I hated feeling like this, I really hoped he was taking care of himself.

"So, are you with Javier now?" I asked.

He cleared his throat. "Kinda."

"Kinda?"

"I haven't been feeling like myself for the past few weeks."

"What does that have to do with anything?"

"Nothing. It has nothing to do with it." He snatched his hat and stood. "I should go."

I walked him to the door. "Before you go, I have a question," I said. He gazed down at me. There was so much pain on his face, so much heartbreak. "Have you always been curious about other guys?"

"No."

I frowned. It didn't make sense. If he was curious about guys, how could he want to have sex with him the first night that they met?

"But you were curious when you met Javier? How'd you know you wanted to try something with him?" I asked.

Trevon paused and scratched the back of his head. "It's... stupid."

"I don't care."

He lowered his voice. "I had a dream about him a few nights before I actually met him."

My heart raced. "What kind of dream?"

"I really don't think you want to know," Trevon said, grasping the door handle.

I shook my head. "No, I need to know, Trevon, please." Not only for my own sanity, but for another reason entirely.

"We were... uh... hooking up."

I sucked in a breath. It was like the ones I had of Eros and the ones Maria had of Zane and Javier. Why were the guys next door suddenly in everyone's dreams?

"Did you just have one dream?" I asked.

He put his baseball cap on and stepped out. "No," he said. Okay, this was getting weirder by the moment. "Thanks for listening to me. I know you didn't have any reason to. I just needed someone to talk to." He nodded. "And good luck with Eros."

I smiled softly. "Thanks."

He turned and walked down the hallway; shoulders rolled forward—looking defeated.

"Trevon!" I called after him. "Take care of yourself."

Chapter Twenty-Five

I sighed and flopped down onto my bed. This was very, very weird.

Ever since Eros, Javier, and Zane moved in, we were all dreaming of them. And these weren't normal dreams. These were intense and intimate dreams that left us wanting more.

But why? Why were we all suddenly thinking of the guys next door?

I rested my head on my pillow, opened an internet browser on my phone, and typed: *What does it mean when you dream about people?*

Hundreds of articles from *Psychology Today*, *Cosmopolitan*, and *Bustle* popped up. I recognized some of them from my Psych 101 class in college when Maria and I had to do a research project on Carl Jung. I doubted that they'd be factual, but I still wanted to know what these dreams meant—even if it was all just a far-fetched theory from Freud or from some psychic who read palms for a living.

Someone knocked on the front door.

I groaned and tossed my phone onto the bed. Who was

knocking this late at night? It was nearly 1am. Maria was out with Zane, and Trevon was long-gone by now.

When they knocked again, I pushed myself off of the bed and walked to the front door. I peeked through the peephole, eyes widening. "Eros," I said, pulling open the door. "What're you doing here?"

He leaned against the doorframe, eyes hazy. "Come out with me."

"Now?" I asked. Don't get me wrong, I wanted to go wherever he wanted to take me, but I wasn't prepared. Mentally or physically. "Nothing's open."

His lips curled into a smile, and he took my hand. "I know a place."

Eros drove us downtown, near Crimson's Nouveau, and parked on the side of the road. He curled an arm around my waist, pulling me into his chest. Instead of walking toward the entrance of the restaurant, he led us down a dimly lit alleyway toward the rear of the building.

Snow was falling around us, flakes sticking to Eros's thick hair. A few men were standing outside in the alley, passing pills to each other. I grabbed onto Eros's bicep. "Where are we going?" I whispered to him, eying the burly men who were now staring directly at us.

He directed me to a grey metal door and banged two times on it with the side of his fist. After a few moments, a man—who looked exactly like those in the alley—opened the door. I squeezed his bicep harder. Where were we?

The man nodded to Eros, and Eros stepped through the door, tugging me in. We walked down a deserted hallway, then down a set of dusty stairs. A single light flickered above us. The low thump of music played through the walls, and I tried to calm my racing thoughts. When we reached the bottom of the stairs, Eros pushed open another door.

I stepped into the room, nearly bumping into a waiter who was dressed in a maroon suit. Eros grasped my hips and pulled me back. "Be careful," he murmured into my ear.

There was a bar in the center of the room, filled with people flirting with each other. Twelve beige cushioned booths sat around the perimeter of the room. Everything was lit with dim red lights which hung off of the brick walls.

Eros guided me through the crowd of people to a booth in the back. All the women were dressed in skimpy little dresses or short skirts, and I felt out of place in my leggings and sweater.

"What is this place?" I asked, sitting down.

"This is The Lounge."

"Why are we here?" I grabbed a menu from the middle of the table and tilted it toward the candle flickering between us.

"Because I wanted to see you."

"How can you see anything in this place?"

He chuckled, the light from the candle illuminating his face. "We can go if you'd like."

"No!" I said, quicker than I meant. I took a deep breath. "I mean, no, we can stay." His lips stretched into a genuine smile, and my heart tightened. I missed that. "So, what is this place?"

I gazed around the room. The Lounge definitely wasn't a regular bar. By the way people were straddling each other and kissing, shooting down alcohol and touching, it looked more like a sex club to me.

A woman at the bar took a sip of red drink, grabbed her friend, and kissed her. Her hands roamed down the woman's body and dipped between her legs.

Jesus.

Eros followed my stare and chuckled again. "It's a place to let loose."

"Why don't you just go to a regular bar? What's so special about this one?"

He pointed to the drink in the woman's hand. "Regular bars don't have those."

I gazed around the room, noticing that almost everyone here had a similar drink. "What are they?"

"They're called Passion Delights."

Well, I knew what I wasn't getting. I was going to stick to my water for tonight. If I had one of those *things*, I would break and beg Eros to do naughty, naughty things to me before the end of the night.

I placed down the menu and leaned forward. "So... why've you been ignoring me?"

Eros's stare remained on me—so dark, intense, and distant. "I've been dealing with family."

"But you've been ignoring me," I said. I understood that he had his problems—we all did—but he had been over the apartment with Maria and Zane. He had time to see them.

He grabbed my hands. "I have."

"Why?"

A waiter walked up to our table and cleared his throat. "Evening Eros." The man was tall, dark, and devilishly sexy. His blonde hair rested on the sides of his face and his piercing blue eyes stared right at me.

Eros swore under his breath and shook his head.

"Haven't seen you around in a while," the waiter said. "Last time you were here was with Luci, wasn't it?"

There it was again. Her stupid name, ruining our time together. *Luci, Luci, Luci.*

Eros clenched his jaw. "We would like to order."

"I see that you've brought a friend," he said.

"We'll take a basket of Fervor Crisps, a Passion Delight, and..." Eros looked at me. "What would you like?"

I pulled my hands away from Eros and rubbed my neck. "Water is fine."

The waiter was staring down at me. "Is she yours?" he asked Eros, not peeling away his eyes away from me.

Eros tensed and sat up taller. "Our order."

The waiter bowed his head slightly. "My apologies."

When he walked toward the bar, Eros turned back to me and grabbed my hands again. "Ignore him."

I nodded my head and drew my finger against this ring. "Why're you ignoring me?" I asked. I wanted to know if it was because of Luci, but I couldn't get myself to say her name. I didn't want to seem like I was jealous—we weren't even exclusive yet.

Hell, I didn't know what we were.

"My family is bothersome," Eros said. A stray piece of hair fell into his face as the faint scent of cinnamon drifted through the air.

I knew that. From Javier, from Kasey, from Eros himself. But I couldn't stop thinking about the conversation that I overheard last week. I wanted answers. "What am I involved in?"

"What're you talking about?"

I took a deep breath. "I overheard your conversation with Javier last week," I said. He pulled his hands away and groaned, leaning back in his seat. "You told me that you'll tell me things later and I want to give you space to tell me when you're ready, but..." My heart clenched. "But I don't want to be lied to or kept in the dark. I don't want to be—doing whatever we're doing— with someone who's keeping secrets from me. I—I don't think I could handle that after what Trevon did."

That was the truth. And, as much as I hated to admit it, my conversation with Trevon made me question everything. He was cheating on me for weeks, and I had no idea. What if Eros was the same way? What if he had secrets that would hurt me too?

He paused and pressed his lips together, then took my hands again. "My family lives very different lives than I do. They don't understand my interests and they don't understand why I enjoy your company." He sighed softly. "I don't have a good relationship with them. They've made me..." He gulped. "They've made me feel a certain way about myself, and I don't want to reopen those memories right now." He rubbed soothing circles against my palms. "I'm—I'm not a bad person." His voice was quiet toward the end.

By the way he said those last few words—so slow, so confused—I didn't think he believed what he was telling me.

I gently squeezed his hands. "I know you're a good person... I just don't want to get hurt."

"I won't let anyone hurt you," he said.

The waiter reappeared with a basket of Fervor Crisps and one Passion delight—ruining the moment. "Anything else I can get you?"

"No," Eros said.

"What about you, dear?"

"No," Eros said again.

Before he returned to the bar, he brushed his fingers against my forearm. "By the way, I didn't catch your name."

I shuffled in my seat. "It's, uh—"

"Leave us," Eros said, jaw clenched.

The waiter hesitated but bowed his head again. "Again, my apologies." He gazed at me. "Sweet dreams, my dear." I wrinkled my nose at his departing figure. Talk about creepy.

When I looked back at Eros, he had nearly drunk half his Passion Delight already. His eyes were closed, shoulders relaxed, lips parted ever so slightly.

I sipped on my water. "What does your drink taste like?"

He reopened his dark, hazy eyes. "Like sex."

"I didn't know a drink could taste that good," I said, trying to lighten the mood. I grabbed a Fervor Crisp from the basket and bit into it, moaning softly. A drunken smirk stretched across Eros's face, and he snatched one too. "These are good," I said to him. "But yours are so much better."

. . .

By the end of the night, Eros was resting back against the booth—completely relaxed. He had finished two Passion Delights, and together we devoured the Fervor Crisps. We took a to-go bag and headed back home.

Every time I glanced over at Eros from the passenger seat, he looked tense. His jaw was clenched, his hand was tight around the steering wheel. It was a stark contrast to when we were at the bar. I placed my hand on top of his, hoping that it would relax him, but he immediately pulled it away. "Don't do that, Dani."

"Are you okay?"

He pressed his lips together and parked in the lot to our apartment building. The veins in his arms were visibly pulsing. "I shouldn't have had that drink."

"Are you feeling sick?" I asked, exiting the car and walking with him to the building.

"No." He stayed a few feet away from me and walked onto the elevator.

What was happening? He was avoiding me like the damn plague.

I stayed quiet and watched the muscles flex through his shirt. My eyes wandered down his body.

"That's not the problem," he said finally.

When the elevator doors opened, we stepped out of the elevator. He walked in front of me, shutting me out. Oh, here we go again. He told me something personal, then acted all distant.

We reached my apartment first. He didn't say goodnight to me, just grabbed his keys from his pocket and continued quickly to his door. I followed him. "What's wrong with you, Eros?"

He clenched his jaw. "It's nothing."

"Don't give me that! I can't figure you out." I pressed my hands against my temples. "I'm tired of you playing with my feelings."

"I'm not playing with your feelings." His voice was stiff.

"You ignore me, you take me out, and when we get home, you're suddenly distant again. What the hell is your problem?"

He turned toward me—eyes dark, wide, and angry. "You!"

I sucked in a breath full of cinnamon. Heart racing.

"You're my problem, Dani."

I pressed my lips together, nostrils flaring. "How the hell am I your problem?"

His eyes flickered to my lips, then he pushed me against the door, snatched my chin, and pressed his fingers hard into my skin. "Everything about you drives me fucking crazy."

My eyes widened. "Well, if that's how you feel then leave me alone." I firmly pushed my palms into his chest.

He shuffled back a few steps but immediately pressed me against the door again. Forehead resting on my own. Lips dangerously close to mine. His fingers brushed against my hips. "I can't get enough of you." His irises were completely black now. He paused, and his eyes flickered to my lips.

Oh, God. He was going to do it. He was going to kiss me.

"Fuck it," he said, pressing his lips to mine in a moment full of passion and lust and want and need.

Chapter Twenty-Six

One minute he was pushing me against the wall pressing his lips to mine, the next he was throwing me down onto his bed and tugging off his shirt.

His hands were all over my body. His hardness was pressing against the front of my jeans. I wrapped my legs around his waist, needing him closer. I had waited too long for this.

I ran my fingers all the way down his sculpted back, brushing them against two scars. He grabbed my wrists harshly and pinned them above me, then fingered the bottom of my shirt and pulled it over my head.

For almost a month, I had dreams of his fingers on my skin, his lips on my chest, his cock between my legs. But I never imagined that it would feel this good.

I ran my hands through his hair, making him groan. A wave of cinnamon engulfed us, and I inhaled the scent—getting drunk off of it.

With one hand, he groped my breast while the other was between my legs, pushing down my leggings. He placed hot, wet kisses down the center of my chest until he reached my bra line. His fingers curled around the hem of the cup, and he pulled it down, sucking my nipple into his mouth and grazing his teeth against it.

I gripped onto the bed sheets, brows knotting together. "Eros..."

He slipped his other hand into my panties and plunged them inside of me, thrusting them in and out. I dug my nails into his back, the pressure in my core rising with each thrust.

"Kiss me," I said, breathlessly. He wrapped a hand around the back of my neck and pulled me toward him, pressing his lips onto mine.

My head felt light, and all I could focus on was him and his fingers between my legs and his lips on my own, the scent of cinnamon, the sharpness of his nails digging into my skin, the pure energy that passed from my lips to his.

"Please... Eros... don't stop..." I asked as he thrusted his fingers quicker into me. The pressure was building up in my core, and when he bit down on my lip, I arched my back, moaned into his mouth, and came.

Wave after wave of pleasure rolled through my body. My mind felt fuzzy. My fingers were tingling. I wanted more.

He placed light kisses down my neck, down my chest, down my abdomen until he reached the waistband of my pants.

"What—what are you doing?" I asked in a daze.

He pulled down my pants, pressed his lips to my clit, and inhaled deeply. His eyes fluttered closed in ecstasy. "You taste so fucking good."

My legs trembled, but he wrapped his arms around them and forced them still. I gazed down at him, curling my fingers into his hair—right where he liked it. His irises darkened even more. They looked as if they were growing and consuming the whites of his eyes.

"Fuck," he said under his breath. He pulled his lips a few inches away from my pussy and dropped his head, so I couldn't see his face. After taking a deep yet shaky breath, his jaw twitched. "Fuck. Fuck. Fuck." He abruptly sat up and turned away from me. "Not now," he said to himself. "Not fucking now."

I sat up, brows knotted together. "Is everything okay?" I asked, gazing at the scars on his back. They looked just like the ones from my dream.

"You have to go," he said. "Now, Dani."

My eyes widened. "No, Eros. I'm not leaving you like this. What's wrong?" I trailed my fingers down his back. Was that drink affecting him? Was he going to get sick?

After what he went through with me at the Halloween party, I wasn't about to let him get sick right here, right now when I could help him. "Eros..."

He jumped off of the bed and rushed to the door, keeping his head low.

I wrapped his sheets around my body and followed him out of the room. He rushed into the bathroom and slammed the door shut. For a few moments, I gazed at it—heart racing. Then, I knocked on it. "Eros, are you okay?"

"Leave, Dani. Now."

"I'm not going to leave you when you're sick."

"Go before something happens."

My brows furrowed together. What was the worst that could happen? He could projectile vomit or something, but that was it. That'd be gross, but I didn't care.

I lightly banged on the door. "Please, Eros. I just want to help."

Another door opened in the apartment, and Zane walked out —shirtless. His eyes widened for a moment and wandered down my body. "Dani, what are you doing here?"

"Eros is sick," I said, nodding to the door.

His gaze flickered between me and the door a few times. "Let me take you back to your apartment," he said, tensely.

"If you fucking touch her Zane, I'll kill you!" Eros said. I could hear his deep breathing from behind the door, and I gulped. I didn't want to leave him like this.

Zane looked me in the eye. "Please, Dani. You need to leave. Eros will call you when he feels better."

I frowned. "Are you sure?" I asked. When he nodded, I sighed and placed my hand on the wooden door. "Feel better, Eros," I said.

He didn't answer.

It was stupid, but I felt a little hurt. He had helped me when I was sick, and he didn't even want me to help him when he was sick.

I retrieved my clothes from his room, gazing around at the sleek interior for only a moment, then walked back to my apartment. My mind was racing with a thousand different thoughts: how I was so close to letting him take me, how I could still smell his cinnamon scent, how I wished that he never got sick, how I hoped that he was alright.

Maria was flipping pancakes when I got home. The early morning sun was gleaming through the windows, soft Christmas music was playing throughout the apartment, she turned around when she heard the door open. "Someone's home a little late."

"I—uh—just had to get some things at the store," I said.

Bacon sizzled on the stove, and she waved the spatula at me. "Why don't you have breakfast with me and you can tell me about the things you bought at the store." She made two plates for us, and I sighed. "I made your favorite!"

My stomach growled, and I cursed at it. She placed our plates at the counter and hopped up onto a stool. "So, how was the date?"

"What date?"

"With Eros." She playfully rolled her eyes at me. "I saw you come home with him this morning."

I grabbed a piece of bacon and broke it in half, letting the grease glisten on my fingers. "It was good."

"What'd you do?" She stuffed a forkful of pancakes in her mouth.

"Stuff."

"Sexy stuff?" she asked. I pressed my lips together, cheeks flushing. "Oh, my gosh. You did, didn't you?"

There was no point in even trying to lie to her anymore. She was going to find out one way or another. Zane would probably tell her that I was in his apartment—half-naked and banging on the bathroom door for Eros to come out.

"Kind of," I said.

She banged her fist on the table, making the utensils jump. "Finally! The sexual tension between you two was killing me. Every time I was around, I thought I was going to go crazy for you." She smirked, rested her forearms on the table, and leaned forward. "How good is he? Is he, you know, well-endowed?"

I shook my head at her and smiled softly. "I don't know. We didn't have sex."

"Ugh," she said, throwing her head back. "Why not?"

"I think he got sick." I didn't want her to pry anymore, so I leaned forward. "So... how are you and Zane?"

She took a long sip of her orange juice. "Thinking about it makes me want to day drink." She stabbed her pancakes. "I was actually starting to like him, and I think he started to actually like me too. But..." She sighed. "Last night he asked me if I would consider an open relationship."

"Oh." An open relationship? That was like what Kasey had with Aarav and Mycah. "Would you consider it?"

She twirled her fork and gazed down. "I'm not sure. I'm not good at the whole relationship thing, I have trust issues and get jealous over the smallest things."

"You don't seem like a jealous person."

"I hide it well." She parted her lips and took a deep breath.

"My dad cheated on my mom when I was little, and it screwed me up. I'm trying to work on it with my therapist though." She gnawed on the inside of her cheek. "But I'm scared."

I walked around the table and pulled her into a hug. "Take a leap of faith and let him know how you feel."

Chapter Twenty-Seven

ros sat on my bed, hands posted on the pillows behind him,
staring right at me with his demonic black eyes. I crawled
over, knelt in front of him, and brushed my fingers
against one of his curved horns. He sighed and pushed his head
against my hand.

I gripped it—its ridged texture tickling my palm—then brushed
my fingers down the side of his face. He cupped my head in his hands
and gazed into my eyes. "I'm sorry," he said.

My brows furrowed together. "For what?"

He breathed deeply, taking my hands in his. For a moment,
there was so much uncertainty in his eyes. "For kicking you out
yesterday."

"It's okay. You were sick," I said like I was actually talking
to him.

"No, I wasn't."

"You-you weren't?"

He paused and gazed down at our hands. His ring was pressed
against my skin and looked as if it was glowing against it. When he
gazed back at me, his eyes were still black. They were so big, so beautiful, so breathtaking.

"I couldn't let you see me," he said.

"What do you mean?"

"I couldn't let you see me," he said again.

I still didn't understand. "I'm sorry... I don't know what you mean." I had seen him almost every day since that Sunday morning when he caught me dancing around my apartment in only my panties.

He placed my hands on his face and moved them across his skin, then to the horns on his head again. His eyes fluttered close in pure bliss as I trailed my fingers up them. "This me," he whispered. His voice sounded so vulnerable.

This him. The him in my dreams? I shook my head. The him in my dreams wasn't the real him—even though a part of me fantasized about it.

I trailed my fingers back down his face and grasped it gently. He reopened his eyes, and I drank in their darkness. Then, I pressed my lips to his.

This him or the real him; it didn't matter.

I wanted him. I wanted him so badly.

I opened my eyes, a feeling of sadness washing over me. Eros was gone faster than I wanted him to be. Hell, I wished that I could stay in dreamland forever and just be with him—the him in my dreams.

Maria had the Christmas music playing again throughout the house. Outside, snow was falling. I rolled onto my stomach and grabbed my phone. I was going to find out what these dreams really meant.

They probably meant nothing. I was probably just thinking too much about him. But there was no hurt in trying. So I searched: *Meaning of dreams.*

Articles about dream interpretations from Freud and Jung popped up. I skimmed through some of them, but they all said the same thing, had the same predictions, gave me same useless information.

I narrowed my search. *Meaning of dreams with same person.*

The first website that came up said that I shouldn't take dreaming of the same person too personally, that I wasn't dreaming of them because I was obsessed, that my dreams only revealed the feelings and emotions that were most prevalent in my life right now.

So, what did my dreams provoke?

Arousal, need, closeness.

It made perfect sense. When I was being ignored by Trevon, I wanted to feel wanted. When Maria was Zane, she wanted to feel close to someone without being committed. And when Trevon was having dreams of Javier, he wanted to experience sex with another man.

Although it all made sense, I wasn't satisfied with the answer. So, I cleared my search and tried again.

Meaning of sexual dreams about the same person.

Again, psychology articles came up, and I scrolled through them, reading the same things. Dreams use our subconscious. They tell about our hidden emotions and desires. Blah. Blah. Blah.

I sighed and wrapped the blanket around myself. I was about to quit, unsatisfied with these websites, when one link caught my eye.

Forget psychology. Here's the real reason you're dreaming of that same sexy guy.

When I clicked on the link, an outdated website popped up. There were ads for exorcisms and Jesus all over the place. The text was a dark blue on a black background, so dark it was almost unreadable. Usually I'd click right off of this kind of website, but I was desperate for answers.

Psychology tells you that your dreams are just manifestations of your emotions, but they don't tell you the whole truth. Some dreams are real. Some people in dreams are real.

Oh, God. Real dreams. Real people. What was I even reading?

They're called incubus demons.

Incubus demons sleep with sleeping women and men and engage in sexual activities. Sometimes that woman or man can remember the dream, other times they wake up in a sweat with no recollection of what happened.

The demons are usually very attractive to get you to fall for them. I've had a personal experience with an incubus demon, and he was charming that I couldn't help but fall for him—in my dreams and in real life.

It's theorized that these demons are just one of seven kinds. The others being greed, gluttony, sloth, wrath, envy, and pride. Demons are thought to be fallen angels.

To get rid of them, perform an exorcism, wear a cross, go to confession, use salt, or get a—

I stopped reading and blew out a breath through my nose. That was stupid. I couldn't believe that people actually believed in that kind of stuff.

An incubus demon. Such a ridiculous thought. He couldn't actually be one, could he?

In his dreams, he had horns and black eyes and an unquenchable thirst for lust. Kasey dressed me as a demon for Halloween—for Eros. What if... what if he actually was one?

I pondered over the thought for a few moments and shook my head. I couldn't believe that I was actually considering this. It was so stupid. Like angels and spirits and ghosts, demons were just mythical creatures. They weren't real.

Kasey walked over to my living room window and stared out at the snow. "You and Eros have such a nice view of the city," she said.

I plopped down on the couch, lost in my own little world. Every time I thought of him, I couldn't shake the feeling that Eros was in my dreams for a reason and that reason was more than just because I had some unconscious feelings that I needed to resolve. "Have you talked to Eros lately?" I asked.

After he kicked me out, I waited patiently for him to call me like Zane said he would. Two days passed, and I hadn't heard from him. I was beginning to think that he was ignoring me again.

She nodded. "Last night."

"Is he feeling better?"

She furrowed her brows, turned around, and pursed her red lips at me. "He was sick?"

I nodded, hesitantly. "Yeah, I was over his apartment the other morning and he locked himself in the bathroom and refused to come out."

Her eyes widened. "Oh—uh, yeah, I think he's feeling better," she said. I drew a finger across my palm, remembering the feeling of his horn on it. I wanted to touch it again. She walked over and sat next to me. "You really care for him, don't you?"

"I do," I said quietly, tightening my hand into a fist.

She sat and grabbed my forearm. "He deserves someone like you. He's had it hard."

"I know."

"He told you?"

I sucked in my cheek. "Not everything, but enough." Enough for now, as long as he didn't start closing himself off again.

She held my hand to her chest. "It takes him a long time to open up. I'm surprised that he's told you about his life so quickly." She paused for a moment, then frowned. "You're my friend, but if you hurt him, I'll make your life Hell," she said sharply.

I tensed. I had never seen her so frightening before.

She dropped my hand and smirked. "So, what were you doing in his apartment?"

My knee bounced up and down, and I looked away. "Stuff." I could feel the heat crawling up my neck.

Her jaw dropped. "Oh, Heavens! One of you caved!" She

jumped off the couch and placed her hands on my knees, staring down at me. "Well, tell me!"

A sudden warmth pooled between my legs, thoughts of the other night running through my mind. "He kissed me," I said.

She raised her hands in victory. "Yes! I knew he wouldn't be able to resist you!" She grabbed my hands and pulled me up. "How'd you do it? Did you use my tips? Oh, I'm so excited!"

I honestly didn't have an answer for her. One moment we were yelling at each other, the next his lips were devouring mine. "I don't know. We spent the night at The Lounge, and then we went home."

"You went to The Lounge?" She smirked. "Did Eros have one of those drinks?" she asked. I nodded. "Well, if he brought you there, he lost this little game a long time ago."

"What do you mean?" I asked.

She shook her head. "Nothing, nothing. I'm just glad you got him."

Kasey pulled me into a hug and opened the door. "You better be keeping me up to date on everything," she said, walking down the hall.

My cheeks flushed, and I nodded. When the elevator doors closed, I gazed over at Eros's door and decided to see if he was home. Two days of not talking to him after *that* was eating me alive. Not only did I want to see if he was okay, but I wanted to see him.

After knocking twice on the door, Zane answered. "Hey Dani," he said. "Eros isn't here."

"When will he be back?"

Zane shrugged. "I'm not sure. Do you want me to tell him that you're looking for him?"

Yes, I wanted Eros to know that I was waiting for him. But I didn't want to seem too attached. He was sending me so many mixed signals, I wasn't sure what he wanted. Interested in me. Ignore me. Interested in me. Ignore me. It was a damn roller-coaster with these ups and downs.

"Uh—" I hoped that he didn't think I was too overbearing already and got turned off. "No," I said, gazing down. "I'll... see him around sometime, I guess." I walked back to my apartment, heart hurting. I didn't know what to do.

"Dani," someone said from down the hall. I looked at the elevators and saw Eros jogging toward me. When he reached me, he grasped my hands. "Finally," he said.

I took my hands out of his and clasped them by my side.

He gazed down at them, frowning. "What's wrong?"

All I wanted was to wrap my arms around him and pull him closer to me, but I didn't want to chase after someone who didn't want me back, who didn't return my messages, who ignored me until it was convenient for him. It sucked.

"Dani, tell me." His voice was soft.

"What's wrong with you? Where have you been? Why do you keep ignoring me?"

"I had to leave for a couple days. I didn't get back until late last night." He hesitated but then grabbed my hands.

After a moment, I frowned. "I was worried about you."

The corner of his lip twitched. "You were?" he asked. I nodded. "I should've called you. I just didn't think you'd worry." His forehead was creased ever so slightly.

He had said one thing, but all I heard was that he didn't think I'd worry about him because nobody else has before. I wanted to tell him that I cared about him, but my head was spinning with all the possible ways he'd react, and I couldn't form a single word.

I opened the door to my apartment. "Do you want to watch a movie?"

He grabbed my hand and walked in with me. "Of course."

Thankfully, Maria hadn't come home yet. I didn't know

where she was, but I was glad she wasn't here with another guy. I couldn't deal with another dry humping under the blankets during a perfectly good movie.

Eros turned on the TV, and I curled into his shoulder—watching him shift through Netflix. I didn't care what we watched, I just wanted to be here with him. He turned on a comedy that neither of us found funny, and I gently closed my eyes—his scent so soothing.

Throughout the movie, I felt his phone buzz in his pocket. It was probably *Luci*, his ex, trying to ruin our night yet again. I snuggled closer to him and closed my eyes. When his phone rang, he pulled it out of his pocket and swore under his breath.

I opened one eye and gazed at the screen.

Luci.

He shifted slightly, and when I didn't move in his arms, he clicked on the answer button. "Lucifer, I'm busy. Call back later," he whispered.

Lucifer?

I couldn't make out what the *man* on the phone was saying.

Eros sighed. "I just want one night that I don't fuck things up with her. Can't this wait?" He paused, swore again, and turned off the phone. He picked me up and brought me to my bedroom. I groaned and curled into his chest, not wanting him to leave again. He tucked me under the blankets and knelt down next to me, fingers grazing against my forehead. "Dani... I have to go."

I opened my eyes and frowned.

"I'm sorry. This is important."

Just one night. That's all I wanted.

"Don't hate me," he said.

I paused for a moment. "I don't."

And when I was watching him depart from my room, all I could feel was my heart racing in my chest. Eros was going to see Lucifer.

Lucifer, not *Luci.*

Chapter Twenty-Eight

I woke up, startled, as someone pounded on our front door. The window was cracked slightly, and a cold breeze was creating goosebumps on my bare arms. I gazed at the bright white numbers on my phone.

2:34AM

Who was knocking this late at night? I rolled onto my side, breathing in the scent of cinnamon on my pillow. Maybe they'd go away.

The banging continued, each one becoming louder and more forceful. I jumped out of bed, slipped into a t-shirt, and jogged into the kitchen.

Light flickered into the room from below the front door. I turned on the light and watched the door shake. Maria stood in the kitchen, frozen to the spot.

"Maria!" I whispered. She turned around, clutching a large kitchen knife to her chest. "Who is it?"

She handed me the knife. "I don't know. You check."

I hesitantly took it from her and approached the front door. The only thing I could hear was the deep, ragged breathing coming from the hallway. I clutched the knife in my sweaty palm.

When I peered through the peephole, I sighed and placed the knife on the side table. "Trevon, what the hell are you doing here this lat—"

Trevon pushed the door open, his bloody hands running through his hair. My eyes widened, and I backed away. His face, his neck, his shirt—blood was splattered everywhere.

"Close the door!" he said.

"What—what happened to you?" I asked, hands trembling. "Are you hurt?" I examined him for any open wounds. "Maria, get him gauze and a towel!" Maria disappeared into the bathroom and came out with a medical kit.

"No, no, I'm not hurt." He paced around the living room, tracking blood and mud on Maria's white carpet. "I—I..."

"You what, Trevon?"

Maria placed the kit on the couch, eyes wide. "Is someone after you?"

He continued to pace around the room. "Oh, God. Oh, God. I really screwed up." He walked to the kitchen, placed his hands on one of the counter chairs, and squeezed. "I can't fucking"—he hurled the chair across the room—"believe it." When the chair hit the wall, it broke into pieces.

We jumped back. "What happened?" I asked. He stopped, the blood dripping off of him and forming a small puddle on the ground. I kept my distance. "Take your shirt and shoes off. We'll wash them."

"No!" A bead of sweat rolled down his neck. "No... I can't." He was sweating profusely now.

"Take it off or I will. You're not going to ruin all of our furniture," I said. Who did he think he was barging into our home at 2AM, waking up us both, and ruining all of our furniture with his blood? I snatched the top button of his shirt.

He grabbed my wrist and dug his nails into my skin. "I said no!" His voice was low and absolutely terrifying, nothing like I had ever heard before.

I pulled myself away from him, clutching my wrist. Blood was dripping down my forearm from the deep nail wounds that punctured my skin.

When he saw the blood, he stumbled back. "I—I'm sorry. I didn't mean to. I don't know what's happening." He pressed himself against the couch, chest heaving up and down.

What was wrong with him? What was going on? Why was he suddenly so angry?

Maria was standing near the foyer, her brows furrowed together. Her arms were wrapped around her small body.

"Trevon, it's okay. Just... just tell me what happened, please," I said.

His beady black eyes darted around the room like he was watching for something or someone. "I don't remember."

"Is this your blood?"

"Dani," he said, voice low and full of fright. "I think something is happening to me."

Mom's pendant began to freeze against my skin. "What're you talking about?" I asked.

With trembling hands, he unbuttoned his shirt. There was blood all over his chest, and what looked like claw marks. He stared at me, tears filling his eyes, and dug his fingers into his chest —breaking the skin.

"Trevon..." I breathed deeply. He continued to dig his nails, about an inch deep, until blood began spewing out. "Trevon, stop!" Tears welled up in my eyes, watching the blood pour out of him. When he pulled his fingers out of his chest, the wound closed slowly—like it had never even been there.

"That's not all."

God, I wished that was all.

He gazed up at me with pitch black eyes. They were darker than Eros's. Then, he parted his lips, showing me a mouthful of fangs.

Maria let out a piercing scream.

This couldn't be real. It couldn't. I shuffled back against the front door. There was a demon in the middle of our living room. I grasped Mom's pendant. It felt like ice against my fingers.

Someone banged on the door, and I jumped away from it. Another one?

"Dani! Are you okay?" Eros asked.

I took a deep breath. Okay, oh, God. It was only Eros.

Trevon stepped toward me, but I could tell that he was trying to hold himself back. "Please, don't answer, Dani. I'm not going to hurt you," he said, staring behind me at the door. His lips parted, and he bared his teeth at us—like he was going to hiss. "If you open the door..." Another bead of sweat rolled down his neck. "I won't be able to hold him back."

Maria grabbed the knife from the side-table but didn't move toward the door, nor toward Trevon.

Eros knocked again. "Dani! Answer the door."

Trevon's chest heaved. He placed his hands on the couch, claws ripping through the leather. He shook his head wildly, like he was trying to get the demon out.

Maria snatched my arm and held the knife in front of us. "What are we going to do?" she whispered.

"I—I don't know."

"I don't want him to hurt us or the guys next door." The knife in her hand trembled.

Even though Trevon was terrifying me right now, I knew he wouldn't intentionally hurt me. If he wanted to, he would've done it by now. But I knew that if we opened the door, he would lose control and hurt someone else. And that someone would be Eros.

I would never forgive myself for that.

This needed to stay contained. At least until Eros went back into his own apartment.

Trevon doubled over onto his hands and knees, then curled into a ball, clutching his head. "It hurts."

Eros banged on the door again. "Open up or I'll come in."

"What are we going to do?" Maria asked again.

I pushed her toward the kitchen. "Go get some garlic or salt or something. I'll keep Eros out." God, I really should've kept reading that article about demons.

She sprinted to the kitchen, and I deadbolted the door and pressed my back against it.

"Did you just lock me out?" Eros asked through the door.

"Eros, I'm busy right now. I'll talk to you tomorrow."

"Are you okay? There's blood on the front door."

"I'm fine," I said. "Maria just got her period! That's why there's blood. Anyway, got to go help her. Bye!" I ran back to the living room, praying to the Heavenly God above that he'd leave us alone because I didn't want him to get hurt like Mom did.

If I could protect someone, it was going to be Eros.

Maria rushed back into the living room with a container of salt. She created a circle around us with it. I didn't know if this would work. Hell, I didn't know what we were doing. I just wanted the old Trevon back. I'd take Trevon the Cheater over Trevon the Demon any day.

We huddled closer to each other, and I wondered if we were supposed to put the circle of salt around us or around Trevon.

Maria was pressing her face into my neck, tears streaming from her eyes. "I'm sorry I haven't been to church in months, but, God, please don't let us die."

After hours of watching Trevon struggle with himself: pacing around the apartment, tearing apart furniture, slashing his skin with his claws, he finally let out an ear-piercing scream and collapsed onto the ground. His claws disappeared into his fingers, and his teeth transformed back into his pearly whites.

Maria sucked in a breath. "What was that?"

I swallowed hard, heart racing. "A demon?"

We stayed in the circle for a good twenty more minutes until Trevon eventually sat up. He leaned against the couch, breathing heavy. Everything seemed to be back to normal—for now.

I cautiously stepped out. "Trevon," I asked lowly.

"I'm sorry, Dani," he said, gazing up at me with sorrowful eyes. "I couldn't control it."

Maria stepped out and rushed to the front door. "I need to get out of here."

"Maria," Trevon said. "Please don't tell anyone!"

She hesitated, but then nodded. "Okay." She disappeared behind the door and closed it.

There was a long pause, and Trevon looked back up at me with tears in his eyes. "I'm scared."

"Me too."

He took one of my hands, squeezing tightly. "Thank you for staying with me."

I took a deep breath and knelt next to him. I wasn't okay, but I'd have to be. We would have to find out how to fix this, because I would not let Eros get hurt.

"What happened last night?" I asked. "Why were you covered in blood?"

He gazed at the ground, his lips trembling. "I—I hurt someone."

"Who'd you hurt?"

"I don't know. I brought him to the hospital..." His voice cracked. "I nearly killed a man last night, Dani! What's wrong with me?"

I wrapped my arms around Trevon's trembling body and held him close. I didn't know what was wrong with him or how a demon could possess someone like him, but I was going to find out.

"We'll figure it out," I said.

"What if we don't?" he whispered.

"We have to."

Chapter Twenty-Nine

"It's your turn to watch him," Maria said when I got home from work. The room was about 95 degrees Fahrenheit—just the way Trevon *needed*—and I almost immediately broke a sweat. She hopped onto the stool at the counter and rubbed her tired eyes.

For the past two days, we'd been watching Trevon non-stop. During the day, throughout all hours of the night, he hadn't left the apartment. He also hadn't shifted into that monster again, but one wrong move and he would snap.

Trevon was sitting on the couch, clenching and relaxing his fists. "I need to go out. I hate being cooped up here."

I placed takeout from Ollie's on the coffee table. "Eat."

He ripped it open and clenched his jaw. "I need real food."

"Well, that's too bad," I said—snapping. All I wanted to do was fall into a deep sleep on the couch and enter Cinnamon Heaven with Eros. Not spend the rest of my night with whatever Trevon was.

"That's it," Maria said. She sat up and scrolled through her phone. "I'm calling someone."

He jumped up from the couch, eyes turning black. His food fell into pieces onto the ground. "No! You can't tell anyone!"

"Well, I'm not dealing with your angry ass anymore." She typed on her phone. "How to get rid of the demon in your apartment."

"Mari—"

She tapped on the screen. "Hmm, look at this. Exorcism."

"NO."

I took a deep breath and placed my hands on his chest. "Trevon," I said as softly as I could. "We're just trying to help you."

He grasped my wrists, and I was afraid that he was going to unintentionally hurt me again. But instead of digging his claws into me this time, he took a few deep breaths—eyes fading to their normal brown color—and sat back on the couch. He rubbed his legs harshly, trying to stay relaxed.

Maria sighed. "There are a few people around here that perform exorcisms. I'll start calling." She hopped off her stool. "Oh, and Dani..." She pointed to my phone as it buzzed on the counter.

I swore under my breath and snatched it. Six unread messages from Eros and three from Kasey. I scrolled through the notifications, not bothering to even unlock my phone.

I sat next to Trevon on the couch and sighed. I hadn't looked at it since the other day. It buzzed in my lap again, and Eros's name popped up on my screen. I hated being a hypocrite for scolding him for ignoring me and then ignoring him. But I couldn't risk him coming over. Hell only knew what Trevon might do to him.

"Answer the phone!" Trevon said. "I'm sick of the buzzing."

I turned off the phone. Maria walked back into the room with a half-smile on her face. "I called three people and explained our situation. One refused to come over, one said that she's busy until tonight, and the other is on his way."

About fifteen minutes later, I was resting my head on Trevon's shoulder—forcing myself to stay awake. I should've picked up Eros's call or texted Kasey back, but how was I supposed to explain this? Eros always knew when I lied. He'd definitely see right through another Maria-got-her-period excuse.

Someone knocked on the door, and Maria hopped up. I wiped the sweat off my forehead with the back of my hand. She gazed through the peephole and opened the door. An elderly man, dressed in a full white collared shirt and a cassock with a gold cross around his neck, shuffled in and bowed his head. "You're the woman who called about the exo—"

"Shush it," Maria said, shutting the door.

"So, where is—" The priest took one look at Trevon, eyes widening. "Oh, dear God." He grabbed the cross and held it between his fingers. "Have mercy on me, Lord."

I raised a brow. This guy was supposed to help us?

His hand was trembling as he stumbled back to the door. "This isn't a demon! He's the devil himself. The devil himself!" The man swung the door open and hurried out.

Maria, Trevon, and I stared at the open door—lips parted. The man ran down the hallway, screaming to the Devil and reciting prayers. I blinked a few times, in absolute shock. Well, that was a total flop.

Trevon wasn't that bad right? That guy must've been an amateur or maybe he was just paranoid.

Maria giggled and then Trevon chuckled and suddenly I found myself clutching my stomach and laughing uncontrollably. Maria whipped a happy tear from her cheek. "Wow, that guy... loads of help."

Trevon sat back down on the couch, still chuckling lowly. "He was terrified."

"Imagine if he actually saw you as a demon," I said.

He bumped my shoulder with his, like he used to, and smiled. "He'd probably shit himself."

For a single moment, everything felt normal again. Like we

were laughing at a stupid movie with white wine and three pizzas. Trevon sitting next to me, his head resting on my shoulder, leg bumping into mine every so often. Not sitting in the scorching heat, terrified of my ex-boyfriend because he was a demon from Hell that could snap at any second.

"He was supposed to be the best around," Maria said. "I don't know how much help this lady will be tonight."

"She's our only hope," I said, grasping Trevon's wrist and squeezing lightly. Our only hope.

By 8pm, I had twenty messages from Eros asking me where I was and eight from Kasey inviting me over to her apartment. I reread them for the fourth time and pushed Trevon's feet off of my lap. He grumbled to himself and shifted on the couch, placing them back on me and falling back to sleep.

Someone knocked on the door, and Maria answered it. Trevon blinked a few times and sat up. A young woman with silver hair stood in the doorway. She had black chalky markings on her skin, and her eyes were a piercing blue.

Without a word, she pushed past Maria and walked into our apartment. Trevon stared at her, eyes wide, and stood up.

"This is the man with a demon?" she asked with a thick Russian accent. She walked around him, looking him up and down. "Hmm."

"Can you fix him?" Maria asked.

"I can," she said. "But you two need to leave. I need space."

I shook my head. "I don't think that's a good idea. He's dangerous."

"Nonsense, nonsense." She waved me off. "I've been doing this for years. Nobody hurt me yet."

Maria and I gazed at each other. I shrugged my shoulders and walked to the front door. I didn't want to leave her alone, but we needed a couple hours to relax, and she was our last hope.

. . .

"This is going to be so bad. We should've never come here," I said, fiddling with my fingers. We stood in front of Kasey's door, and I already could smell Eros's faint scent.

She knocked twice. "It'll be fine if you would just act calm," she said, leaning closer to me.

Kasey opened the door, eyes wide. "Dani, I didn't think you'd make it," she said, a hint of annoyance in her voice. Her gaze shifted from me to Maria, and she smiled. "You must be Maria."

Eros stood by the window with a glass of red *wine* in his hand, talking to Zane. Soft classical music was playing over everyone's chatter. Eros inhaled deeply and gazed over to the door. I walked into the room with Maria, trying my hardest to think of an excuse that he would believe.

"Dani," he said, hurrying over and grabbing my hand. Maria awkwardly walked over to Zane and sat next to him on the couch. She hadn't mentioned him since she told me he wanted an open relationship.

Kasey placed a hand on my back, ushering me in. "Where have you been? You've been ignoring us. And..." She scrunched up her nose. "Why do you look like someone straight out of Satan's kingdom?"

Damn Trevon. Making me look like Hell in front of Eros.

"I've been busy," I said.

"Busy with what?" Eros asked.

Think, Dani. Think. I avoided eye contact with him and said the first thing that came to mind. "Trevon stuff."

His grip on my hand tightened. "What do you mean 'Trevon stuff'?"

"Um..." I peeled my hand out of his and rubbed my neck. Damn, it felt as hot as our apartment in here. Kasey narrowed her eyes at me while Eros waited—quiet impatiently—for my answer.

If Eros found out that Trevon was staying with us on his own, he'd think that something was going on between us. Hell, he probably already thought that.

"Kase, can Eros and I talk in your spare room?"

She raised a brow. "I expect to hear this at some point."

I nodded and walked with him to the other room. The moon was gleaming through the windows and hitting the side of Eros's face. He was staring at me, so intensely with his piercing green eyes, that I couldn't think straight. I fiddled with my fingers. "Trevon is—uh staying with Maria and me."

"Why? You two broke up." He shook his head and moved his ring around his index finger with his thumb. "I thought we were... a thing."

A *thing*. We never officially labeled our relationship, and I wasn't sure what being "a thing" meant to him. Friends with benefits? Boyfriend-girlfriend?

I grabbed his hand and squeezed it lightly. I couldn't tell him the truth, but I didn't want to lie to him either. "He's not well," I said.

"What's wrong with him?"

"I—I can't tell you."

"Why not?"

"I want to, I just can't." I swallowed hard. Trevon trusted us with his secret, and I knew that he didn't deserve it, but I wasn't going to blab to everyone about it. This wasn't his fault. "You have secrets too that you don't feel comfortable telling me."

"I don't have secrets that involve ex-lovers."

My fingers grazed against his ring, and I looked him in his eyes. "I promise that nothing has happened between us."

He forced a smile—which looked more like a grimace—and I felt like shit. Trevon just had to ruin this *thing* I had with Eros with his demon problem.

"Okay," he finally said. He grabbed my hand and led me back to the living room, then he grabbed my waist and sat me next to him on Kasey's couch. While everyone drank and talked and laughed around us, we sat in dead silence.

His arm was around me, but all I could think about was Trevon. I hope to God that the lady could help. I didn't want to come home to a bloody mess that I'd have to clean up. And—if I had to dispose of a body—I didn't know how I'd do that.

Eros leaned closer to me. "Tell me what you want me to do to you."

"What're you talking about?" I asked.

He grazed his hand against my knee, then up the inside of my thigh. And, with his other hand, he brushed a hand over my bra through my shirt. "Tell me what you want me to do to you right now."

My cheeks flushed. "Nothing," I said, pressing my knees together. I took off my grey cardigan, trying to cool myself off. Here I was thinking of a hundred different ways to hide a murder and Eros wanted to tease me.

"Tell me," he said.

"I have too many other things to worry about. I don't need the stress of being caught fooling around with you," I said. But that didn't mean I didn't want it. Three days and two nights of non-stop Trevon had done more than stress me out.

His fingers brushed against my inner thigh. "I think you like the idea of something." He leaned in closer, his breath fanning my neck.

I gulped, eyes fluttering closed. "No." Yes.

"Trying to hold back your moans as I make you cum over and over again." His fingers trailed up and down my thigh.

Oh, God.

"Tell me, Dani, do you fantasize about being fucked in public?" he asked. My only response was a shaky breath that I couldn't hide if I tried. He brushed his fingers against the front of my pants, touching my wetness. "You do, don't you?"

Damn. I needed to get out of here.

"I'm going to get something to drink." I hopped up and hurried to the kitchen. A bottle of red wine was sitting on the counter.

Lord, this was my best excuse to drink. Trevon was a demon. Eros was trying to get into my pants. And I was terrified that there was a dead woman lying on my living room floor.

After one long gulp, I rested my elbows on the counter and closed my eyes. Calm yourself, Dani. Don't think about all the things he could do to you, all the things you *need* him to do to you —just so you could relax for a fraction of a second. Now is not the time nor place.

When I finally thought that I could control my desires, I reached into my back pocket for my phone, so I could check on Trevon, but it wasn't there.

"Looking for this?" Eros asked from behind me, voice chillingly quiet. He placed the phone on the counter in front of me. "You told me you weren't seeing Trevon." He stepped closer, so he was pressing against my backside—trapping me.

Damn it. Damn it. Damn it.

"I'm not," I said.

He wrapped an arm around the front of my waist and slipped his fingers under the waistband of my leggings. Oh, God. Not here. Not now.

"Why the fuck does he want to take you out for dinner then?"

Cinnamon.

"What—what are you talking about?" I asked. He began to rub fast, rough circles around my clit.

I grabbed onto the side of the counter to steady myself and gazed down at my phone. Trevon's last message read: *Thanks for the other night. Everything is taken care of. Can I take you out to dinner to repay you for everything you've done for me?*

"What is he talking about, Dani?"

"I don't know why"—he plunged his fingers inside of me— "he wants to bring me out."

Eros gently grabbed a fistful of my hair and pulled it back. "Don't lie to me. You're terrible at it."

He thrusted them harder into me, and I gripped the counter for dear life. "I—I'm not."

"Tell me or I'll make you cum so fucking hard that you won't be able to stop yourself from moaning in front of everyone here."

Pressure built in my core, and I clenched around him.

"I—I told you... I just helped him because he was sick." I squeezed my eyes shut and bit my lip. It felt so good. I didn't want him to stop.

He tugged harder on my hair.

"I promise, Eros. Please, stop. You're... you're going to make me cum." My legs trembled underneath me. He continued thrusting his fingers into me. "Please, you have to believe me. I'm not lying."

After another moment of absolute torture, he smirked against my neck. "I know."

He knew? He knew, but he didn't stop.

With each thrust, my core continued to tighten. So good, yet so damn wrong.

"Then stop, Eros! You said you wouldn—" I parted my lips, brows knotting together. Fuck. I was going to cum.

Eros pounded his fingers into me, shoving me against the counter with each thrust. He slapped his hand over my mouth. I buckled forward and moaned into his hand, eyes rolling back.

Holy Hell.

My core was pulsing over and over as I released myself onto him. Waves of ecstasy were rolling through my body. I inhaled deeply. "What was that for?" I asked. "I told you the truth."

He pulled his hand from my pants and pushed himself off of me. "That was to make sure you knew that you're mine." And, without another word, he grabbed my wine, walked out of the kitchen, and stared at me from the couch.

I gazed around the room, hoping that nobody saw. That was... a lot.

Kasey was chatting with Aarav—staring right at me—lips in a smirk. Just by looking at her, I could tell that she knew everything that had just happened.

Fuck. I closed my eyes and took a deep breath. I was going to Hell, and this time I wasn't joking. Hell was real, it was all fucking real.

Chapter Thirty

"Are you jealous?" I asked on the ride home with Eros. Maria had insisted that I drive with him—not her—because she wanted us to spend quality time together, but I really think she just wanted to flirt with some other people who showed up at Kasey's.

Eros stayed quiet, his hand tightening on the steering wheel. Under the dim streetlights, his ring was shining brightly. "No." He took a deep breath. "It's not in my nature to be a jealous person... I just don't understand why he's staying with you."

I sighed. Trevon's secret was going to be harder to keep to myself than I thought it would.

"He just has to." I grabbed his hand resting on the gearshift. "If it makes you feel better, you can stay the night with me." My words shook as I said them because I didn't know if it was too soon to sleep over each other's places.

"What are we, Dani?" Eros asked.

"What?" I laughed nervously. God, I didn't expect him to just come out and ask that. I wasn't prepared to answer that kind of question yet.

Eros pulled into the lot to our apartment building and parked. "What do you think we are?"

"What do *you* think we are?" I asked, playing with his ring. The shiny dark metal molded to his finger almost perfectly.

He pulled his hand away and faced me, his green eyes nearly glowing in the darkness. "I asked you first."

"I—uh... think we are a lot of things."

"Look at me when you talk, Dani," he said.

My heart raced, and I looked over at him. What did I think we were? Well, that answer was probably much different from what I hoped we were.

"Calm down. It's just a question."

"If it's just a question, then why can't you answer it first?"

He chuckled and shook his head. "Be confident. You feel what you feel, and you need to be honest with yourself. It's the only way you'll ever be happy."

There it was again. Him telling me to choose happiness—even if that meant giving him up.

I parted my lips. "I think that we're..." I swallowed my insecurities, ready to be vulnerable *and* happy. "I hope that we have something more than this physical attraction. I—I feel something between us, and I think you do too, I just don't know what it is."

He just stared at me for four, five, six moments. Completely silent. His face was void of all emotion, and I gulped.

"But it's totally okay if you don't. I'm just being stupid and speaking nonsense and—"

He pressed his lips to mine, his fingers trailing up my forearm and creating a sea of goosebumps on my skin. I sat still for a moment—overwhelmed. The kiss was soft and gentle and full of love and I never wanted it to end. So, I closed my eyes and kissed him back.

His fingers laced through my hair, and he pulled me closer to him. Pressing his lips harder to mine and slowly devouring me.

And, in that moment, I knew one thing and one thing only: I wanted us more than anything I'd ever want.

After another moment, he pulled away, leaving us both breathless. His eyes were a clear green. There was no tension in his face, except in his lips which were in a tight line. "I want you to be sure, Dani."

I was sure. I hadn't been surer of anything.

"Are *you* sure?" I asked, a smile on my face.

He chuckled. "You're so weird."

"What? I need you to be sure too!"

A lopsided grin stretched across his face. "I'm sure." He took my hands. "Please just think us through. I need you to make the right choice for yourself."

"What is there to think through, Eros?" I squeezed his hands and laughed to myself. "I don't think that anything you can say or do would surprise me at this point."

He paused. "Just *every* moment that we've been together."

I sucked in my cheek. When I read that article the other day, I didn't think that demons existed but after Trevon changed into that *beast* I knew that anything was possible. I even wanted to ask him about it, but that meant I needed to reveal Trevon's secret. And I wasn't about to do that—yet.

If Eros ended up just being human, he'd freak out about Trevon staying with me. He'd might even call the police, get him arrested, or—worse—get him killed.

Instead, I nodded. "Okay."

He brought my hand to his lips and kissed the top of it, just like he had done the first day I met him when all I wanted was to stay away from him because the attraction between us was too overwhelming. Look at us now.

"Stay with me tonight," he said.

"In your apartment?" I asked. He nodded. "I—um... Maria doesn't feel comfortable staying alone with Trevon."

"Well, it's good that Zane is staying at your place tonight, isn't it?"

"He is?" I asked.

"He is now."

"No, Eros, I don't want to be a bother. It's okay. I don't have to stay—"

"Dani, it would make *me* happy if you stayed with me."

And—because I wanted to—I nodded my head. "Okay."

While Eros looked for Zane, I stripped off my clothes in his room. Though dull, the black walls and grey décor looked sleek at night when the city-lights gleamed on them through three wall-length windows. The only color in the sea of blacks and greys was the gold throw blanket, handing off the edge of his bed, and a golden apple that sat on his black metallic side-table.

I gazed at the city and unclipped my bra, letting out a sigh. After the last few days, the simplest things relaxed me. I hoped that the demon was exorcised from Trevon because if it wasn't, I didn't know when I'd be able to enjoy another night with Eros.

The door opened behind me. "He's not her—"

I gazed over my bare shoulder, watching Eros's gaze drift down my body. "Are you just going to stare at me?" I asked, the corners of my lips curling into a smirk.

He stepped back. "Sorry."

I played with the ends of the throw blanket and smirked. "Don't go."

After Kasey's party, I couldn't get Eros off of my mind. I wanted to pick up where we left off. With him between my legs, his fingers inside of me, his lips hovering under my ear, making me beg for him.

He stepped back into the room and shut the door behind him. "Make me want to stay." He leaned against the door, one ankle crossed over the other, dark eyes fixed on my hips.

"I don't have to make you do anything," I said, turning around. "You already want to."

His gaze slowly traveled up my body until it reached my chest. "You really like teasing me, don't you?" He undid his belt buckle.

I stepped closer to him. "Sometimes."

He grabbed my wrist, drawing me to him until I was pressed against his chest. "All the time," he said. He placed one passionate open-mouthed kiss on my lips, then laid wet and needy ones down my neck to my bare breast. I pushed my hand into his jeans, fingers grazing against him. He was hard for me already.

He sucked my nipple into his mouth, teeth grazing against it. I clenched. "You're so fucking sexy," he said. He tugged on my nipple, and I arched my back and moaned. "I love the way your body reacts to me."

I pushed him away and knelt in front of him, toying with the buttons on his jeans. He stared down at me, lips parted, brow furrowed, eyes hazy as hell. "Dani," he said under his breath. I slowly pulled down his pants and underwear, the head of his cock springing out.

My eyes widened at it. Here I was thinking that Trevon was big.

He pushed a hand through my hair and gently caressed the top of my head. I wrapped both hands around the base of his cock and sucked it into my mouth, tongue swirling around his head. I gazed straight up into his darkening eyes and took the rest of his inside of me until he hit the back of my throat.

"Fuck." He curled his fingers into my hair.

I bobbed my head back and forth on him, and each time I reached its base, he'd push his hips closer to me, so I'd take even more of him into my mouth. He continued to curse under his breath, muscles tensing. "Fuck. Fuck. Fuck." He threw his head back. "Get up, Dani. Get up now."

He snatched my arm and forced me to stand. Within a

moment, he had spun me around, pressed his cock against my backside, and thrusted his fingers into my panties, then into me.

"Oh, God," I said, squeezing my eyes shut. I clenched around him, a wave of cinnamon suddenly striking me. "Please don't stop." I reached behind me and grasped his cock in my hand, stroking it.

I just wanted it inside of me, filling me completely.

"More, Eros," I said. "Please, I want more."

I turned my head to gaze at him, but he grabbed the back of my neck, forced me to turn back to the wall, and held me in place. "Stay like this."

His breaths were heavy and ragged against my ear. I continued to stroke his cock, and he loosened his grip on my neck. I turned to face him again—hungry for his lips on mine—but I only had time to catch a glimpse of something sharp and black protruding from his head before his grip tightened on my neck, forcing me to face the wall.

"I said to stay like this," he scolded.

Oh, God. Oh, God. Oh, God.

He continued to pound his fingers into me, adding another one, until I could barely hold myself up any longer. "Cum for me," he said harshly in my ear.

And, just like that, my legs were trembling. I clenched harder on his fingers, pressed my forehead against the wall, and came for him. Like he wanted me to.

All I could smell was his cinnamon scent. All I could feel was the pure adrenaline rushing through me. And all I could think about were his horns.

After a few moments, he pulled his hands out of my underwear and placed it on the wall next to me. "Fuck, Dani." His nails dug into the back of my neck. I placed my palm on top of his hand on the wall, brushing my finger over his knuckles.

My eyes widened when I saw the paint chipping right under

Eros's fingers. Holy Hell. His nails were sharper than Trevon's were.

"Can you let go of my neck?" I whispered.

He took a deep breath. "Give me a second." After another deep breath, then another, he finally loosened his grip. I turned around—expecting to see a more frightening creature than Trevon—but it was just Eros. No horns. No claws. No black eyes.

The vein in his neck pulsed violently, and his eyes were hazier than I'd ever seen them. He excused himself to use the bathroom but didn't return for a while.

When he came back in, I was lying on his bed, staring at the ceiling. A billion thoughts were racing through my head. This couldn't be real.

The bed dipped, and Eros slid under the blankets with me, wrapping his arm around my waist from behind. He pushed a stray piece of hair behind my ear. "Are you okay?"

"Yes, why?" I said, but I wasn't okay.

"I just..." He hesitated. "I just wanted to make sure."

We laid in silence, neither one of us actually sleeping. It started to snow outside again, and I would've thought it was beautiful against the city lights, but I couldn't think of anything besides Eros.

"What's bothering you?" he asked, lips against my ear.

"Nothing."

"Don't lie to me." His fingers curled into my hips.

I couldn't believe that this was real life. I couldn't believe that I was really going to ask this. I gulped. "Do you believe in the irrational?"

"What do you mean?" he asked.

"Like supernatural stuff, ghosts and vampires and... demons." I whispered the last word.

He tensed. "I don't know. What do you think?"

"I don't know either," I said. But I did.

Demons were real, and one was lying right next to me.

Chapter Thirty-One

"So, do you think it actually worked?" Maria asked.

I placed the bag of popcorn into the microwave, leaned against the counter, and gazed into the living room. Eros and Zane were sitting on the couch, talking amongst themselves. Besides the glare of the paused romance movie on the TV screen, the room was dark.

Hell, everything seemed dark since I discovered that Eros was a demon. The way his eyes shifted between a piercing green and a reflective black, the way he could turn into one of the monsters from Mom's stories in a single moment, even the way he looked at me with that devilish smirk.

Chillingly terrifying, yet undeniably erotic.

"Hopefully," I said. "Did Trevon seem different when he left yesterday?"

"He said he felt better."

The microwave beeped, the scent of butter filling the apartment. I took out the bag and walked with Maria to the living room. "Let's just hope," I said quietly to her.

While Maria sat a whole cushion away from Zane, I curled into Eros's arm on the loveseat. He was rubbing the black metallic surface of his ring with his thumb like he had done last night after I asked him about demons.

"Oooh, what do we have here?" Maria glanced over at us, a mischievous glint in her eye. Eros brushed his hand against my shoulder, fingers dragging lightly over my skin and giving me goosebumps. "What's going on with you two? You're always either fighting or flirting. This is different."

I gave Maria a side-eye. "I'll tell you later."

Eros pushed a strand of hair behind my ear. "Why don't you tell her now?"

"Why don't you tell her?" I asked, narrowing my eyes.

"She asked you."

These two were determined to embarrass me in any way that they could. I sighed and turned back to the paused movie. "Eros and I are... a thing."

Zane raised a brow at Eros, and Maria just smirked—like she'd been waiting for this since that Sunday morning when she brought him over. "And what does that mean?" she asked.

I rubbed my palms together. "It means that we are... a—"

Someone pounded on my door, the knocks hard and frantic. "Dani!" Trevon said. Dam it. "Please open up!"

Maria stared at me with wide eyes and I stared back with the same alarmed expression. It didn't work. It couldn't have if he was back again. Trevon still had a demon inside of him, and that same demon wanted only one thing the other night: to hurt my Eros.

When I leapt up, Eros snagged my waist and pulled me back down. "Don't let him ruin our night." His voice was sour.

Trevon banged again, and the hinges on the door shook.

"I have to. I'm sorry." I pulled myself out of his grip and hurried to the door with Maria. I really, really, really hoped that I was wrong about this. Maybe he was just excited to see the two lovely women that let him stay in their apartment while he was possessed by the devil. Not frantic and covered in blood with the stench of hell lingering on every inch of his being.

For a single moment, the thought of telling Eros crossed my mind, but there were many reasons I was against it. First, Eros didn't know that I knew about him and he was hiding himself for a reason. Second, Maria might've knew that Trevon was a demon, but she didn't know that Eros was a demon—and who knew if Zane was also one; that would freak her out more. Third, I felt inclined to protect Eros from Trevon.

That was probably the stupidest reason of all of them, but it was true. Trevon stayed calm when I was with him. And, if that priest was right and Trevon was possessed by the devil himself, I would have a hard time keeping him from tearing Eros apart, especially when I knew Eros would antagonize him.

"What are we going to do?" Maria said quietly to me. "He can't come in here!"

I glanced back at the guys who were watching us from the couch. "Well, we'll have to calm him down."

Trevon was wrath, pure fury, and rage. Nothing like Eros's lustful nature.

Maria and I slipped out of the room and slammed the door behind us. Trevon was on the ground and leaning against the wall, knees to his chest. His head was between his legs, and he was tugging harshly on his hair.

"Trevon," I whispered, crouching next to him. I took his shaky hands away from his face and resisted the urge to cower away. Blood dripped from a hundred of his fangs onto his chin and rolled down his sweaty neck.

This wasn't his fault, Dani. He didn't choose this. Don't show him your fear.

"Trevon," I said again, softer this time. He snatched my wrists —like he didn't even recognize me. "It's okay, Trevon. It's me, Dani."

After taking a few deep breaths, his fangs slowly started to disappear into his mouth.

Someone opened the door, but Maria pulled it closed. "Are you okay?" Eros asked from behind it.

"We're fine!" Maria shook her head. "I can't believe that I'm helping this loser," she said under her breath.

"I thought you said you were better," I said to Trevon.

Trevon clasped my hands tightly in his. "I was, but this morning I lost control again."

"You can't keep doing this."

"Dani, I'm not trying to. You have to believe me." He sounded so frightened.

"Did you hurt anyone?" I asked. He grimaced, and I closed my eyes. God, was this the shittiest situation to ever be in. My ex demon boyfriend who wanted to kill my current demon boyfriend and who also had no control over himself and snapped at the smallest things, showing up at my apartment while I was watching a sweet romance movie with that current demon boyfriend. Wonderful.

Eros said something else, but I couldn't hear him. Instead, I pulled Trevon to his feet and stepped close to him. "As soon as we get inside, go right to the bathroom. Don't even look in Eros's direction. We will talk about this later."

Trevon wiped the blood off of his chin with the back of his hand. I licked my finger and rubbed the deep red stain off of his neck. Why the hell was I doing this again?

When he was ready, Maria opened the door, and we walked in. Eros leaned against the counter, eyes dark and arms crossed over his chest. "Feeling better?" Eros asked Trevon, annoyance dripping from each word.

Trevon kept his chin tucked but nodded, trying to walk past Eros. But Eros, being the damn guy he was, placed a hand on Trevon's chest and stopped him. "Is that blood on your chin?" His muscles were strained against his grey v-neck. Great, not only do I have one demon to take care of... but now I have Eros.

I could feel the rage in Trevon, even caught a glimpse of a fang.

He would lose total control in a moment, would try to rip Eros to pieces. Dig his claws right into his chest, let the blood gush out. Bit right into his neck with those fangs, stop his heart.

I grabbed his arm and pulled him away from Eros. "Stop it," I scolded, glaring right up into his dark eyes. "He's sick. Let him go lie down."

He looked strained for a moment, like he wanted to protest but his eyes softened just a bit when they looked into mine. "I just want to make sure he's alright," he said tensely.

"Eros, please," I said.

"Dani." He dropped his hand from Trevon and clenched his jaw, any sign of softness drying up. "He shouldn't be here."

"Why?" I asked, testing him. "Tell me why he shouldn't be here."

"He's... he smells like..." Eros growled lowly, nostrils flaring, and stormed to the couch where Zane was lounging still.

I clenched my jaw and lead Trevon away. Once he was safely in the bathroom, I stood by the door and sighed. Maria was fetching clothes from her room for him, and Eros and Zane were talking to themselves again in the living room.

"Did you feel that wrath on him?" Eros asked quietly. I tilted my head in their direction.

Zane sighed. "If he's hanging out with Javier still, he's bound to be covered in wrath. It'll be seeping from his veins soon, if he's not careful."

"He had blood on him," Eros said. "Coated on him. I could smell it."

Zane paused for a moment. "You think Javier is hurting him?"

Eros blew a breath through his nose. "He smells more like Satan than Javier to me, but who knows."

Trevon opened the door, and I stepped away. Lucifer and Satan were supposed to just be monsters from Mom's stories— but Eros and Zane were talking about them as if they were normal people leading normal lives in a normal world that they called

Hell. Who would be next? Beelzebub, the green king of envy. Mammon, the prince of jewels and riches. Or—her favorite—Asmodeus, the sorcerer of temptation.

Everything I had thought was a mere fairytale was becoming truth. And I didn't know whether I wanted to ask for more or hide in the crook of someone's shoulder and wish this away.

Chapter Thirty-Two

My bedroom door opened, and I sat up on the bed. "Eros," I whispered. I had been waiting for him.

After Trevon's interruption earlier, I knew he wouldn't be able to stay away. Just like at Kasey's he was here to make sure I knew that I was his—not Trevon's.

He stepped into the moonlight which was streaming through my bedroom window. His scent of cinnamon was forcefully strong but not strong enough to bewitch me like he had done so many times before.

All I wanted to do was dig my fingers into his thick muscle, touch him like he had touched me so many times, and tell him that I knew his little secret.

This was real. This was Eros.

So damn frightening yet the only thing that I wanted.

I grabbed his wrists and pulled him onto the bed with me. "Come here," I said, my hand rubbing up his bare abdomen and curling around the back of his neck. "I want you."

Human or demon, it didn't matter to me. I would prove my want for him one way or another. Everything would be so much easier when he knew that I knew.

When he had crawled between my legs and pressed his hardness against my core, I let him tease me. His breath warming my neck, his fingers running down my sides, his horns brushing against me. "Dani," he whispered, grinding himself harder into me.

"Yes?" I asked, breathing him in.

He grasped my chin in one of his hands and pushed the other into my underwear, finger slowly running down my fold. "You're so wet for me already." He pressed a finger against my entrance, teasing me. "I bet you can't wait for me to be inside of you." He pushed his finger harder against me, and I did want him inside of me. "Your tight pussy clenching around my cock as it thrust in..." He pushed it inside of me, and my pussy wrapped around it. "... and out..." He pulled it out. "... and back into you..." Back in. "So fucking slowly until you can't handle it."

I breathed in his ecstasy, reached between us, and grabbed his cock through his briefs. "You're the one that can't wait to be inside of me," I said, fingers slowly trailing down his jaw. I rolled us over and grinded my hips against his hardness. "For weeks you've been thinking about it, haven't you? About how good my hands would feel wrapped around your horns as I ride you. About your teeth leaving love-bites down the side of my neck so everyone can see that I'm yours. About your finally being inside of me after months of torturing yourself around me."

He gazed up at me with hazy black eyes and placed his hands on my hips, but I grabbed them, pinned them to the pillow next to his head, and intertwined my fingers with his. "No more torturing yourself, Eros. It's my turn," I said. I pressed my lips to his.

It was the perfect distraction.

I left hot, needy kisses down his neck. "I want you to take me," I whispered, tightening my fingers around his. "Any way that you want." His ring dug into my palm, and I grinded my hips harder against his. "Anywhere that you want." I slid the ring off his finger —without him noticing—and slid my hand out of his, hiding the ring under my pillow.

When it was secure, I sat back up and smirked down at him, hips still moving back and forth. In the morning, the ring would be there. Evidence that Eros had spent night after night with me, and that I enjoyed every moment we spent together.

He wrapped his hands around my waist. "Look at you," he said, eyes hazy. "The things I want to do to you." He shook his head, the corner of his lips curling into a smirk. "They're sinister."

"Tell me," I said. His hardness was pressing against my panties.

He sat up and trailed his lips up the side of my neck. "I want to dig my fangs into every inch of your flesh." His fingers dipped between my legs. "And fuck you until you're trembling." He wrapped a hand in my hair and pulled roughly on it. "I want to hear you scream and beg and whimper my name."

Chapter Thirty-Three

When I hid Eros's ring under my pillow last night, I expected to wake up with a giddy feeling. I thought it'd feel like Christmas morning again, when I used to wait for Mom to finish her coffee before I dragged her to the Christmas tree to see what Santa and his flying reindeer brought me.

But I didn't feel anything giddy. I knew exactly what was under my pillow, and I was terrified.

Even after asking Eros about demons, he didn't want to tell me his secret; he continued to hide it from me. And, besides that, I had so many questions that I didn't even know I wanted answered. How would Eros react? Would he still want us or was our relationship best as it was? If he still wanted us, would I be able to survive the depths of Hell if he asked me to go?

One of my windows was pulled all the way open, letting a cold breeze blow in. I cocooned myself in my comforter, stood next to my bed, and stared at the pillow. Maybe I should leave the ring under it and pretend that it was never even there. Things were going well, and I didn't want to ruin them.

I paced around the room, watching white puffs of air form in front of my face and gazing at the snow as it fell and melted on my windowsill. Though my room must've been freezing, I felt extremely hot, like my body was igniting from the inside out, heating every inch of my skin, setting my fingertips on fire.

I wanted to stop thinking about that stupid ring, but I couldn't. All I could think about was what would happen when Eros found out that I knew his sinful little secret. Would he finally stop holding back? Would he fuck me senseless as he promised? I pressed my legs together. Would I be able to handle all of him?

There was only one way to find out.

Before I could stop myself, I hurled my pillow to the other side of the room. I gazed down at the bed, and my heart nearly stopped. His ring rested perfectly against my grey bed sheets, glowing like his eyes.

A few moments later that giddy feeling appeared.

No more trying to fit the pieces of Eros's puzzle together. No more doubts. No more waiting for him. This ring was the only evidence I needed.

I grabbed the ring and held it in my hand. It vibrated in my palm, pulsating back and forth and back and forth. So much energy trapped within such a small piece of jewelry.

The black metallic transformed into a garnet red right in front of my eyes, and when it did, I felt like the wearer of this ring had the strength to destroy the strongest, to tempt the purest, to bring the entire world to its knees.

This ring wasn't powerful. It was power.

Without sparing myself a moment to control the sudden impulses inside of me, I tugged a shirt over my head and headed straight to Eros's apartment. Two months ago, the thought of a demon fucking me senseless would scare the hell out of me, but now I was craving it—more than I'd ever craved anything in my life.

He didn't answer on the first knock, so I knocked again. I

could just feel his hands on my body, his breath on my neck, him keeping all of his promises to me.

"Javier, if you stole that fucking rin—" Eros said, yanking the door open. He was fastening a towel around his waist, beads of water dripping down his bare chest. When he saw me, he parted his lips—and I could just taste the cinnamon on them already. "Dani, what are you doing here?"

I didn't want to wait any longer. I stepped inside his apartment without an invitation and pressed my lips to his.

"Dani... have you... seen... my ring?" he said pulling away only slightly to speak between kisses.

Tingles ran up and down my arms. This was it. I pulled away and held out my hand between us. "Do you mean this?"

He gazed down at the red ring sitting on my palm. "It must've fallen off during the movie," he said.

"That would explain why it was in my room, huh?"

He tensed. "Right..."

I pushed the ring back on his finger, watching it turn from red to black before Eros pulled his hand away. If he wouldn't admit that he was a demon to me, then I was going to get it out of him and I was going to have fun doing it.

My fingers danced along his abdomen, and I undid his towel and let it fall to the floor. Eros didn't move, he just gave me his infamous smirk. When I pressed my lips to his and gripped his dick firmly in my hand, he growled lowly into my mouth, picked me up, and took me to his bedroom.

Eros laid me on his bed. "Someone's awfully frisky this morning."

"I want you," I said running my hands through his hair.

He placed soft, wet kisses down my neck, his stubble brushing against my soft spot. "I want you to do something for me first," he said. He trailed his fingers down the center of my chest, then over one of my nipples through my thin shirt, making it hard. "I've been thinking about it for the past week."

"And what is that?" I asked. My head was feeling hazy already, and we hadn't even started.

"Touch yourself," he said against my ear.

I clenched. "Touch myself?"

He sat up, darkness clouding his green eyes, and pressed his hardness into me. "Can you do that for me, Dani?"

Heat rushed to my core. "I—uh…" I swallowed hard. This was not how I expected this to go. I wanted to be the one in control—even for just a few moments. "Are you going to watch?"

His fingers trailed down the insides of my thighs. "Yes."

I gulped. This was what I wanted. This was how I would get him to turn. I took a deep, shaky breath and leaned against his headboard. He curled his fingers around my shorts and panties and slowly slid them down my legs, gaze following.

I pushed one hand between my legs. I couldn't believe that I was actually going to do this for him and let him watch.

His one simple request had made my pussy wet already. I closed my eyes, enjoying his scent as my fingers touched my clit.

"Spread your legs," he said. I gulped nervously and let my thighs rest against the bed. "Wider."

I pulled my legs farther apart and rubbed my fingers harder against my clit, a wave of pleasure rushing through me.

"Look at me," he said.

When I opened my eyes, he was intently watching me and stroking his cock. His hand moved slowly over every inch, and I held my breath. From the smooth swollen head to the girth of his hard cock, I couldn't peel my gaze away from him. I furrowed my brows and moaned. God, I wanted him inside of me.

He swore under his breath, eyes filling with darkness. It was working.

I continued to rub my clit, fingers moving faster. I wanted his head between my legs, breath warming my core. Him thrusting me against the headboard, fangs digging into my shoulder. I squeezed my eyes shut. Fuck.

He grabbed my chin. "I said to look at me, Dani."

A surge of pleasure rushed through me, nearly sending me over the edge. "Oh my God," I said—not taking my eyes off of his. The corners of them were black now, and all I could imagine were those damn horns on his head. "I want you inside of me," I said.

Another rush of pleasure ran through me, and I clenched again—my pussy throbbing. "Please Eros."

He watched me, pupils dilated. "Keep begging like that, and I'll give it to you."

My fingers grazed over my nipple through my shirt, and I arched my back and moaned. "Oh, God, Eros... please. I can't handle this any longer." I felt like I was in the clouds, my head was in such a fog.

He stood, tugged me to the edge of the bed, wrapped his arms around my legs, and pressed himself against my entrance. I gripped onto the edge of the bed, fingers digging into his silk sheets.

The scent of cinnamon hung so heavily in the air that I couldn't think. He took his cock in his hand and rubbed it against my wetness. "Eyes on me, Dani." I gazed up at his bold black eyes and didn't look away when he began to push himself inside of me.

My pussy clenched as he shoved himself all the way inside of me. He rested his forearms by the sides of my head and groaned in my ear. "Fuck, you're so tight," he said, kissing just below my ear. One of his hands was holding my chin, the other was rubbing my clit in small torturous circles.

I sunk into the sheets. I was in Heaven. Pure fucking Heaven.

Eros stood back up, grabbed the hem of my shirt in a fist, and yanked it off my body—ripping it at its seams. His eyes were black without any trace of white. He was so terrifyingly dangerous, and yet it only turned me on more.

I clenched myself around him in excitement, legs shaking, and we both knew that I was close to cumming for him already. He gazed down at my breasts, watching them bounce as he thrust into me. His breaths becoming increasingly quick and ragged. He squeezed his eyes shut, then reopened them. "Fuck."

My heart pounded in my chest. He was going to shift.

He slowed his pace. "Dani, I—I can't." He swallowed hard, unable to keep eye contact with me. "I'm sorry."

"Don't stop, Eros."

"I have to," he said. But before he could pull out of me, I ran a hand through his hair, pricking my finger with the tip of his horn. He grabbed my wrist. "Dani, stop."

"Don't stop," I said again, this time more sternly. I ripped my hand out of his and grasped his hair again.

He snatched both of my wrists and pinned them against the bed. "I said to stop. You don't know what you're doing." The vein in his neck pulsed violently.

"I know exactly what I'm doing," I said. When his black eyes met mine, he loosened his grip, giving me a chance to pull my hand out of his. I grabbed his jaw. "Fuck me like you said you would last night."

"What're you talking about?"

I ran my thumb against his lips, noticing the fangs he tried to hide. "Your fangs devouring me. Hard, fast, and merciless, Eros."

He paused for a long moment, eyes darkening and lightening —like he was trying to hold himself back. He parted his lips slowly, watching me gaze at the fangs in his mouth. I clenched around him, wanting them on me.

When he realized that I wasn't going to run away screaming, he stood up and thrust himself hard into me. "That's how you want it? You want me to be merciless with you?"

"I want you to tear me apart."

He gently grazed his fingers up the column of my neck, then harshly wrapped his hand around my throat and squeezed, thrusting into me at the same time. My core tingled. "More," I said, tugging on one of my nipples and moaning.

"Dani, don't," he said again. "I will be rough with you and won't be able to sto—"

"Is that all you've got?"

Suddenly, his jaw and cheekbones sharpened, his nail lengthened into claws, and his horns grew from his head, lengthening until a demon stared down at me.

Pressure built inside of me, both pain and pleasure. It felt as if his cock was growing—longer and thicker—even more than it was before, stretching my insides beyond my limits. But he didn't seem to care anymore. He continued to pump in and out of me, ruthlessly.

Holy Hell. I grasped onto the bed sheets, the pain quickly turning to pleasure. He was right, this was too much.

He turned me over, pulled my ass into the air, and snaked a hand up the front of my neck. I gripped onto his arm for support and arched my back, core tightening when he shoved himself inside of me from behind. He curled one arm around my waist and rubbed my clit.

Each thrust was harder than the last, pushing me closer toward the headboard. The bed shook under us, and I tried to say his name, but I couldn't get the word out. All I kept thinking was...

Cinnamon, cinnamon, cinnamon. God, I wanted more cinnamon.

His fingers continued to move wildly, sending a wave of pleasure up my body. "Cum for me, Dani," he said. I squeezed my eyes shut, screamed out, and released myself around him, trembling in his hands.

A flood of emotions washed through me—the strongest being lust. I collapsed in his arms, not being able to move.

After a few more thrusts, he threw his horns back, pulled out of me, and came on my ass. I breathed deeply, lying on my stomach, and sighed, feeling completely satisfied for the first time in my whole life. That was the best sex that I had ever had—by far.

I rolled onto my back and gazed at the demon in front of me.

A million thoughts were racing through my mind. But instead of saying any of them, I shuffled up to the headboard and shielded my body with a blanket.

After *that*, I didn't know what to feel. Hunger. Desire. Pure anxiety.

He stared back at me, not moving. "Dani..." Strands of dark hair laid across his damp forehead. Just like my dreams, his horns were curved and had small ridges around them. It was true. This was really him.

"I'm sorry," he said.

I knelt on the bed, holding the blanket around me. He still didn't move, but his breathing quickened. I lifted my hand, fingers grazing against his horns, then against his cheekbones, then against his swollen shoulder muscles.

He was different but damn amazing.

Demonic power radiated from him, even now when he was standing in front of me—naked and bent with nervousness.

"Why?" I asked, gazing into his eyes. "Why're you sorry for who you are?"

He gulped, and I could tell that he was trying to breathe evenly. His fingers curled into the bed sheets. "Because I'm a monster to you."

"Monsters are heartless and violent, Eros." I pushed a strand of hair off his forehead. "They're cruel and they hide behind the faces of good people. You are not heartless nor cruel, especially not to me."

His eyes softened, and I wondered how someone who was supposed to be so evil and scary could comfort me so much.

"Why didn't you tell me?"

"I needed to be sure that this was what you wanted." He paused. "Is this still what you want?" He broke eye contact with me and shook his head. "You can say no. Don't be afraid to say no."

I brushed my fingers against his chin, lifting it so he was

looking at me. "You told me to choose happiness, and I chose you."

He hesitated for a moment, then smiled. Not one of his infamous smirks, but a true, genuine smile. And I smiled back at him.

Eros was happy.

Chapter Thirty-Four

"So, tell me more about this whole demon thing. Are there really seven different types? Which are the nicest? Do I get to meet any other ones? Is Kasey an incubus too?"

Eros grazed his fingers against the small of my back, leading me through the crowd at The Lounge, and chuckled. "One question at a time."

Lemon, pine, strawberries, chocolate—I inhaled each tempting scent as we passed the men and women flirting at the bar. Each smell was more mesmerizing than the last, but none compared to cinnamon.

I scooted into the same booth that we had last time and smiled. "I'm just curious."

Eros slid in next to me and wrapped his arm around my back. "I know." He placed a kiss on my forehead. "It's cute." His lips lingered, and when he finally pulled away his eyes were hazy. "You always smell so goo—"

"Look at the lovely couple." The waiter from the other night placed a pitcher of water between us. He pulled out a small notebook, flipping to a clean page. "Back again." He smiled. "I bet your parents would love to meet her, Eros."

Eros clenched his jaw, fingers digging into my shoulder. "We'd like to order."

The waiter's eyes glowed—deep, black, and lifeless. "I guess you don't agree."

"Get us another waiter."

He smirked. "Why is the great and powerful Eros holding back? Afraid you'll scare her off if you show her who you really are?"

I pressed my lips together and leaned over the table. "He asked for another waiter."

The waiter turned to me, eyes reddening as they lingered on Mom's pendant in the center of my chest. They blazed like the pits of Hell—not that I actually knew what Hell looked like yet. "Oh, Little Blessed One, don't you speak to me like tha—"

Eros snatched the waiter's neck and jerked him close. "Talk to her like that again, and I'll take whatever's left of your pathetic souls." When he pushed him away, there were deep red claw marks in the waiter's neck. "Now, get us another fucking waiter."

The man grasped the sides of his neck and scurried away through the crowd. Music thumped softly through the bar. People were downing those Passion Delight drinks like they were water. Eros grabbed my hand.

"Now, which question do you want answered first?" Eros asked with a smile.

I leaned forward, my heart racing. "If Hell is real, is Heaven real too?" I asked. Maybe there was a chance—a sliver of hope— that I would get to see Mom again. "Because if it is, I want to go. I want to see my mom. She has to be up there. She was everything good."

Eros's light expression suddenly turned grim. "Your mother..." He spun his ring around his finger and exhaled. "Heaven is not what everyone thinks it is. It's not all good people." He shook his head. "I can't tell you where she is or how to get up there because demons cannot reach the Golden Gates without wings," he said, and I frowned. "But I will do everything that I can to keep you safe from people who stole your mother from you. I promise that one day I will get you the closure that you need."

He gave me a weak smile, and I gave him one back. "Okay," I said softly. "Okay."

A woman in a little black dress walked up to our table. She gave Eros a flirty smile and even had a seductive glint in her eye, but Eros didn't spare her a glance. When she looked at me, her blue eyes sparkled. "Good evening," she said.

"Hi." I smiled and leaned closer to her. She smelt like roses.

Her fingers brushed against mine. "What would you like tonight?" she asked, leaning over to give me a clear view of her cleavage.

"Heaven," Eros said shaking his head. He lifted his finger, telling her to stand. "Don't seduce her."

Unlike the previous waiter, she nodded respectfully at Eros and took our drink orders. We both asked for Passion Delights—because I didn't care about winning or losing any game anymore—but she only returned with one for Eros. Passion Delights were only reserved for a select few *people*, and by people she definitely meant demons.

I watched her retreat to the bar, then gazed at Eros. "What's so special about Passion Delights?"

He sipped it, then inhaled deeply. "They give incubus or succubus demons a kick."

"A kick?"

"It makes them more sensitive to someone's arousal."

My cheeks flushed, and I sipped on my plain water. "So, if I was aroused right now, you'd know?"

"I can always tell when you're aroused." He tapped his ring on the glass, making it clank.

"You can?"

He chuckled and sat back, gazing at the bar. "I could tell that our waitress turned you on."

I gulped and glanced at her. Her blonde curls bounced on her shoulders as she walked back and forth behind the bar, pouring sex-crazed demons more Passion Delights. For a moment, her eyes met mine, and I dug my nails into Eros's thigh. "She's attractive, but that doesn't mean she arouses me."

He trailed a finger down my cheek. "So, given the chance, you wouldn't want to fuck her?"

My eyes widened at the thought. "No, I'm dating you."

Eros smirked. "That's not what I asked," he said. I took a long sip of my water. Was it getting hot in here or was it just me? Eros sat back. "If we weren't together and you met her at a bar, would you go home with her?"

I pursed my lips. "Come on, Eros. I don't sleep around with people I meet one time."

"Look at you, getting so defensive over it."

"I'm not getting defensive over it."

Eros leaned closer to me, his fingers slipping under my dress. "You're wet just thinking about it."

I pushed his hand away, cheeks flushing. Damn him. Why did he always have to put me on the spot? Didn't he know that I was an anxious mess all the time? I cleared my throat and tried to push away the thoughts of the waitress. "So, the other night when you ordered a Passion Delight, did you intend on losing the game?"

He shrugged as if losing meant nothing to him. "I knew I wasn't going to be able to resist you for much longer." He curled a finger around my hair. "You don't even have to try. It comes so naturally to you."

I snorted. Hell, no. I had to learn the tricks from Kasey, had to repeat them hundreds of times so I wouldn't forget them.

Eros chuckled and leaned closer to me. "But, let's be clear, I did not lose."

I playfully slapped him on the chest. "What? I totally beat you at your own damn game. Admit it."

He took another sip of his Passion Delight and shook his head.

"I will not. I had you curled around my finger since the day I met you."

Well, there was no denying that one. He hooked me on cinnamon like an addict. I smiled, thinking back to that Sunday morning. I was so naïve, thinking I could ever resist someone like him for the rest of my life.

I brushed my fingers over his ring. "You could haunt anyone," I said. "Why did you choose me?"

"First, demons don't haunt people. We're not ghosts," he said, eyes cloudy.

I smiled. "Sorry—possess then."

"Second, you chose me."

"What do you mean by that?"

"Come on. You don't think other demons haven't tried to possess you before me?"

I clutched Mom's pendant. Other demons? Like Javier or even Kasey? My nose wrinkled. "I don't remember others."

"That's because you didn't let them possess you." He leaned forward onto his elbows, ring shining under the dim table light. "In order to be possessed—in order for a demon to take full control of your body and your emotions—you have to agree to it."

"Who would willingly be possessed?"

"You." He chuckled and ran a hand across my back. "You wanted me to make you cum, so you told me that you wanted me. You gave me possession of you."

"Sneaky," I said, nodding. "That's how you did it."

"That's not sneaky compared to most. If you didn't like something, other demons wouldn't care. They would've continued using your body for their needs," he said. I gazed around at the other demons in the bar, lingering on the male waiter. He seemed like one of those types. Using people until he didn't need them anymore. Hell, Javier was that type—using Trevon for his own needs, letting him become a damn demon, throwing him out when he was finished.

"So"—I glided my finger across his ring, watching a streak of red follow my finger on its black canvas—"if I didn't want to do anything with you or if I wanted you to stop, you would?" I asked, and he nodded. "How do I know you'll stop?"

"If you don't like something, say *heaven* and I'll stop."

"*Heaven*," I whispered to myself. The word sounded bittersweet—like the past few weeks of sinning had sealed my fate for an eternity in Hell, but Mom was standing up in the clouds, calling my name for me to come home someday.

The candle between Eros and I flickered against his glass, and I smiled—thinking back to the times when Mom used to drink red wine while we binge-watched cartoons on Tuesday nights in the living room. My five-year-old self would always inch close to her, bat my lashes, and ask for one tiny little sip. Desperately wanting to know what the big deal was about those fancy cups and the sour smelling happy juice inside of them.

Eros pushed his Passion Delight in my direction. "You've been eyeing it all night."

My eyes widened. "Really?"

He chuckled. "One sip."

I gazed around to make sure nobody was watching, then took a larger-than-intended sip. It burned the back of my throat, the sourness making my nose wrinkle. "This is gross." I placed the glass on the table and pushed it back to him. "I don't know how you get a kick out of that."

"It'll hit you," he said, standing. He grabbed my hand, tossed some type of paper money—*Joss* he called it—onto the table, and led me out of The Lounge. Instead of taking the route back to the car, we walked along the sidewalk, watching small snowflakes melt on the ground.

A bus pulled up to the corner of Sixth and Penn, and Eros

grabbed my hand, pulling me towards it. "Come on. Let's go somewhere."

"Where? Are we just leaving the car her—"

"Trust me, Dani," he said, tugging me along before the bus pulled away. "We'll come back for the car later."

The bus was crowded even for a Friday night. Eros guided me to the back, near the last pair of exit doors, and I held onto the handrail as the bus lurched forward. "Where are we going?" I asked again.

Eros stood behind me, one hand on the handrail beside mine, the other on my shoulder. "Patience," he said. I sighed and gazed out of the window, watching Dr. U's office building whizz by us. We were headed outbound toward the Liberty Bridge.

The bus stopped a few more times, letting more people on. Eros tapped his fingers on my shoulder, his breath on my neck.

"Shouldn't you be watching for the stop?" I asked. "And not me?"

He chuckled and pushed a strand of hair behind my ear. "We're not getting off at a stop."

"Then where are we—" I grasped the rail tighter, my core suddenly tightening and pulsing quickly. What the—

"You okay?" Eros asked against my ear. His fingers were trailing down my sides.

That drink, that damn drink was doing this. And Eros knew it would. I took a deep breath, trying to suppress my growing excitement.

"Oh, my God."

The bus stopped again, and even more people crowded on. I scooted against one of the exit doors, heart pounding. Why were there so many people here tonight? Everyone's body heat was making me so hot, I just wanted to strip off all of my clothes.

I shifted my gaze from the people on the bus to my reflection in the door windows. Stay calm, Dani.

Eros's black eyes reflected off the windows. He pressed his

hardness into my backside, rubbing it against my ass, and I clenched unwillingly. "What are you doing?" I whisper-yelled. I tried to face him, but he grasped my hips and held me in place. "People are going to see!"

"I won't let anyone see you the way I do," he said against me. Then he paused and gazed toward the crowd behind us, making direct eye contact with few people. Suddenly, the bus filled with noisy chatter and the overwhelming aroma of several scents. Men and women with seductive glints in their eyes—who I had no doubt were demons—pried eyes away from us and directed them toward themselves.

Eros curled an arm around my torso and pressed his fingers against my pussy through my dress. I grasped the handrail tighter, my knuckles whitening. "Eros, please."

He pushed me closer to the door until my chest was plastered against it. "Please what?" He continued to rub me while he undid the top button or my dress, revealing my cleavage. I grasped his hand as he unbuttoned the next one, hand slipping inside of my top. He trailed his fingers across my bare skin and over my nipple. "Not wearing a bra tonight?" he asked shaking his head. "What did I tell you about teasing me? Do I need to teach you a lesson?"

I shook my head. "No... Eros, please. I won't do it again," I said. He pinched my nipple, and a wave of pleasure washed over me.

"You need to learn to be a good girl." He unbuttoned the next button.

"Stop, Eros. Somebody is going to see!"

"Calm down and they won't." He undid one more button and my breasts fell out of the top. I squeezed my eyes shut, praying to God that nobody was watching. He curled a hand around my neck and pulled me away from the door to gaze at my reflection in the glass.

I watched his fingers dance across my skin, from breast to

breast—toying with my nipples. Then he pressed his lips to my ear. "You're craving my cock, aren't you?"

"No, I—I'm not." I took a deep breath, my core clenching.

He chuckled and pulled his hand off of me. I sighed and closed my eyes in relief, pulling my dress closed. Thank God that was over because I didn't know what I would do if—

My eyes widened when I heard the faint sound of a zipper. I didn't have time to turn around before Eros lifted the back of my dress just enough for him to slide his himself underneath.

Oh, my God. He's going to fuck me. Right here, in front of everyone.

I clenched again, pressing my fingers into the glass window. He pushed himself against my wetness.

The bus stopped again, and some others came on. Eros pushed me closer to the door as people pushed into him.

"Eros, please, someone will see!" There was no way in Hell that someone wouldn't see us fucking in the middle of a crowded bus. But when I looked around, they were all staring lustfully at the demons disguised as humans.

He wrapped his hand around the front of my throat and pulled me close. "Tell me that you want it," he said. But I wasn't going to beg in front of everyone and risk someone finding out, so I sucked in a deep breath and hoped that this ache in my core would suddenly disappear. "Beg for me," he said, rubbing his fingers roughly against my clit.

Damn it.

I squeezed my eyes shut, feeling his cock poke at my entrance. "Please, Eros," I said. A sudden rush of pleasure warmed my core. "Please give it to me."

He pushed himself inside of me slowly and groaned. "You're so wet." He thrusted himself deeper and stilled. I dug my nails into my sweaty palms. This wasn't happening. This really wasn't happening.

He pulled my hands away from my top, letting it fall open just enough to see my breasts in the reflection of the glass. "Look at these," he said, groping one. He rolled my nipple between his fingers and tugged on it. "I'm going to have fun with you."

I grabbed the handrail, trying not to make a sound as he continued to tug on my nipples. Waves of pleasure were coursing through me already, and he hadn't even started fucking me yet. "Eros," I whimpered, gazing at his black eyes through the reflection.

He trailed his fingers up my neck, gripped my chin, and brushed his thumb against my lips. "Shh, shh, shh. Don't want anyone to hear you yet, do you?"

Yet? I didn't want anyone to hear me at all.

After chuckling sinisterly into my ear, he thrusted himself hard into me, watching my breasts bounce. I pressed my lips together, a muffled moan escaping my throat. Oh, my God.

He stilled. "What did I tell you?" He drew a finger around my nipple. "Do you want everyone to watch me fuck you?" My brows creased, and his grip on my chin tightened. "Huh?"

"N—" Again, he thrusted himself into me without warning, fingers harshly rubbing my clit, and I moaned—unable to stop myself.

Eros smirked against my ear. "I'm going to make you scream." He continued to thrust himself into me, hand pressing on my lower back and making me arch. My breasts were nearly pushed against the door. People brushed against me—backs turned—as the bus continued down the road.

With each thrust his pace quickened, and I wondered how the hell someone hadn't seen us yet. Maybe they had. All I knew was the pressure in my core was so intense I could feel my pussy quivering. His size expanded inside of me, and I let out a soft moan.

"Fuck, Dani," he murmured against my ear, pulling me off of the door and watching my breasts bounce again. "Beg for me. I wanna hear you beg."

I shook my head. Not here. Not now. If I opened my mouth, I wouldn't have control over what came out of it.

But Eros was having none of it. He pressed his fingers into my lips. "Beg," he said more forcefully. When I didn't answer, he grabbed a fistful of my hair. "I can make everyone on this bus turn around and watch you get fucked or we can continue like this. Your choice. If you don't beg, I'll choose for you."

"Eros," I breathed, pussy clenching. "Please."

"Louder."

Someone was going to hear me. They definitely were going to hear me.

"Please..."

He furiously rubbed my clit, and I could feel myself teetering over the edge. Just a few more moments, and I would—

"What don't you understand about louder?"

After one more deep thrust, I cried out. "Please, Eros." Waves of pleasure hit me hard, and I grabbed onto the handrail for dear life, my legs trembling. My brows were furrowed together, and I rested my forehead against the window. Holy Hell.

When I was finished, Eros wrapped his arm around my torso and pulled me to him. "Good girl," he said. He pulled out of me and redid the buttons on my dress until all of them were clasped together.

He zippered up his pants and whistled. Everyone turned back to the positions they were originally in. I breathed heavily, leaning against the door.

This was sin. We were sin. And I loved every second of it.

Chapter Thirty-Five

After not making eye contact with anyone for the rest of the bus ride—thinking that if I did, they'd know what just happened—Eros and I headed back home. I lit the vanilla candle on my side-table and peeled back the curtains so we could see the city lights in the dark.

Eros laid on the side on my bed, head propped up on his hand. "Did you enjoy that?"

I gave him a half-smile, still feeling weak. Sinning with him had me more excited than it should have. Every day Hell was becoming more tempting.

"Tell me more about what it's like to be an incubus," I said sitting on the bed next to him.

"What do you want to know?"

I wanted to know everything—more about the Kingdom of Lust, more about the path to Hell, more about sinning. But, instead, I said, "How many lovers have you had?" And I nearly slapped a hand over my mouth when I did. He'd probably had hundreds, while I'd only slept with cheater-turned-demon Trevon and a lousy kid in high school who thought that 10 seconds of jackhammering would make me cum.

All emotion faded from his face. "I've had many sexual partners—too many to count, to be honest with you."

I played with the hem of the blanket. "Is that... normal? Kasey has an open relationship, and Zane told Maria that he wanted one too."

He sat up, thumb playing with his ring. "Yes, it's normal to have multiple partners at the same time. Most sex demons participate in open relationship, and it's common to practice polyamory."

My heart nearly dropped. Of course, they would desire more than one partner. They had needs. But did that mean Eros was seeing someone else right now too? I didn't want to believe it, but after Trevon cheated on me, I couldn't shake the thought of being with a man and not knowing if he had someone else on the side.

"Oh," I whispered, my gaze falling to the bed. Maybe I should've waited to tell him that I was sure I wanted us, until that lustful feeling went away, and I truly understood what came along with dating a demon.

It wasn't just amazing sex. It was wondering if I was the only one in his life or if he had been hiding someone else from me this whole time. It was wondering if I could ever compare to any sex demon that Eros slept with before me. I was just human after all.

And he *was* being more suggestive than usual today with that waitress. Maybe she was his lover or maybe he wanted to gage whether I'd be okay with him seeing other people.

"Dani, I—"

"No, Eros. It's okay. You-you don't have to explain yourself." My eyes watered as I stared at the city lights which looked so bright against the darkness outside.

"That's not—"

I held my hand up and pressed my lips together. "Please, I don't want to hear it. It'll break my heart." I grabbed Mom's pendant in my hand and squeezed it harder than I ever had before and stood. "Maybe we aren't a good idea. I can't get into that type of relationship right now and—"

He grasped my face in his hands, thumbs brushing over my cheekbones. "Dani! Listen to me." His eyes were a piercing green. "I don't want a polyamorous relationship."

"You don't?"

"And, please, don't think that I've been fucking someone else this whole time. Yes, I've had multiple partners at once, but only when everyone was comfortable with it. I've honestly only desired one partner at a time."

We sat in silence, just staring at each other. His eyes shifted through a hundred shades of green—each a different emotion—and finally settled into a soft emerald. "When I was a child, there was a couple in the Kingdom of Lust who only had each other for partners and wouldn't take anyone else. At that time, I thought that being committed to one person was best because I had experienced thousands of years with polyamory and didn't understand love."

"You had never experienced love in a polyamorous relationship?"

He grabbed my hand and squeezed it. "Not personally," he said. But I knew that it could happen. Kasey had a strong relationship with Aarav and Mycah. "I guess it was just the world I grew up in, seeing my parents around different people—never really happy with any number of them." His frown deepened. "One day I'm sure that I could care for more than one person at a time, but right now I just need to learn how to care again, and I want to care about you."

This man. I drew him into a hug and smiled. I loved this side of him.

When I pulled away, he was tense. "You're okay with that?"

"What do you mean?"

"You're okay with what I told you—" He hesitated. "That I only want one partner, right now?"

"Hell, yes," I said. And—to my surprise—the words 'right now' didn't bother me like I thought that they would.

A smile flashed across his face for a brief moment, but then it vanished and turned into something much darker. "In the Kingdom of Lust, it's seen as a disgrace if you only take one romantic partner. My parents hated me for it." He pressed his lips into a thin line, suddenly becoming quiet. The only sound in the room being the candle crackling in the corner. "They punished me," he said quietly.

I clenched my fist. They hated his decision so much that they punished him for it? That was rotten.

"How?" I asked, after relaxing my fist. I didn't want to bring up painful memories, but Mom always told me that people acted off of past experiences and I wanted to know what they did so I could care for him the way he needed to be cared for.

He stared me right in the eyes, leaned onto his forearms at the edge of the bed, and pulled his shirt over his head. The two parallel scars on his back were a deep red; it was the first time that I could really see his scars for what they were. "First," he said—voice quiet. "They cut my wings."

"You... you had wings?" I whispered, imagining him with immense charcoal-colored wings stretching from one side of the bed to the other. My fingers trailed alongside of the raised red skin, and he winced. I immediately pulled my hand away. "I'm sorry."

"Don't be. I just... didn't expect that." He gazed back at me. "Most people flinch away from them."

I crawled closer and hugged him from behind, planting my lips on his cheek. "Don't feel bad about them."

"They're a daily fucking reminder of how much of an embarrassment I am to the Kingdom. How could I not feel bad about it? A lord with no wings, who only enjoys one partner at a time and that partner is—" He tensed and shook his head. "Forget it."

My brows knotted together. Did I make this worse for him?

"Your scars make you who you are, Eros. And if you think that anybody who shames you for them is worth torturing yourself over, you're wrong."

He grabbed one of my hands, still facing away from me, and stayed quiet. When his breathing evened out, he dropped his head in shame. "They banished me from the kingdom."

I clenched my fists. They shamed him, stole his sacred wings, and banished him from his own kingdom. They deserved to have angels rain down upon them. They deserved to relive all of their sins but feel absolute agony for them—instead of getting off on destroying their own son.

"Have you been back?" I said, trying not to relish in my cruel thoughts.

"No. When I go back to Hell, I stay in the Kingdom of Pride with Lucifer."

My fingers grazed against the side of his cheek. "Are you happy?"

"Am I happy?" he asked himself, like he hadn't asked himself in such a long time. "I'm happy now that I can be who I want to be and with who I want to—"

My door was slammed open, and Trevon barreled in with black eyes and razor-sharp teeth, soaked in blood from head to toe.

Chapter Thirty-Six

I leapt up—heart racing. Damn it.

Eros pushed me behind him, horns growing from his head and eyes turning black in less than a second. "What the..."

Trevon's beady little eyes flickered from me to Eros, and a tint of red rose within them. He lurched forward, snarling.

Oh, my God.

Before Trevon could reach Eros, Eros stepped back—nearly knocking me out of the way—grabbed Trevon by the neck with his claws, and held him in the air. Trevon dug into Eros's wrists with his own claws, making blood pour out of the open wounds. He flung his body in every direction, but Eros held him in place.

When Trevon's face turned blue, I gulped and rubbed my sweaty palms together. If Eros didn't let him go, Trevon would die. And as much as I didn't want him in my life, I didn't want him dead. This wasn't his fault.

I yanked on Eros's wrist. "Eros! Stop. He can't control it."

Eros turned to me, body shaking. "You knew about this?" he asked harshly. I nodded my head, gaze remaining on Trevon as Eros hurled him to the other side of the room. He smacked against the wall—hard—and pieces of drywall fell next to him. I ran towards him, something inside of me aching to help him, but Eros snatched my waist and held me back.

Trevon charged at us, and again Eros swiftly placed me behind him and snatched his throat.

"Eros don't hurt him! I can stop it, please. Let me help."

Eros's eyes burned with rage—an emotion that didn't suit him well. "You've been around him like this?" he asked. I pressed my lips together, trying not to show the menacing demon standing over me my fear. "Why didn't you tell me?"

"I just found out about you!" I yelled at him. "Now, let me help." I pulled on his wrist and actually pulled Eros away. Trevon was still lashing out, body thrashing, but I placed my hands firmly on the sides of his face. "Trevon, look at me." He turned his head, looking toward the door. "Please Trevon," I said softer.

When I finally got him to look at me, the tint of red vanished from his eyes, and I sighed in relief. He reeked of blood and wrath but placed his hands on mine and trailed his fingers down my slender ones, taking a deep breath through his mouth.

Eros growled, causing Trevon to snap his gaze back to him and start squirming again.

"God, damn it," I said. I tightened my grip on Trevon. Eros was the one triggering Trevon to act this way, even if he wasn't trying. "Eros, can you leave?" I asked. "Please."

Eros stepped closer, eyes pure darkness. "I'm not leaving you here with him."

Trevon stepped forward, but I placed my hands on his chest and pushed him back against the wall. "Eros, please."

"I'm not leaving." He took another threatening step. "I let you try to fix him, and it didn't work."

My eyes widened, and I spun around—keeping one hand on Trevon's chest. "It worked! You just ruined it." I clenched my jaw, and Trevon pushed against my hand. If Eros didn't leave soon, I didn't know if I could calm him back down. "Leave now," I said to him.

Eros's black eyes were dancing with white little lights as he stared at me. He bared his fangs at Trevon, then stormed out of the room.

When he left, I lightly stroked the sides of Trevon's face. This better calm him down, because if it didn't, I would have to let Eros do whatever he was planning with Trevon.

After five minutes of just staring at him in pure angst—aching to grab Mom's necklace that was becoming colder and colder against my chest—he stopped thrashing around, and his eyes faded to brown. He slid down the wall. "Shit," he said.

I took a deep breath, inhaling the strong scent of vanilla, and crouched next to him. "Why'd you go ballistic on Eros?"

His muscles twitched at the mere sound of his name, but he crossed his arms over his chest and stayed still. "I don't know why."

"Well, get yourself together," I said, standing. I didn't know if I'd be able to ever calm him down again. This time was harder than the last, and it was bound to just keep getting worse. "And don't come out of this room until I say so."

I slipped into the living room, when I knew he wouldn't shift again. Eros paced around the room in his human form, brows creased. Zane leaned against the counter with a confused expression. And Maria stared wide-eyed at both of them. "What's going on?" she asked.

"Don't, Dani," Eros said, warning me not to say a word.

I flared my nostrils, feeling drained from dealing with Trevon. "She already knows," I said, harsher than I meant.

Zane pushed himself off the counter. "You knew about this?"

Maria furrowed her brows. "I knew about what?" she asked. I nodded to Trevon's bloody jacket on the counter—the most obvious thing in the entire room—and her lips formed an 'O'.

"You mean…" She held two fingers above her head, mimicking devil horns.

I slapped a hand over my face. Eros rubbed his forehead and mumbled something under his breath.

Maria stepped closer to me. "I thought we were keeping it a secret."

I shrugged. "Eh." It didn't matter anymore. Eros was a demon. Zane was a demon. Kasey was a demon. Everyone was a goddamn demon nowadays.

Zane turned to Eros. "Who do you think sent him?"

Eros stared at me for a few moments, as if he was thinking hard about something, then looked at Zane. "The Chains is the only way to find out."

My eyes widened. "The Chains? You're going to lock him up in chains? In… Hell?"

"Don't worry about it," Eros said, just brushing me off.

I shouldn't have cared. Trevon was dangerous, and if he were in chains, he wouldn't be able to hurt anyone else, but a feeling of pity sat heavy inside my heart. This wasn't his fault, and this past week he'd fought against the evil inside of him.

I crossed my arms over my chest. Maybe I was always compelled to see the good in people because I wasn't sure why I seemed to care so much about Trevon going to Hell. But I cared—a lot. "Don't tell me who or what to worry about. I'm perfectly capable of doing that myself," I said.

Eros stood across the room, biceps flexed, his eyes darkening into black pits. Maria screamed and shuffled backward. "You're one of them too?" She plastered her back against the wall, gaze flickering between Eros and me. "Dani! Why aren't you freaking out?"

"Maria, don't get mad, but—"

"You knew about this, didn't you? Oh, my gosh. When were you going to tell me? Next thing, Zane is going to be one too." She looked at Zane who scratched the back of his neck. "OH MY

GOSH. You know what? I can't do this right now." She stuffed her mascara stick, her phone, and a bag of Lindor chocolates that Dr. U gave me last week from the kitchen counter into her purse and hurried to the door.

"Maria, wait!" Zane ran after her, but she slammed the door in his face.

Once he followed her out, Eros began his stride down the hallway toward my room. I wrapped my hand around his forearm and dug my heels into the ground. "Eros, please, I don't want him to get hurt down there."

"You don't want him to get hurt?" He shook his head, lip curled in disgust. "Do you know how much danger you've been in with a fucking wrath demon living in your apartment with you?"

Yes, but I wasn't about to tell him that.

"He hasn't hurt me once. What makes you think that he'd hurt me now?"

He clenched his jaw and pulled his arm from my grasp. "Because my family would do anything that they can to break me, even if that means killing someone I love."

My lips parted, and everything that we were fighting about seemed to vanish. All of my worries and all of my doubts were nothing now.

"You love me?" I whispered, shock running through me. Eros froze. His black eyes softened, and I found that strange comfort in their darkness again. I tried to steady my breathing, but it was no use. "Do you?"

Eros gulped. "You make me happy," he said quietly. "Something I haven't felt in a long time." His voice nearly cracked toward the end. He gazed down for a moment at his ring. "And, with you, I don't have to hide who I am. I feel free and my heart feels full and I don't have to try too hard. It all comes so naturally."

I smiled.

He grabbed my hands, intertwining our fingers. "But I don't

know what love feels like. I know a lot about lust and flirting and fucking, but I don't know the first thing about love anymore. This feeling scares the Heaven out of me... Is love supposed to do that?"

Was love supposed to smell like cinnamon? Was love supposed to have black eyes and curved horns and a heart that I wanted for my own? I didn't know what love looked like or what it was supposed to do anymore either.

"What are you afraid of?" I asked softly.

He gazed at the floor, brows furrowed together in pain. "I don't know."

"What are you afraid of, Eros?" I asked again, wanting him to admit this fear to himself, because that was one of the first steps in overcoming it.

We waited in silence.

"I'm afraid of you," he said. "I'm afraid that you'll meet others like me and be turned off or—worse—you'll be turned on. I'm afraid that you won't like my style of living or that others will try to hurt you..." His voice faded. "I'm afraid that eventually you'll think I'm worthless too."

My heart hurt. His parents really screwed him up, and I hated them for that.

"Eros." I brushed my hand across his cheek. "I can't promise you that we're going to have a perfect life, but I can promise you that I'll never stop trying to show you your worth."

He leaned into my hand and placed his over mine, eyes fluttering closed for a moment. "Dani, please, let me chain him. Just so I know that you're safe."

I played with his fingers. "Will it hurt him?"

"No, it'll just get rid of the demon inside of him."

"Okay," I said. "As long as it doesn't hurt him. He didn't ask for this."

Eros paused for a moment, then shook his head. "You truly care about people. You forgive them. You're harmonious and divine. Too good for me."

I playfully rolled my eyes. "And I suppose that you're just this merciless demon who likes to tear people limb from limb and eat their rotting flesh. That *definitely* sounds like you."

"Well, I do like eating you."

I scrunched up my nose and shook my head at his infamous smirk. "Enough of that, we have to help Trevon."

Chapter Thirty-Seven

"I can't believe I let you talk me into this," Eros said, standing in front of a supernatural black mist which was swirling around in the center of the living room. He had pushed the couches and coffee table into the kitchen to create the portal to Hell while I retrieved Trevon from my bedroom.

I shrugged as if talking Eros into bringing me to Hell was nothing. "I just wanna see what Lucifer's kingdom is like."

Truth was that I wanted to help Trevon and wanted to see if Mom's stories of Hell were real. Was Hell everything people thought it was? Was it filled with deceit and violence and acts of terror?

Trevon shook his head next to me, the veins in his arms and neck pulsing violently again. "I don't want to go, Dani." He kept his gaze on me. "Why... how will this help me? I can barely survive with this—" He snapped his head to the side, eyes nearly rolling to the back of his head, but then took a deep breath.

"That's why, Trevon," I said. "The Chains will help you." I cupped his face in my hands. "If I didn't believe that this would help you, I wouldn't let Eros bring you there."

Eros squeezed his way between Trevon and me. He grabbed

my hand and snatched the back of Trevon's neck. "Close your eyes."

"What do you mean? What's going to happen when we—"

Gusts of wind blew from the portal into my living room, making the curtains fly in all different directions. Eros pulled us into the portal, and I decided not to close my eyes because everything looked so surreal. Blurry objects. Hazy memories. Distant voices. All on a mesmerizing black backdrop. I couldn't peel my eyes away from it if I tried.

We walked in further, and everything became clear. To my left, a woman who resembled Maria was smashing a bat into storefront windows in the city center, knocking antiques off of the shelves. To my right, a man who resembled Trevon was cutting a woman to pieces and storing her flesh in my kitchen fridge. And, straight ahead of me, a woman who looked exactly like Mom was pressing a knife to her own neck, watching drops of blood trickle down it in our old bedroom mirror as I watched from the bed—clapping.

My heart raced, and I shivered in fear. Someone grasped my hand and pulled me closer to them. I thought it was just Eros, but then another hand grabbed my shoulder, jerking me in another direction. Before I knew it, demons swarmed around me, baring rows of jagged teeth in my direction and reaching for me with their shredded flesh of arms.

"Dani!" someone yelled. It sounded so distant.

I needed to get out of here, but I couldn't move. A demon reached for me, claws digging into my forearm and tearing my skin apart. I clutched my wound with a shaky hand.

Someone pulled me backward, and I bumped into a hard chest. Eros pushed away the demon, slid his hand around his neck, and snapped it. And, without another word, he pulled my face into his chest so I couldn't see anything else. I inhaled his cinnamon, relaxing only slightly in his arms.

Damn, I'd never do this again. This was a mistake.

After a few more moments of listening to hissing and growling, we stopped. I reluctantly opened my eyes to see us standing in front of another portal. Inside of it, there were two demon guards. I sighed in relief, heart still pounding in my chest. Whatever we just went through was gone, at least for now.

"Brace yourself," Eros said, pushing me into the hole. I somersaulted through the air a few times and struck the cold, hard cement on the other side. I posted my hands on the ground, trying to catch my breath. Maybe I should reconsider this whole Hell thing. If I had to see that again, I didn't know—

Someone cleared his throat, and I gazed up at the two icy-eyed demons standing over me. "Was Lucifer expecting someone?" one asked the other.

"A succubus, but not..." He looked me up and down, eyes narrowing in a nasty stare as they landed on Mom's necklace. "... her." He crossed his pale arms over his chest. Their horns were curved like Eros's—but smaller and were made of blue ice.

"What is she?"

The other one hissed and snatched my neck, nails digging into my flesh. "State your business."

Suddenly, Trevon tumbled through the portal and smacked belly-first onto the ground. I squirmed in the demon's hold, fingers desperately trying to peel his away.

Eros strolled through the mist. No awkward tumble or fall, just a casual stroll—like this was normal. But when he saw my legs dangling in the air and me gasping for air, he growled. "Put her down now!"

The demon immediately released me, and I fell to the ground with a thud and clutched my neck. Hell. I really shouldn't have come. I haven't even been here for a whole minute and I have already almost been choked out.

Both demons bowed to Eros. "Sorry, Lord Eros. We didn't know she was yours."

Eros wrapped his arm around my waist, picked me up, and placed me at his side. "We're going to The Chains."

"You're allowed to pass, but…" the one that choked me said.

"But?" Eros asked, challenging him.

"But—um…." He scratched the back of his horn, gaze everywhere except on us. "She must stay here."

The other demon stepped forward. "Commander Lucifer's orders. Any new human or demon must be approved by him before entering the kingdom."

Eros's fingers dug into my side. "Tell him I'm here with Dani. He'll let her though."

"Commander Lucifer is-is busy," one said. He kept glancing in my direction and looking away. When Eros growled, the other guard stepped forward. "But we're sure that we can find him."

One of the demons called for a female guard to deliver a message to Lucifer. While we waited for her to return, the two demons stood deathly still next to each other. Every so often, they'd glance at Eros and gulp fear.

The female guard returned and nodded. "Commander Lucifer allows her to pass along with the prisoner."

Eros grabbed my hand, snatched Trevon off of the floor, and pushed past the guards to the door. Well, what a warm welcome that was.

As soon as we walked outside, I gasped at the sudden coldness. The stories Mom told me about Hell—at least Lucifer's Hell— were true. Lucifer's Kingdom was far from flames and fire. It was pure ice. Chillingly frightening like he was.

Tiny icicles dangled from frost white trees. A soft layer of snow laid atop a chalky stone fence that stretched on for miles. Two blazing blue suns floated in the sky and above a castle made entirely of ice. I gaped at it and clenched Mom's pendant which was burning on my chest. Glacier-like mountains surrounded the castle, giving it an eerie feel.

"It's cold in hell," I said. Usually, I didn't like the cold, but this was something I could stare at for years and never get tired of.

Eros chuckled and tugged me along. "Only in Lucifer's Kingdom." He nodded to the castle and leaned closer. "I'll take you there sometime. You'd love it inside."

We trudged down a clear path that snow didn't seem to accumulate on—or even touch seeing that it was dry stone—until we reached a heavily guarded stone building. Before we entered, Eros grabbed my hand. "These are The Chains. Are you sure you want to go in?"

I nodded and inched closer to him. Yeah, sure, I'd be alright. We were at a prison for demons. Nothing could be worse than what I went through in that portal. Nothing.

The guards opened the doors for us to enter, and the lights flickered on. Hundreds of iron cages were stacked on top of each other throughout the room. Demons rattled them and stuck their arms through the bars to reach for me. All I could smell was fresh feces.

Eros grabbed my hand, and we walked through the prison.

"Come here, little girl."

"Let me taste you."

"A sacred little sinner, you are."

One held half a human arm in his hands, his beady eyes trained on me. "Confess your sins to me, and I will cleanse you of them." He bit off a finger, and I nearly puked.

Holy Hell. I should've brought a cross.

Eros leaned down. "Don't listen to them. They prey on your fear," he said.

I gulped and thanked God herself when we moved away from the foul-mouthed demons and stopped in front of an empty set of cages. Eros pulled Trevon into one of them and clasped a silver chain around his neck and wrists.

Trevon sat on his knees, staring at me, unaffected. Then, suddenly, he let out a piercing scream—his body jerking up. His body moved in ways I had never seen before—back arched almost a hundred and eighty degrees, shoulder blades popping out of place, head rotating in a terrifying circle like an owl.

He hastily bear-crawled on his fingertips towards the bars that the chains were attached to and pulled, bending them. Every curse word imaginable was coming out of his mouth, and I cringed—never before hearing such vile things from him.

Moments passed, and Trevon stopped completely. He stood to his feet, standing two to three feet taller than both Eros and me. His body was being stretched, and I could see every one of his ribs, nearly bursting through his skin.

He seized back and forth, and I grabbed Eros's forearms. My God, I was wrong. Things could get worse down here.

His eyes rolled to the back of his head and black blood seeped from them. I screamed and leapt forward to help Trevon in any way that I could, but Eros caught me and held me back. "You said that this wouldn't hurt him," I said, tears streaming down my cheeks.

His eyes turned black and his teeth lengthened into sharp fangs. The veins in his neck dilated so much that I thought they would burst. My heart was aching. How could this be happening? Why was this happening to him?

"Why did you lie, Eros?" I asked. He was in so much pain, and I could feel every bit of it.

Despite my best efforts to hold Trevon one last time, to tell him that everything would be alright, to try to comfort him when I knew a demon was terrorizing his body, Eros held me back.

In the next moment, Trevon fell onto his hands and knees, choking. He clutched his throat as a bulge—the size of a bowling ball—appeared in it. Two sets of sharp red claws pulled his lips apart from the inside, and what must've been a demon pushed his head through Trevon's mouth—stretching it until the corners of his lips began to rip open.

The demon leapt out of Trevon's body, and Eros snatched it. Trevon's eyes returned to their normal brown, and he smacked against the cement.

I wrapped my arms around him, cradling his head to make

sure he wasn't hurt. When I turned him onto his back, I gazed at his face where his mouth was ripped open and doubled over him. Blood dripped down his cheeks, chin, and neck as tears ran down mine. I couldn't believe this. This was nearly too much to handle.

After a few moments of trying to steady my ragged breathing, I gently rested him on the ground and turned back to Eros. I wanted us all to get out of here right now and never come back to The Chains.

Eros was standing in front of a cage which had Trevon's demon on the inside. The demon had deep scar wounds, a long-pointed tail, and dark beady eyes. I didn't know much about Hell, but it was clear that he wasn't from this kingdom, especially not with that fiery red skin.

"Kingdom of Wrath," Eros said to me. He stepped closer to the cage. "Did Sathanus send you?"

"Satan? Who listens to that livid fool anymore?" The demon grasped the chains and pulled on them. "Let me out!"

"Who sent you then?" Eros asked.

The demon curled his sharp tail around my wrist and yanked me right against the cage. "That bastard knew this would happen all along." His beady eyes were fixed on me. "He knew I'd be chained to this fucking wall in this fucking kingdom!" The demon released me, and I grabbed my wrists. He pointed to Eros. "Your brother is going to fucking regret his very fucking life."

Eros lunged toward the cage, hands grasping the metal bars. "Javier sent you?"

"I've had enough of your fucking voice!" The demon turned away and smashed his head into the cement wall on the other side of the cage. Talk about anger management issues.

Eros pushed himself off of the cage bars and stormed away, hitting me by accident. He gently grasped my elbow to steady me. "Sorry," he said softly. He took a deep breath and pushed a strand of hair behind my ear. "Are you okay?"

I nodded. Yeah, *okay*, sure. Let's just get out of here.

"We have to go. I need to talk to Lucifer," he said, grabbing my hand.

I tugged on his arm when we passed Trevon whose face was pale. "What about Trevon?"

"We leave him here for now. Being possessed by a demon leaves him more susceptible to another possession, and..." He frowned at Trevon. "My parents and Javier will think to use him again to get to me. He's safe in here."

I didn't want to leave him here like this—especially with those wounds. "But what about his injuries? We're just going to leave him in this jail with nobody to take care of him."

"You hear that," a demon with glowing green eyes said from the cage above Trevon's. "She cares about the human boy."

"He's going to rot to the bone down here," someone else said.

Eros placed a hand on my shoulder and squeezed. "He'll be alright. I'll get someone to heal him," he said with a look that gave me so much reassurance that I actually believed him. "Lucifer has some of the best healers in all of Hell."

I clasped Mom's pendant, giving Trevon one last lingering look, then walking out of that disgusting prison.

My hands didn't start trembling until we were half-way down the path toward the portal room. That was a lot. Too much almost. Demons from all those different kingdoms, their foul language, their disturbing laughter, and those menacing looks in their eyes—looks that I had only ever seen in passing on Earth.

Every now and then, there'd be someone with a red or yellow or green tint in their eyes, but I'd always, always, always think that I was seeing things. But this was real, and it was more frightening than the bedtime stories I'd beg Mom to tell me.

Eros pushed a strand of hair behind my ear. "Are you really okay?"

"Honestly?" I said. "That was terrifying, and not a place that I ever want to go to again."

He chuckled. "I hope you mean The Chains and not Hell itself."

I gazed around us at the realm of ice, admiring its beauty. Even kingdoms like this had vile places like The Chains. "Hell isn't all bad," I said. "Just parts of it." Like the creepy demons who wanted to rip me limb from limb and sing me terrifying lullabies.

Eros opened the portal room door for me. "The Chains and the Portal can be intense for newcomers, but you'll get used to it. On the bright side, you made it through one of the most terrifying places in this kingdom." Eros turned to the two demons who were watching us nervously. "Tell Lucifer to meet me at The Lounge tonight. I have information that I need to share with him." He grabbed my hand and led me to the portal.

"Close your ey—" I squeezed my eyes shut before he could finish, ready to get out of here. He didn't need to tell me twice.

<h1 style="text-align:center">Chapter Thirty-Eight</h1>

The waitress from the other night stood behind the bar, wearing a low-cut bodycon dress and flirting with a pair of women on the other side. Unlike the rest of the women here, she showed only a bit of cleavage—but it was enough to be tempting.

I gazed at her for a few moments, then turned back to Eros who was sitting next to me. We were back at The Lounge, waiting for Lucifer, and I was doing everything that I could to keep myself calm.

It wasn't Lucifer that made me nervous, but Mom's stories of him that did. A fallen angel with cold eyes and a passion for deception.

"Is he scary?" I fiddled with my fingers and leaned closer to Eros.

"No," he said. "But you might think so."

I sipped my white wine. Well, Dani, there was no going back. Since Eros traveled to his kingdom often, I was bound to meet him eventually. Maybe after getting to know him, I'd be more comfortable. After all, Eros seemed to look up to him.

"What kingdom does he rule again?" Pride, obviously Pride.

"Pride," he said, raising a brow. "Why do you keep asking me?"

"Is he... arrogant?"

"I am," someone said from behind me. Low and devilishly demanding.

My eyes widened. Great job, Dani, embarrass yourself in front of Hell's most powerful ruler. Before I could hurt my pride more, I turned around and sucked in a breath.

Mom told me the ugly stories of Lucifer, but I never imagined he'd look so sexy. He was the epitome of his kingdom—icy blue eyes, platinum locks that hung loosely by the sides of his face, incredibly sharp and chilling features.

Lucifer arched a brow. "So, this is Dani?"

I smiled awkwardly at him, nervous that he was staring at me and only me. Not sparing Eros a single glance, not admiring the beautiful people around us. Me.

God, I wanted to say something, but what could I say to a commander of Hell? Do I ask him about the weather down there? Oh, hey Lucifer, I thought that Hell was hot but...

Eros interlocked our fingers, a big smile on his face. "Yes, this is her."

"Well..." Lucifer sat across from us, extended his arm, and took my hand in his. He held my hand for a moment longer than he should've, and I noticed the scars running across his knuckles. "It's nice to finally meet you."

I parted my lips to speak, realizing that I still hadn't said anything. "I'm—um. Hi."

Damn it, why was I so awkward?

He chuckled. "Don't worry about it, darling. I have that kind of effect on people." His gaze flickered to Eros. "She is quite adorable. I'll give you that." Then he rested his arm on the back of the cushioned seat and leaned against it. "So, why'd you summon me?"

Eros sipped his Passion Delight and sat up. "Javier sent a wrath demon to possess a human."

The light from the candle between us flickered across Lucifer's face. "Demons from Wrath always possess humans."

"He's been staying with Dani."

Lucifer took a long and deep breath and grabbed a waiter by the elbow as he walked by. "Get me the strongest drink you have." He paused and gestured to Eros's Passion Delight. "But none of that shit." The waiter nodded.

"He lashed out on me this morning," Eros said.

"Javier..." Lucifer eyed me. "... knows?" he asked. I furrowed my brows at him. Knows what?

"You think he's that smart to figure it out?" Eros leaned back in the booth, trying to look nonchalant—but by the way he continued to twirl the ring around his finger, I could tell he was worried.

"To the average demon, it might not be apparent, but I could tell as soon as I saw her. You could tell. There's no reason Javier wouldn't be able to tell either. He's not as smart as us, but he's definitely not stupid." Lucifer gazed at the ring, then at me. "Does she—"

"No," Eros said.

I narrowed my eyes at Eros. "Do I what?"

He clenched his jaw and started speaking in a different demonic-sounding language across the table at Lucifer. It was hushed, but by the way they continued to glance at me, I knew I was the topic of their conversation.

Damn demons always keeping secrets from me. I slumped against the seat and watched the candle flicker. The waitress from earlier set a blue drink in front of Lucifer and smiled at me. "Can I get you more wine? Maybe something else?" She brushed her fingers against mine. "You can come behind the bar and pick it out yourself."

Lucifer and Eros stopped talking and looked over. I swallowed that sinful feeling I was getting in the pit of my stomach and shook my head. "No, thank you."

When she walked away, Lucifer looked at Eros. "You know what this means."

"Enlighten me," Eros said with annoyance in his voice.

"Javier is trying to get rid of you. Since his father is King of Wrath and his mother is Queen of Lust, he wants to rule the two kingdoms when they step down. Right now, he's heir to his father's throne and you're heir to your mother's. You're the only thing standing in the way of his desires." Lucifer crossed his arms over each other, biceps bulging, and rested them on the table. "I wouldn't be surprised if your parents were involved."

Eros knocked back the rest of his drink and wrapped his arm around me. "I'm not heir to the throne."

"Your parents eliminate you, their first born who is the keeper of the ring..." He gestured to Eros's black ring. "... and the only demon in the kingdom that knows the secret that could destroy their rule."

Eros's jaw tightened. "And Javier is next in line for the throne. My mother's son, a demon who possesses the true way of the incubi," he said.

There was a tense silence for a few moments while Eros and Lucifer stared at each other. I gently placed my hand on Eros's arm, wanting to soothe him.

Lucifer sat back and sipped his drink. "You know what you have to do, don't you?"

Eros sighed and rubbed a hand over his face. "I hoped that it wouldn't come to this so soon."

Lucifer waved a dismissive hand in the air. "Yes, you were. That's why you summoned me. You have the woman. Now, all you need is the kingdom."

Eros leaned back in the booth. It was like he couldn't sit still tonight. "Lust will never follow me."

"The kingdom was hysterical after they banished you. Many would follow if you reclaim your place."

"Which entails?" Eros asked.

Lucifer leaned across the table, and I inhaled the scent of apples. "Don't be stupid. The only way you can do it is by eliminating Javier and your parents."

Eliminating as in killing? My eyes widened. Eros had joked about killing before, but I never saw him really do it. I thought it was a joke, and I—sure as Hell—never even thought I'd be a part of a plan to murder anyone.

"And what happens then?" I asked, speaking directly to Lucifer for the first time tonight. My heart was racing at the dreaded thought of death. Killing to gain power and place in a society seemed so wicked.

Lucifer smirked at me. "You will be the Queen of Lust."

"Queen of Lust," I whispered, tasting the words on my tongue.

Mom would've never approved, but God did it sound tempting.

I took a deep breath. I could barely even speak properly in front of demons. I'd be terrible at the whole lust thing—flirting with anything that moved, the demons, the visitors, humans. My nose wrinkled.

Eros placed a hand on my thigh and squeezed gently. "Stop overthinking it." He rubbed small circles on the inside of my bare thigh, and I leaned against him. Well, that was one way to get me to stop thinking.

"You will do it at the annual dinner that the Kingdom of Lust holds," Lucifer said.

Eros pondered the thought for a moment, then shook his head. "They won't let me in."

"They will if you bring Dani," Lucifer said. I was going to be there while it happened?

"Dani will not be coming." Eros's voice was stern.

"Either you bring her or find another woman to take—someone of importance."

Eros placed his elbows on the table, fiddling with that ring again. "I'm not putting her in harm's way. It's bad enough that my parents will be there, but Javier's father will also be there."

Lucifer chuckled. "Satan, the King of Wrath." He shook his head. "I'll accompany you then. Haven't seen my old *friend* in a long time."

"You'll come?" Eros asked.

"I'm not going to pass up the chance to watch the true ruler of Lust claim the throne."

Eros stayed quiet. I watched his eyes darken and become distant—like he was playing out scenarios in his head. When his eyes shifted back to their green color, he sat up. "What do you want for it?"

Lucifer took another sip of his drink. "You always think I'm trying to get something out of our deals."

"You are, aren't you?"

He tilted his head, lip curling into a smirk. "I'm sure we can negotiate."

Eros continued to rub soothing circles on my inner thigh. "Negotiate what?"

Lucifer paused for a moment, gaze lingering on me. "It's a win-win for all of us," he said. I furrowed my brows as Eros dug his fingers lightly into my thigh. Lucifer's smirk widened. "I know you're opposed to polygamous relationships, but you can share every now and then, can't you?"

I fidgeted in my seat, core clenching.

I could've blamed my excitement on Eros's mesmerizing scent of cinnamon or the dominant, yet strangely appealing way Lucifer held himself. But neither of them were the reasons for the innate need I had to sin at that moment. It was me. No matter how wrong it was, no matter how much I told Eros that it would only be us—if that's what he wanted—I couldn't deny that I was turned on by the mere thought of being with both of them tonight.

Lucifer chuckled. "I think Dani likes the idea." He turned toward Eros, but kept his gaze trained on mine. "You want to please your woman, don't you?"

From the corner of my eye, I saw Eros glance between us—just feeling the tension. I squeezed Eros's hand and looked at him. The thought of both of them in bed with me was driving me crazy, but Eros was enough.

"Eros already pleases me," I said. More than anyone ever had.

Eros picked up his Passion Delight and took a long sip of it, eyes becoming hazy. I tried suppressing my arousal, so he couldn't sense it, but it was no use. Just thinking about it made me wet.

"Dani," he said. "What would you like?"

"I-I want to do what you want," I said, gazing into his dark eyes and smelling the intoxicating aroma of cinnamon and apples.

"She's already turned on by the mere idea," Lucifer said. "You are too."

Eros grazed a finger against my cheek, and I looked at him. "What do you want?" His fingers lightly brushed against the inside of my thigh again. "Tell me, Dani."

I glanced between the two men, and I could already feel the warmth pool between my legs. There was no point in denying it. "Okay," I whispered.

"That didn't answer my question," he said, voice low. Lucifer smirked at us from across the table, ice eyes captivating me.

Was he really going to make me say it in front of Lucifer? This was so damn embarrassing. I shifted in my seat and pointed to the corner of the room. "Can I tell you over there?"

"You'll tell him here," Lucifer said.

Eros moved his hand further up my leg—getting dangerously

close to the hem of my skirt—and brushed his nose against my ear. He grabbed a fistful of my hair in his hand and tugged it back, trailing his lips up the column of my neck. "What do you want, Dani?"

I squeezed my legs together, but he pushed them apart, fingers rubbing the outside of my panties. My brows knotted together, and I looked at Lucifer who was staring us.

"Both of you," I said.

As if on cue, Lucifer stood and slid into the booth next to me. "Are you sure this is okay?" I asked, but Eros's lips were already on my neck. Lucifer placed his hand on my thigh and leaned closer to me. He brushed a finger against my chin and moved my lips to his.

He mumbled something, but I honestly couldn't comprehend what was going on. My mind was buzzing with excitement.

Eros continued to rub his fingers against my panties. "Relax, Dani. Enjoy this."

Lucifer pressed his lips against mine, so needy like he'd been waiting a lifetime to kiss me while Eros plunged his fingers inside of my pussy. I clenched around him. I couldn't wait for them to be inside of me.

I placed my hands on their thighs, slowly trailing up. They were both hard.

"Get a Lust Room!" the annoying male waiter yelled from behind the bar.

Eros pulled away from my neck, eyes dancing with darkness. "We're in a sex bar for Hell's sake. Fuck off." He scooted out of the seat, picked me up, and walked toward the bar with Lucifer.

The waiter dangled a pair of maroon keys from his finger, smirking. Lucifer snatched them and led us into a back hallway. Doors were open and demons were walking from room to room. Fucking on top of beds, on floors, against doorframes. My eyes widened. Some rooms were occupied by only a few demons while others must've had ten or more in them.

Lucifer held open a door at the end of the hallway. Eros let me down inside of it, and I walked around—gazing wide-eyed at everything. There was a large oak bed in the center of the room, a velvet armchair in the corner, and a dresser to the right of it. Tattered ropes and chains and all sorts of toys hung from hooks on a wall.

"Do they clean these places?" I asked, drawing my finger across the comforter.

Eros rummaged through the dresser and pulled out a bottle of lube, and I wondered just what I was getting myself into that we needed *that*.

Lucifer grabbed my waist from behind. "Yes," he murmured against my ear. He gently pushed my chest down onto the bed, pressed his hardness against my ass, and looked over at Eros. "Eros is going to watch as I fuck his woman, aren't you, Eros?"

Eros stalked over to us, eyes black. Instead of crawling onto the bed with me, he sat down on the armchair, kicked one of his ankles onto his knee, and started to untie his shoe. So damn slowly. It was like he wanted to watch.

Lucifer pulled my underwear down slowly, his fingers grazing against my thighs, then leaned over me and grasped a handful of my breast through my bra. "Fuck," he groaned. The corner of Eros's lip curled as Lucifer kicked off his pants and pressed his hardness against my ass.

Oh, dear Lord, forgive me for my sins.

Eros leaned back against the chair, stroking his cock through his pants. I pushed my ass against Lucifer, wanting him inside me. He rubbed his cock against my wetness, and I clenched.

"Fuck her already. I bet her pussy is aching for it," Eros said. He stood and undid the buttons on his shirt, letting it hang loosely off his shoulders.

Lucifer's nails dug into my hips. I arched my back and pushed myself closer. He slowly pushed himself inside of me. Eros kicked off his pants and walked over to us, cock in hand.

Holy Hell.

He crawled onto the bed in front of me. "Look at me, Dani."

I gazed up at him, my brows pulled together as Lucifer wasted no time pounding into me from behind. Eros rubbed his cock against my lips, and I opened my mouth—wanting him inside of me too. He pulled away smirking. "Beg for it."

I whimpered. "Please, Eros." My pussy clenched. "I need it."

Eros pushed the head of his cock onto my lips and grasped my chin. "I said to beg."

"Please, I—"

He pushed his dick between my lips, slowly thrusting his whole length down my throat. I bobbed my head back and forth on him, my tongue swirling around his head, as I clenched around Lucifer, the feeling of being filled exciting me.

Lucifer yanked the bottom of my dress up and Eros pulled it over my head. He snatched the clasp of my bra and undid it, watching my breasts bounce out of it. Eros pushed himself back inside of me until he hit the back of my throat, and I gagged.

He trailed a finger down my jawline, and I gazed up at him through teary eyes. "Good girl," he said, lightly snaking his hand around my throat. His gaze traveled down my backside, watching Lucifer thrust into me. "Arch your back," he said.

I did as I was told, and Lucifer groaned. Eros smirked at him, his hazy eyes traveling up his body. Lucifer quickened his pace, roughly thrusting in and out of me.

Oh, Hell. Just like that.

I closed my eyes. Holy—

Eros snatched my chin. "Look at me when you cum." He groped my breast with his other hand, pushed his hips closer to me, and pinched one of my nipples. I clenched harder around Lucifer, wave after wave of ecstasy rolling through me, and I came.

Eros released himself inside of me, his warm cum sliding down my throat.

Lucifer pulled out, and I collapsed onto the bed, my chest rising and falling. Oh, my God. That was crazy. He placed his knuckles against the bed on either side of me and leaned over. My eyes closed, a feeling of exhaustion washing over me, but it was quickly replaced with another surge of hunger.

Eros laid down on the bed and pulled me on top of him—my back against his chest. "We're not finished with you," he said. He drew my legs apart and rested them on either side of his thighs.

Lucifer grabbed the lube from the armchair and squirted some into his hand. Eros pressed his lips to my ear, and I turned my head so I could kiss him.

We were in bed with the devil, but all I wanted to do was pull him closer.

The bed dipped below us, and Eros groaned softly against me. After a few moments, he readjusted himself, so his cock was pressing into my backside. He pushed some hair behind my ear and said, "This might hurt." Then pressed his lips against my temple. "If it's too much, you know your safe word."

I nodded my head, grasping his arms below me. My mind was in a fog, vision seeming cloudy. Eros grabbed my ass and pushed himself against its entrance.

"Eros," I breathed, feeling nothing but pressure. "I—I don't know if I—"

He pushed himself inside of me. I took a deep breath, brows knotting together in pain. Lucifer crawled between our legs and rubbed my clit. I dug my nails into the bed sheets, wanting to displace all the discomfort.

Eros dragged his fingers across my nipples. "It'll go away soon," he whispered. Once he was all the way inside of me, he stilled. "You're going to enjoy this."

For a moment, I was aching, nearly on the verge of screaming to the high heavens for him to stop, but then his lips were back on my neck, his stubble was brushing against my soft spot. I was squirming, and my pussy aching to be filled.

Lucifer rubbed his cock against my wetness, then pushed himself inside of me. I moaned and threw my head back, clenching around them.

Eros began to slowly thrust himself in and out of me, moving faster and harder with each thrust. Lucifer thrusted himself into me, just off rhythm with Eros. He watched my breasts bounce with each thrust, eyes icing over.

Holy.

I moaned louder, not caring about who was listening through these walls. The entire bar could know that these two were fucking me, and I wouldn't care.

Eros snaked one arm around my waist, fingers rubbing my clit. Pleasure warmed my core. Lucifer dipped his head and sucked my nipple into his mouth, teeth grazing against it. He bit down—quite hard—but that didn't matter anymore. My legs were trembling so much that I released myself on him.

Lucifer pulled out of me. "Open your mouth," he said, crawling over and wrapping a hand around my neck. I parted my lips and stared up at him. He pulled me closer, pushed his dick onto my bottom lip, and came into my mouth. He pressed my lips together, thumb grazing against them. "You're so fucking sexy."

When Eros pulled out of me, I drew my shaky legs together and leaned back against him. Oh, my God. Why'd this feel so damn good?

Eros got off of the bed. "Stand up, Dani."

I shook my head. "I—I can't," I breathed. The steady ache in my core, the thrilling feel of their hands running all over my body, the insatiable hunger for them—it was all too much. But I was hooked on cinnamon and apples like they were drugs, unable to come down from the high Eros and Lucifer had unknowingly put me in.

Lucifer pulled me to the edge of the bed by my ankles, wrapped his hands under my legs, and picked me up.

"What are you doing?" I asked, wrapping my legs around his torso. Eros brushed a hand against my ass, pulling it apart, and they positioned themselves at my entrance once more. "Oh, no, no, no, no, no. I can't do this again."

"Oh, darling. Wait until you get to Hell." Lucifer lightly squeezed my thighs.

Was everyone just fucking nonstop in Hell like this? Would I ever get used to thi—Eros pushed himself inside of me, and my eyes closed. Yes. Yes, I could definitely get used to this.

I wrapped my arms around Lucifer's neck and trailed a finger up one of his icy horns. Lucifer thrusted into me too, and I couldn't stop my legs from shaking. I couldn't make it stop, nor did I want to.

They continued to thrust into me, and I sat there helplessly in Lucifer's arms. Eros fondled my breasts, his fingers lightly grazing against my nipples. I was hopelessly aware of every sensation, every touch, every thrust, every breath, and it was torturing me.

My mind was foggy, vision hazy. All I could think about was how close I was to cumming again.

They both thrusted into me at the same time, and I threw my head back. Having my third toe-curling, leg-trembling, mind-numbing orgasm of the night.

When I had fallen limply into Lucifer, unable to hold myself upright, Eros scooped me into his arms and placed me on the bed. They both laid next to me, Lucifer trailing his fingers over my hip bone, while I stared up at the ceiling and gasped for breath. I pressed my knees together to try to stop the throbbing between my legs. "I think that I'm dying," I said.

Eros chuckled. "How did you like your first real taste of Hell?"

"Oh... I loved it," I said. If this was what being with Eros was going to be like all the time, I think I was bound to be happy for the rest of my life. Living in this ecstasy—who wouldn't love it?

"Have we turned you into a sinner?" Lucifer asked.

I half-hearted laughed. Mom used to call me her perfect little angel. Oh, how I could only imagine what she would think about me now. I was far from angelic; I was lust itself. Filled with it. Bathed in it. Born in it. Fucking in it.

"No," I said. "I've been a sinner."

Chapter Thirty-Nine

"I t was a pleasure getting to know you," Lucifer said after Eros drove us back to his apartment. He stood in front of a portal to Hell in the center of Eros's living room. "I look forward to next time, Dani."

Eros curled an arm around my waist, resting his chin on my shoulder. "Meet us here in two days for the dinner party."

Lucifer gave us one last lingering look and stepped into the portal. When he left, the portal closed up as if it had never even been there. Eros sauntered to his kitchen and pulled out two wine glasses from the cabinet. He was wearing a forest green sweater that hung comfortably on his body, and he was more relaxed than I expected him to be after that.

He popped off the cork to a bottle of wine and gazed over at me. "You're quiet."

My mind and body were both numb from the past three hours, I didn't even know what to say. If I knew something like that was going to happen tonight, I would've prepared. Maybe did a little workout so I could keep up with two demons who were hell-bent on fucking me over and over and over again.

After he placed a glass of wine in my hand, he led me to the living room. He sat on the couch and pulled me onto his lap. "Relax," he said. "I know that was a lot for you." His fingers trailed up my arms, and he began massaging my shoulders. "How are you feeling?"

One of the living room windows was open a few inches, letting a cold breeze into the room to cool me off. I leaned against him, closing my eyes. "Good." Really good. I just had questions.

"Why did you agree to that?" I asked. I should've asked before it happened, but I was too caught up in the moment that I couldn't think straight. "I thought you only liked one partner at a time and didn't want something like that."

He tensed, his fingers pausing. "I just... wanted to gauge your reaction for... the future."

"What do you mean?" I asked.

"Nothing," he said too quickly, rubbing my shoulders. He was hiding something. Again.

"What are you not telling me?"

"Nothing."

I placed my hands on his. "Please Eros, trust me."

He stayed quiet for a long moment. "It's too dangerous to tell you now. Once I get everything sorted out with my parents and Javier, I will tell you. I promise."

I knew that this whole family thing was bothering him, but I didn't want to be lied to. It hurt more than anything to know he was keeping something big from me, and that something meant being with many other people in the future.

"We should talk about the rules in our relationship," he said.

"Um, okay." I sipped my wine. "What kind of rules were you thinking about?"

He took my glass of wine and placed it on the coffee table, then sat me next to him. His lips were set in a small smile, and his dark eyes were comforting. "I think that if—when we rule the Kingdom of Lust, we should keep our relationship closed." When I furrowed my brows at him, he continued. "I mean, we shouldn't see anyone else romantically until we think otherwise."

"I thought that's what you wanted to do."

His cheeks grew the faintest color red. "It is, but you may feel different once you become queen. It's a different world down there, and relationships with more than two people get messy in Hell. There are demons that are envious, wrathful, greedy, prideful, slow, hungry, filled with desire. They'll backstab, kill, and cheat to get what they want." He paused. "All I'm saying is that until our kingdom is strong and stable, we should refrain from other romances."

"Okay..." I said. This man was so confusing. No open relationship. Three some with Lucifer. No open relationship. Was I missing something?

He shook his head and chuckled. "Dani, you're so innocent. I think you're getting this all confused. I don't mind sex with other people once in a while, just no feelings. If you want us to share a bed with someone—like Lucifer—for the night, I'll most likely agree to it, but it's not something I'm looking for everyday or even every other day honestly."

Whew. Okay, that sounded so much better. If I ended up in a romantic relationship with another person and Maria found out or—worse—Dr. U found out, I wouldn't hear the end of it. But having sex—especially sex *that* amazing—with other consenting people, I didn't mind.

"Do you have any rules that you want to talk about?" he asked, grasping my hands.

There was one thing that had been bothering me, and I wasn't sure how to ask it without appearing jealous. But after taking a deep breath, I gazed down at Eros's ring—feeling drawn to it—and brushed my finger against the darkness. "Are you going to be having sex with other people when I'm not with you?"

Tonight, I learned that his sex drive was extremely high. What if I couldn't please him the way he needed me to? I didn't want to come home one day to find him in bed with someone else—even if there were no feelings attached. Trevon had little control over cheating on me—since he was under Javier's lustful spell—but it still hurt. I needed Eros to be honest with what he needed.

He placed a finger on my chin and lifted it until my gaze reached his. "I am faithful to you, Dani. Only you. I will not have sex with someone else, unless you're there and/or you're okay with it. And, honestly, I prefer to only have sex with someone I'm romantically attracted to."

I smiled and slowly nodded my head. Okay, I could do this. We could work.

Dr. U flipped through a file at her desk, the overhead light reflecting off of her glasses. I peeked my head into her office and knocked. She looked up from her work, her eyes growing wide. "Dani! What're you doing here this late? It's nearly 7 o'clock on a Friday."

There were a lot of reasons that I was here. I held up a brown paper bag from Crimson's Nouveau and smiled. "I wanted to bring you something before the office closes the next few days for Christmas."

She closed her file and gave me a soft smile. I handed her the bag and sat across from her, gazing out the window. It was a terrifying kind of dark outside tonight and reminded me of the night Mom was murdered. We were walking down Fourth Street on Christmas Eve, listening to *Joy to the World* which was playing in the city center a few blocks over. Mom was twirling me around, her blonde hair blowing into her face. We were happier than we had ever been.

And then she saw a woman across the street, stopped dead in her tracks, and kissed my forehead, telling me that she loved me more than anything. I tugged on her hand, wanting to get to the ice-skating rink before it got too packed. She gave me a smile, her lips twitching, and looked at the woman again who was hurriedly crossing the street at the crosswalk. Even in the darkness, that woman's eyes were a piercing red.

Mom told me that we would have a race to the rink, that she'd give me a head start. So, I sprinted as fast as I could down the road to the rink that I'd been to a thousand times before and stopped when I noticed that she wasn't following me.

I couldn't remember what happened next, just that Mom was lying on the ground not moving and the woman was standing over her and I was screaming at the top of my lungs.

Dr. U was coming out of her office, briefcase hanging off her shoulder, when she found me. She crouched down to my level and asked me what was wrong. At the time, I didn't know, but I knew that something wasn't right, so I just pointed to Mom and the woman with red eyes a block away and clutched the necklace that Mom put around my neck earlier that night. Dr. U looked over to them, fear clear in her eyes, and grabbed me.

Before I knew it, she was running down the street with me to the police station, taking me away from the only family I had. When I got to see Mom's body on Christmas morning—at the time we were supposed to be at church—I pushed a strand of her blonde hair from her face and told her a bedtime story.

"Fervor Crisps?" Dr. U asked, pulling one out of the brown paper bag. "I love these!"

I grinned. "You've had them before?"

"Of course!" She bit into one and sighed. "*You've* had them before?"

"Eros makes them."

Her eyes widened, and she slowly chewed. "Eros, as in the man you're dating?" she asked.

"Yeah." I nodded. "I'm going to visit his family for the holiday and am nervous."

She placed the Fervor Crisp on a napkin and dusted off her hands. "You're going to see his family?" While she had become comfortable with my relationship with Eros, she suddenly looked hesitant. "You're moving rather quickly, but..." She sat up, took my hand, and smiled. "You'll do great. I know you will. You've turned out to be the strongest woman I know."

We gazed at each other for a few more moments, and I closed my eyes. Hoping that I had made Mom proud like I had Dr. U.

After a few seconds of silence, I stood. "Well, I don't want to hold you up. Have a good Christmas. I'll see you next Monday."

I tugged on Mom's pendant and walked to the door. I'd see her if I survived Hell.

"Dani!" she said before I walked through the doorway. I turned around to see her smiling weakly at me. "Be careful."

Chapter Forty

If I was going to visit the Kingdom of Lust, I was going to make an unforgettable first impression.

I shimmied into a long red satin gown that Eros brought over this morning and smoothed it out. It was as bright as Kasey's lipstick, clung to every one of my curves, and had a plunging neckline that showed way more cleavage that I was used to.

Music was playing softly on the speaker in the living room. Maria peeked her head into the bathroom. "You look amazing!" She walked in—still wearing pajamas—and brushed her fingers against Mom's pendant. "And your necklace is nearly glowing!"

My cheeks warmed. "You're not going to the party?" I asked. "Didn't Zane invite you?"

She sighed. "He did, but I don't want to see Javier, and demons freak me the fuck out."

"Are you sure?" I asked. It'd be nice to have some support there tonight.

"Zane said he was leaving the party early to come over, so I'm just going to stay in," she said. I raised my brows. Maria, staying in? That was a first.

"So, you and Zane... you're fine?" I asked, smiling.

She grabbed my hand, cheeks flaming, and pulled me toward the front door. "Yes, but I'll tell you about that later. You can't be late to a party in Hell," she said.

After visiting Dr. U's office last night, I had told Maria that I was going to Hell to visit Eros's family. Of course, I only told her the essentials—that I'd be amongst a bunch of sex demons, having a lovely dinner with Eros's disgustingly rude parents, trying not to embarrass myself—and made sure to leave out the part about Eros actually killing his parents and seizing the kingdom.

That part scared me the most. Not only was I going back to Hell, but this time I was going back to Hell with my boyfriend who was going to murder his family to take back his throne.

Maria opened the door and pushed me out. "Have fun and good luc—" She stopped half-way, her gaze traveling from me to the hallway behind me.

I glanced over my shoulder. Lucifer stood at Eros's door, smirking in our direction. His icy eyes lingered on me. Maria's mouth fell agape. "Holy fu—" She pulled me back into the house and slammed the door. "Who is that?"

"Lucifer."

She leaned closer to me, her voice quiet. "Lucifer, as in the guy you had a threesome with?" When I nodded my head, her eyes widened. "You get it, girl. He's so sexy!"

"Thanks, Maria," I said, playfully rolling my eyes at her and opening the door again. She wished me good luck, knowing just how much I was fearing this whole night. I pulled her into a hug. If the plan failed, I didn't know when I would see her next. And— even though she was annoying sometimes—I was terrified that I'd *never* see her again.

Since yesterday morning, I'd felt that something wasn't right, that I shouldn't go tonight. But I was going because Eros was counting on me and Eros deserved to be king.

Lucifer was still waiting by Eros's door when I finally left the apartment. His white hair rested messily by the sides of his face, and his eyes were icier than last time. "Stunning."

"You don't look too bad yourself," I said.

Eros opened the door. A red tie was hanging loosely around his neck, and his soft hair was parted to one side. So many succubi and incubi would be all over him tonight, trying to pry him away from me.

He pulled me inside and pressed his lips to my ear. "If we didn't have to deal with my family tonight, I'd already have that dress ripped off of you." His fingers trailed over my cleavage. "Everyone is going to be all over you tonight."

I pulled him closer, ignoring Lucifer's playful groan at our affection, and fixed his tie. When I was finished, he grasped my hand and held it to his chest. "I can't wait to show everyone how amazing you are," he said.

I hoped that's how the night would go—making a damn good impression in the kingdom he was banished from—but nothing ever went to plan. Eros pulled away to fix his hair in the mirror one last time, and I grasped my necklace, suddenly filled with so much doubt.

Something was bound to go wrong. I could feel it.

"Are you ready?" Lucifer asked, standing in front of a portal.

I clenched the pendant in my fist, accidentally ripping it off of the chain. My eyes widened at the *V*-shape piece of metal in my palm. "Oh, my God." I broke it. The one thing that I needed to survive tonight broke. What was I going to do? I needed Mom with me. I couldn't sit at dinner with a table full of demons without her to keep me calm. I—

"Dani," Eros said. He placed his hands on my shoulders and gazed down at the pendant. "Calm down. It's fine. You're fine."

"But—but my necklace." I held my hand toward him.

"We can fix it," he said.

"No." I shook my head. "Last time it broke, it took weeks for

Trevon to fix it. We can't fix it now." I ran my hands through my curls. "What am I going to do?"

Lucifer stepped forward. "There is a jeweler in Pride who can fix it for you while we're at dinner. He's exceptionally good at all things jewelry, even handcrafted that ring Eros has on his finger."

"But I—what about Mom?"

Eros squeezed my shoulder. "You'll be fine without her, Dani. It'll take less than a couple hours for him to fix it."

I gazed between the two men and reluctantly handed the pendant to Lucifer, hoping that I'd see it again. It was one of the few things left of Mom.

"I'll meet you there," he said. He stepped into the portal and disappeared.

Eros took my hand. "Close your eyes," he said. I squeezed my eyes shut. I would not make the same mistake as last time. I didn't have Mom to protect me.

When Eros told me to open my eyes, we were standing in a portal room in an unfamiliar kingdom. The room was fairly large with soft egg-white walls and two red velvet couches on either side of the portal. The lights were dim, and there were two guards dressed in suits with black horns and reflective eyes. Lucifer stepped out of the portal behind me, nearly bumping into me. He rested a hand on my lower back.

"Lord Eros. Commander Lucifer," one guard said.

The other eyed me but returned his gaze to Eros after a moment. "You're the last to arrive. Everyone is waiting for you in the castle."

The Kingdom of Lust was much different from Pride. The sky was a light pink with white feathery clouds. Beds of roses lined the white stone walkways which lead to a towering castle.

Lucifer placed his hand on Eros's shoulder. "This is all about to be yours."

Eros gazed around us, taking in the sight of *his* kingdom, and nodded. He looked so stoic and strong, and I was glad one of us was.

While we walked to the castle, Eros repeated that I must stay with Lucifer at all times—even when he went to do whatever it was that he was going to do. He didn't tell me the specifics, and I didn't want to know. Times like this, when your lover was going to kill his parents and seize the Kingdom of Lust's throne—in Hell —it was best to remain ignorant.

What I did know was that the three of us were going to pretend that Eros had finally accepted life as a *true* incubus through a partnership with Lucifer and me, which meant that I had to flirt with both of them all night long. And that wouldn't be a problem.

I linked arms with Eros and walked up the staircase to the front doors of the palace. Demons were already drunk off of Passion Delights on the front steps—flirting, kissing, touching. They were doing it all, and I only wished that I had Mom's necklace—my security net.

A few succubi batted their lashes at Eros, but he brushed by them. He didn't even look at them when they called his name.

When we reached the top, another two guards nodded at Eros. "Lord, Commander." They looked at me, then at each other. "Who is this?"

"She's my date," Eros said.

"Our date," Lucifer corrected, grabbing my hand. If this was going to work, we couldn't make any mistakes.

"You share the human girl?" The guards looked at each other and laughed. "The Great Lord Eros who was shamed for only wanting one lover, now is sharing a woman with a comman—"

Eros grabbed his throat, pressing him up against the stone door. "If you have a problem with it, tell me."

The guard shook his head. "No, no, Lord. I was just in disbelief."

When Eros released his grip, I squeezed his bicep tighter. Tonight was only going to get worse. He stepped over the man and opened the door himself.

Lucifer placed his hand on my lower back. "Stay by my side," he said.

I took a deep breath and stepped into the room. We would walk out of here with the Kingdom of Lust or we wouldn't walk out of this castle ever again. I could feel it.

The lights were dim inside. Demons were dancing, grinding, and flirting with each other. Some were nearly naked, others were clothed. The palace kind of reminded me of The Lounge, if it had hundreds more people and they were all demons.

Horns of ice. Dresses of gold. Red curled tails. Green scarred skin. There were demons from all the kingdoms here. But, despite their differences, one thing was the same amongst all of them: when Eros walked in, everyone stopped.

They shuffled to the side, creating a path for us to walk through. The succubi stared at me and whispered, eyeing my hand on Eros. I rubbed my sweaty palm on my dress, hoping that they didn't notice how nervous I was.

I had never been surrounded by hundreds of people who were more beautiful than I would ever be. And—by the way they held themselves with so much confidence—there was no doubt in my mind that they could please Eros more than I could ever.

"Dani!" someone said. Kasey pushed through the crowd—red lipped and dressed in black stilettos—and jogged over to us. Her eyes were dark, her horns sharp, she was breathtaking. She pulled me into a hug. "I'm so glad that you made it!"

"Not even going to say hello to your brother?" Eros said from beside me.

She playfully pushed his shoulder, then bowed to Lucifer. "Commander. I didn't think you'd be here with Eros and Dani."

"I'm their date," he said.

There was an uproar of whispers, and I tried to ignore it. My heart was pounding way too hard in my chest. I glanced around to distract myself and locked eyes with the one person I wish I hadn't. Javier.

He sat at a long table, staring directly at me, and smirked. I gulped nervously, trying to pull my gaze away from him. I hated to admit it, but he was much more attractive in his demon form. Sculpted frame, large horns, dark eyes tinted red.

An older demon sat next to him, tail curling around a succubus's waist. A pair of scars laid diagonally across his face. They both whispered back and forth.

Eros must've seen them too because his grip on me tightened. We continued through the crowd of whispers to the table.

"Eros, I didn't think you'd actually make it." A petite woman approached us, her voice a bit distasteful. She had hair like Kasey's and piercing eyes like Eros. "Look who it is, Dear."

A tall man walked up beside her. His gaze flickered from Eros to Lucifer. "Son." The man nodded stiffly. "Commander. I don't think we invited you."

Lucifer smirked, tapping his fingers on my lower back like he was amused. "I was invited by Eros as his and Dani's date."

If I thought that my heart was racing before, I was definitely about to have a heart attack when Eros's dad looked me up and down, his mother following suit. She curled a finger around a strand of my brown hair and watched me closely. I stayed still, absolutely terrified. "She's pretty, Eros."

"She is," his father said.

Eros paused and pulled me away from his mother. "But?"

"But?" she said with a strained smile on her face. "Why do you think I want to say more?"

"Because you always have more to say."

His mother shook her head and curled into his father's arm. "I'm just surprised. That's all."

I tried my hardest to have a neutral expression, but everything she said sounded so fake, rehearsed even. No wonder Eros didn't like his parents.

Eros stared at her, his face void of any emotion. "Surprised about what?" he asked tensely.

"She's not a demon," his father said.

"And you're seeing her *and* Commander Lucifer." She held out her hand for Eros to take, but he didn't. So, instead, she slapped him playfully on the chest. "I should've known. You've been spending so much time with him lately and none here with us."

"You banished me, Mother."

She waved her hand, dismissively. "Oh, that's silly talk. Now that you've accepted the true incubi way your banishment shall be lifted. You can spend more time here in the palace."

"I don't wan—"

I dug my nails into his bicep to get him to shut up. If we were going to do this—no mistakes. That's what he told me, and I planned to keep it that way. I didn't want to die, and I didn't want him to die either.

"Why don't we have dinner?" Eros's mother asked, shuffling her husband to the table.

"Yes. Dinner," Eros said.

Once his parents sat at the head of the table, next to Javier and the other demon, there were two chairs left. Lucifer sat in one and Eros sat in the other. He tugged me into his lap, lips brushing against my ear. "When we rule, I'll make sure you have a seat at the head of the table."

<h1 style="text-align:center">Chapter Forty-One</h1>

Servers filed in through a door with platters of food and bottles of Passion Delight and dark red wine labeled Sanguio. As soon as the waiter popped the cork on the Sanguio to give to Javier, I wrinkled my nose. It smelled so vile.

Javier and the man sitting with him grabbed glasses. The older man gazed across the table at me, then drank a long sip—eyes turning red—and placed it down. "Eros, glad to see you've made it with your *pet*."

I clenched my jaw. The man held a certain familiarity and power in the way he spoke and held himself. He reminded me of Trevon when he was possessed. He must've been from the Kingdom of Wrath, possibly the Commander of Wrath himself, Sathanus.

A waiter placed a plate of food in front of him and nearly knocked over his drink. He slammed his fists against the table, and I jumped. Yep, definitely from Wrath. I turned away from him.

Javier cleared his throat. "Dani."

Oh, great. Here we go.

"How's my dear friend Trevon doing? I'm assuming you two

aren't together anymore since you're here with two of Hell's finest."

I balled my hands into fists under the table. He had some nerve asking about Trevon, especially because he was the reason for our breakup and for him being possessed. I took a deep breath through my nose and bit back my anger. It would be exactly what he wanted. "He's doing fine," I said. "Thanks for asking. Maria is doing well too."

Sathanus snatched his drink from the table. "Lucifer, I didn't think your pride would let you sink so low to have a human pet."

Lucifer placed his elbows on the table and leaned forward, brow arched. "Still trying to get under everyone's skin, Sathanus? Seems like you could use your time doing something more useful like, maybe, actually commanding your kingdom instead of burning everything to the ground."

After slamming his fists against the table, Sathanus stood. His eyes blazed red. "I will not take this disrespect. You and the pet were not invited here." He glared at Lucifer with so much hatred. "Remove them this instant or I will."

My heart raced, and I suddenly got flashbacks of Trevon freaking out on me that first night. Eros placed his hand on the inside of my thigh and rubbed it gently, trying to calm me down.

I gazed at the meat on the center of the table and tried to control my breathing. God, I should've brought a cross.

"Dani and I were invited by Lord Eros," Lucifer said.

I didn't know which commander was scaring me more—Sathanus who was about to flip the table or Lucifer who was frighteningly calm right now.

Some succubi sashayed over, pushed Sathanus back down, and sat on his lap. His eyes still blazed, but when he snaked his arms around the women's tiny waists, the color faded.

Eros's father cleared his throat and placed his Passion Delight on the table. "We don't call pets by their names, Commander," he said to Lucifer. "She's a pet, and that's all. Call her what she is."

"She's not a pet," Eros said, tensing.

His mother laughed. "Eros, baby, she isn't anything more than that. Why don't you get yourself a true succubus? Someone who could actually please you."

Damn these people. I could please Eros. I could please him, couldn't I?

She stood and leaned over the table, flashing her cleavage to everyone. I turned away in disgust. "Girls!" she said, flicking her manicured finger behind us. Two succubi walked up to us.

One sat on Eros's other leg and pressed her breasts against his chest while the other ran her fingers up and down his horns.

Eros tensed, and his eyes darkened just enough for me to tell that he enjoyed how she touched him. I pressed my lips together and stared at the table. Could I really please Eros?

He dug his fingers into my side and shoved the woman off of his lap. "What the fuck are you doing, Mother?" He stared at the two succubi. "Get the fuck away from me." He was seething, and I felt like our whole plan was ruined.

Lucifer pulled me onto his lap, placing his hands on my waist and holding me to him. Eros stood and slammed his hands against the table. "Why do you insist on fucking with my life?"

"You will sit down now," his father said. "Or you will be escorted to the portal with your filth of a pet."

Javier smirked across the table, and I had the sudden urge to hurl my fist at him.

"If you want your banishment to be lifted, you will sit," his mother said.

I brushed my fingers against his and noticed that he didn't have on his ring anymore. He looked down at me with black eyes, growled in frustration, and sat.

The girls hovered around us while we ate. I watched them lightly graze their fingers against the back of Eros's neck, lean a little too close to him, and even speak in those damn seductive tones that could work on anybody.

Lucifer leaned closer to me, lips against my ear. "You need to eat."

I snatched my fork and stabbed it into the lasagna, because I wasn't about to eat whatever kind of meat was sitting in the center of the table that Sathanus couldn't stop devouring.

After eating about half my plate, I glanced up to see Javier staring at my breasts. I wrinkled my nose. What a damn disgusting—

Javier looked me in the eyes. "Eros," he said. "I don't see what your problem is. You have Commander Lucifer and the pet as your lovers. If you've truly accepted the way of the incubi, you shouldn't have a problem letting a couple beautiful woman sit on your lap."

I hated that man. Hated him so much.

Lucifer gripped my waist a little tighter, so I couldn't move. "He doesn't have a problem with it. In fact, girls!" He motioned for them to come closer. "Why don't you escort Eros to a Lust Room?"

My eyes widened. What the hell did he think he was doing? When Eros refused to go—and he would—this was all going to get much worse for the three of us.

Eros took a deep breath and stared at me as the demons sauntered over to him, swaying their hips from side to side. They were so damn sexy. I didn't know how anyone could resist them.

They wrapped their filthy arms around my Eros.

"Make sure you girls do a real good job. He's been tense lately." Lucifer winked at them.

They wouldn't have to because he wasn't actually going to go with them. He wouldn't. He told me he wouldn't do anything I wasn't comfortable with. There was no way he'd let them take him to a Lust Room.

Eros looked away from me and stood.

The girls giggled into his neck, their lips trailing up the sides of it. I sat there with my brows furrowed. No, no, he wouldn't go. He was just going to push them away again.

He looked at Lucifer, then turned away—not sparing me a single glance. And, in that moment, I didn't know what to think. All I could do was watch hopelessly as he walked down the hall with his arms curled around their waists.

<h1 style="text-align:center">Chapter Forty-Two</h1>

I had been hanging onto a thread of hope that Eros wouldn't actually do anything with them, but when I heard that door shut my heart broke. It was like Trevon all over again, but worse.

Lucifer rubbed my thigh in a soothing way and leaned close to me. "It'll be okay," he whispered.

I didn't even want to be here anymore. All I wanted was to curl up in my bed with Maria's arms around me and cry. For Mom, for Trevon, for Eros. It was stupid but I couldn't help it.

I felt broken.

Dinner continued in silence, and I was sure that everyone just wanted me to hear the moans coming from the Lust Rooms. Lucifer tried to reassure me that there were many Lust Rooms here, but I didn't care. Every minute that Eros wasn't here with me hurt.

He was probably shoving them against the walls, thrusting into them, making them beg the way he always made me do. And I was stuck looking at his asshole of a brother and wondering why I ever agreed to this.

When dinner was over, Lucifer pulled me up. "Smile, Darling."

I hurried to the other side of the room, not being able to listen to those damn screams any longer. "What is there to smile about? I'm in Hell and my boyfriend is fucking two girls in a Lust Room right now."

He grabbed my hand, grimacing. "What did Eros tell you the other day?" he asked. I shrugged. "Don't do that," he said.

"Don't do what?" I asked.

"Didn't Eros tell you that he didn't enjoy fucking someone he's not romantically attracted to? That he's only faithful to you?"

"Yeah, but—wait." I stopped walking. "How'd you know about that?"

He gazed down at me with those icy blue eyes. "He tells me everything."

I crossed my arms over my chest. "I wish he'd trust me."

"If he didn't trust you, he wouldn't have brought you here. He needs you to understand. He's in a hard position right now. One wrong move down here and we all die." After a few moments, he arched a brow. "Are you ready to help him?"

"How am I supposed to help him? He's not here?" I asked.

Lucifer shook his head and smiled. "You know, when Eros told me about you, he never mentioned this little attitude you have. I'm starting to really like it."

"This is not the time for jokes, Lucifer."

We stared at each other for a few moments. Strands of his white hair hung loosely by his face; his jaw was as sharp as ice. "Well, then, let's get on with the plan. First piece of business, you're going to flirt with Javier."

I blew out a breath through my nose. "You're kidding me," I said. He shook his head, his annoying aroma of apples drifting to me. "Eros would never want me to flirt with him. We both hate him."

Eros told me to stay with Lucifer and to avoid Javier. Javier was pure wrath which meant danger—which really meant that he could hurt me more than he already has.

Lucifer placed his hand on the small of my back and lead me through the crowd of demons. Kasey waved me over from the make-shift dance floor, but Lucifer kept on pushing forward. "Do you want to help him or not?"

"He would not want this," I said. I didn't know what Lucifer was trying to pull because it was out of character for Eros to agree to something like this.

"You must."

I stopped in the middle of the fuck-fest that was happening on the dance floor. "Eros might trust you Lucifer, but that doesn't mean I have to."

Well, Dani, you trusted him up to this point. You just made yourself look stupid.

Lucifer clenched his jaw. "I'm here to help the true leader of this kingdom claim the throne. Trust me or not, I'm on your side." He lightly placed his hand on the back of my neck and steered me through the crowd. "Do you want to help Eros?"

There was a bar on the other side of the dancefloor with light pink accent lights under it. Javier was leaning over it, talking to the woman on the other side. I shook my head. "I can't flirt with him. I'm terrible at it. Why don't you find a succubus to distract him?"

"No." Lucifer stopped. "You are going to flirt with him because he wants *you* and has been staring at *you* the whole night."

A few mahogany tables stood in front of the bar. Lucifer placed his drink down on one, then grabbed my hands in his. "Listen, I don't know where Eros is right now. He could be in that Lust Room or he could be somewhere in the palace. This wasn't part of the plan," he said. I closed my eyes. "I can tell you that he cares for you and is doing his best to keep you safe, but you have to do the same. If you don't at least try to distract Javier, he will look for Eros. And if Eros is in the middle of enacting our plan, then he's screwed which also means that we're screwed."

All I wanted was to run right out of the kingdom, throw away being Queen of Lust for a normal life as a human, continue my internship under Dr. U, and become a psychologist just like her, but I couldn't. Not only were there guards in every corner of this castle, but I loved Eros.

I loved him, and that would be my downfall.

If I left and he died, I wouldn't forgive myself. We would deal with this whole complicated situation later. I had to do the one thing I never thought I'd do.

Flirt with Javier to keep Eros safe.

I was going to hate myself for it, but I wasn't going to let Eros die. It wasn't who I was.

Okay, Dani. You can do this. Just distract him. It'd be easy.

Javier leaned over the bar, chatting up the bartender. One hand was stuffed into his pocket, the other was holding his Passion Delight. The cuffs of his shirt were rolled halfway up his forearms.

I stepped in his direction, but Lucifer grabbed my arm and pulled me close. "Do what you have to do—*anything* you have to do—to distract him. Do you understand?" he asked. I went to reach for Mom's necklace and swallowed hard when I remembered it wasn't there.

I had to do this all on my own.

Lucifer nudged me and sat at a table where he could easily watch. I kept my gaze low as I approached the bar—trying to gather all the confidence I had left in myself—and slid onto a stool a few feet away from Javier. I pursed my lips, pretending to look at the drink menu.

Once I felt his gaze burning into me, I glanced at him, eyes lingering longer than they should've to let him know that I was interested. His eyes were black pits tinted with the darkest color red. An odd combination that looked so wrathful, yet so alluring.

Javier strolled to me, his finger gliding against my bare back from shoulder to shoulder, making me shiver. "Lonely?" he asked. He rested his forearm against the bar and leaned closer to me.

I gazed at him through my lashes. "What makes you think that?"

He brushed his fingers against my elbow. "Eros has been gone for a while now, probably still fucking those whores."

Stay calm, Dani. He's just trying to get under your skin.

"Well, I'm just his pet. Nothing more," I said. The words came out harsher than I wanted them too. I turned back to the menu. Passion Delight. Vodka with Passion. Red Sangia with a dash of Passion.

Javier smirked and sat next to me. "Really?" He placed his hand on my knee, fingers digging into it lightly. "Because to me it seems like Eros treats you like a queen. Always defending your honor." He inched closer, and I could smell his intoxicating peppery scent. "I bet he worships your every move, doesn't he?"

Flirt, Dani. Step up your damn game.

I turned in my seat to face him and watched his gaze flicker to my breasts. "He does, but..." I lightly brushed my foot against his, heart racing.

"But?" he asked, fingers rubbing circles on the insides of my thighs. His eyes were so captivating that if I wasn't careful, I would fall under his spell too.

I blushed and glanced down, pulling myself away from him. "No." I shook my head. "No—forget it."

Javier paused, his finger stopping and digging into my mid-thigh. "But you want to be treated like a pet, don't you?"

I sucked in a shaky breath and pressed my knees together. I didn't want to be a pet, but since the other night with Lucifer—since my first night with Eros even—I was slowly discovering my love for lust.

Everyday something new excited me. First it was Eros, standing in my bedroom with black eyes and curved horns—too tempting to pass up. Next, in public while we took a leisurely ride in the bus. Then our threesome with Lucifer. And, now, as I flirted with Javier I realized that there was a world of desire down here and I knew nothing about it—but I wanted to.

This was what Javier wanted, and it had to be what I wanted from him right now too in order to keep him distracted.

Javier walked behind me, placed one hand on my hip as the other trailed up my body and roughly grabbed my chin. "You *are* a whore, just like I thought." His breath was on my ear. "My brother never really knew how to treat a woman the way she wanted to be treated in bed."

God, I really wish Lucifer never let me do this alone.

His fingers lightly traveled down my neck to my breasts. He ran them across the tender skin, so gently that I closed my eyes and pictured it was Eros teasing me, not him. Then he shoved me against the bar, so close that I could just feel my breasts about to fall out of my top.

"I should let every incubus have a turn with this perfect little body," he said. "I bet you love being filled, don't you?"

I gulped.

He snatched my chin again. "Don't you?" His voice was harsh.

"Yes," I whispered. "I love it."

He chuckled and stuck his fingers into my mouth. And I, shamefully, wrapped my lips around them.

Forgive me, Eros.

Javier chuckled against my ear. "What a good fucking whore you are. I think I'll keep you to myself for tonight. But tomorrow you'll get passed around until every incubus and succubus gets their share of you." He pulled me off of the stool. "Come with me."

I dug my heels into the ground. Oh, no. This was not part of the plan. I was to stay here and distract him. Not go with him to God-only knows where inside this castle and have him do *things* to me that I didn't want to think about.

When I didn't move, he clenched his jaw. "Come with me," he

said, his eyes turning a deeper red, and his peppery aroma almost becoming overwhelming. So wrathful. So damn terrifying.

Lucifer was leaning back in his chair and staring at me with an empty glass in his hand. This was not what Eros would have wanted.

Javier followed my gaze and frowned. Despite my best efforts to stay at the bar, he dragged me in Lucifer's direction. "Lucifer, I'm taking your whore for the night. Hope you don't mind. I'm sure Eros doesn't."

As if I were nothing to him, Lucifer stood and swung his suit jacket over his shoulder. "Have fun with her."

My eyes widened. This wasn't right. Javier was about to take me to a Lust Room, and Lucifer—Eros's greatest friend in Hell— was just going to let him. He said that I had to do anything to distract Javier. But sex with Eros's brother? Eros would never agree to something like that.

I surveyed the room. Guards of Lust and of Wrath were posted at each door. Eros's parents were watching my every move from the dinner table. I couldn't run, and, even if I could have, I wouldn't be able to fight off Javier. He was too strong for me.

He pulled me along, heading directly for the Lust Rooms. At this point, I just wanted to make it out of here alive. I didn't want to die in the hands of a demon, especially Javier.

So, I followed him in absolute terror. When we passed Lucifer, Lucifer's fingers brushed against mine, and he pushed something into my hand. I furrowed my brows, balled my hand into a fist, and continued walking.

Whatever it was, I could feel its immense power pumping through me. Energy transferring from it to me. It was small and cool and felt exactly like Eros's ring.

But why did Lucifer have it? What was I supposed to do with this? I didn't have pockets, nor did I have time to stuff it some- where secure. So, before Javier could notice, I slid the ring on.

The ring clamped down onto my finger, squeezing so tightly I thought that it would turn purple, then the metal itself burrowed into my skin until only the thin outer band and the newly added pendant, shaped like a *v*, was visible.

Javier placed his palm on the back of my neck and led me down a hallway. It looked nearly identical to the hallway at The Lounge, except the doors were far bigger and were spaced out much more. When we approached the end of the hallway, Javier pulled a key out of his pocket.

I had to think of some way to get out of this mess. Maybe I could flirt with him for a long time, play hard to get, hopefully buy myself some more time.

Javier pushed his key into the knob. "All of my mother's children have a Lust Room, specifically for their use." He nodded to a room a few doors down and diagonal from his. "This is the first time I've seen Eros's door closed in years."

The door *was* closed, and I tried not to imagine who or what was behind it. Thinking about Eros wouldn't help me now.

Javier pushed his door opened and nodded into his room. I gazed back one last time toward Eros's door and gulped. Sorry for this, Eros.

His door was suddenly swung open, and Eros stormed out of it and down the hallway in the opposite direction from us, shirtless. I wanted to call out for him to come and get me, but when I noticed the scratch marks on his back and the red bruises on his neck, I could barely move, let alone open my mouth to say anything. At that moment, my whole heart shattered.

Chapter Forty-Three

This couldn't be real. This wasn't the Eros that I knew. He wouldn't cheat on me, and if he had to do it, he would've told me because he knew how much I hurt after Trevon. Eros loved me and cared about me and yet there he was walking down the hall with proof on his body that he really had sex with those two succubi.

My chin quivered, and I stormed into Javier's room.

Fuck him. What was this all for now? To make Eros king and throw me to the side like I was nothing to him? Even if there was a sliver of a chance that he would have to do this to seize the throne, I would've liked a warning. Something. Anything.

The door shut behind me. "You're not jealous, are you?" Javier asked.

I pushed back my tears. "No," I said quietly, staring at the chains hanging from the ceiling next to the king-sized oak bed. "I'm not jealous." There was a mirror on one side of the room, and I could just imagine Javier getting off watching himself torture women and men in here.

I felt betrayed. Hurt. Furious. Wrathful.

He loosened his tie and began to unbutton his shirt. "I guess

you were only a pet to him. Just someone he could use to get off."
He let his shirt hang loosely off his shoulders.

The sensible part of me knew that Javier was trying to rile me up, and it was working.

"Take off your dress," he said.

So many foreign emotions were rushing through me. Anger. Jealousy. Disgust. I'd never felt this demonic before. But one emotion flowed through my veins, so intensely, that it felt natural.

Lust.

"Take off your dress," Javier said again firmly.

Would this make me feel better in the weeks to come? No. Would it make me feel better now? I'd have to see.

I reached behind me and unzipped my satin dress, letting it fall to the ground. His gaze traveled down my body, lingering on the lacey lingerie set I put on earlier. At the time, I thought that Eros would be the one to take it off of me when we got home from Hell. Now, it would be Javier.

He stalked toward me, eyes a mahogany red, and unbuckled his belt. When he drew his fingers around my waist, I closed my eyes. It felt so wrong.

Without speaking another word, he spun me around, pushed me onto the bed, and pressed his hardness against my backside. I felt disgusting. He grabbed a fistful of my hair and thrusted his fingers into my panties, rubbing me roughly. "One minute you're sitting in my brother's lap, the next you're wet for me."

Pressure built in my core, and I closed my eyes. There was no going back from this, no trying to repent for my sins. I was in Hell, and I was going to stay here, whether it was my choice or not.

Javier left sloppy, rough kisses down my neck, then my shoulders, then my back. He pushed his hips further into mine until he was pushing against my entrance, and I clenched.

A feeling of disgust washed through me, and I tried to ignore it.

"What do you want, Dani?" he asked.

Not him. I didn't want him.

He grasped my jaw, his mouth against my ear. "What do you want?" he asked again, so wrathful.

I squeezed my eyes shut and shook my head, another feeling of disgust running through me. No matter how much I wanted to forget Eros and just survive down here, I couldn't do this.

Javier's palm collided with my cheek, making my cheek tingle. I clutched it, my head tingling.

"I said to tell me what you—"

I pushed him off and onto the bed beside me, threw one leg over his, and snatched his chin in my hand. "Don't you dare slap me."

"Start acting like a fucking pet and I won't have to." Javier grasped my wrist, trying to yank it away from him. But instead of letting go, I tightened my grip. "What are you doing?" He pulled on it more, but I refused to release him. "No wonder why Eros cheated on you. Not only are you a whore, but a crazy one."

My heart was pumping with pure adrenaline, and I was so damn tired of everyone tonight. I'd been put down, cheated on, tossed to the side like I was nothing. I wasn't about to listen to another word this no-good scheming piece of—

There was a loud crack. Javier's eyes widened, and he grasped for breath. "Wha-what are you doing?"

I suddenly was overcome with a craving for pepper, a desire for mahogany eyes, and a power too strong to control. My hands shook, and Javier's lips looked so damn delicious. I could just taste the energy inside of him.

My mind felt foggy, and everything about him seemed to become much sharper in my vision. The vein violently pulsing in his neck, the shape of his fangs in his mouth, his long and curved horns. There was only one thing I wanted to do.

I pressed my lips to his, feeding off his rage and desire. All I could feel was his wrath and his lust pumping into me, his fingers digging into my skin and setting it ablaze, an intense throbbing in my core. He felt better than Trevon and Eros ever did.

Javier squirmed under me, his claws digging into my wrists, but I didn't let go. I liked this too much.

When his arms fell limply at his sides and the power between our lips ceased, I pulled away from him and took a deep breath.

Oh, my God.

I could feel fiery passion swimming inside of me. It felt so good that I wanted more.

Underneath me, Javier wasn't moving. His ugly and dull grey eyes were half-opened. I sat up taller, trying to find a pulse on him. And when I couldn't, I gulped. Did I... did I just kill him?

The door swung open, and Eros stormed into the room. "Javier! I'm going to fucking kil—" He stopped when he saw me, eyes wide. "Dani," he breathed.

Well, at least Eros found his fucking shirt.

Lucifer leaned against the doorframe and clapped. "Well, there it is. The moment we've all been waiting for."

"I'm kind of busy. Why don't you leave me alone?" I said, turning back to Javier. I didn't know exactly what I was busy with, but it sure as Hell wasn't going to be Eros or Lucifer.

There was silence, then Eros growled. "What happened to the rules, Dani?"

Lucifer placed a hand on Eros's shoulder. "Don't get her angry. She doesn't know how to control herself yet."

I leapt off of the bed and stormed toward him. "Why don't you tell me that? Tell me why you were leaving your Lust Room with scratches and bruises all over your body." When I stepped toward him, he stepped back. "Huh? Do the rules not apply to you? Did you tell me that stupid excuse about wanting only one partner so you could fuck whoever you wanted behind my back?"

He held up his hands. "Dani, calm down. Breathe for me, please."

"You do not tell me what to do."

Delicious black eyes. Mouthwatering scent of cinnamon. I could feel desire clawing its way up my throat. And, this time, his lips looked so tasty.

I lunged for him, but Lucifer pulled him out of the way. "Shit, this is not going how we expected."

My mind replayed the image of Javier underneath me, my hand wrapped lustfully around his chin as I pressed my lips to his, inhaling the power between us.

I wanted Eros, and I wanted him now.

He continued to back away from me with his hands in the air. "Dani, please. Listen to me. You need to take a deep breath. I need you to calm—" I lurched forward again, but he ducked under my arms, placed one arm around my neck and the other on my hip to steady me, and said, "Dani, please listen to me."

I struggled against him, wanting to just turn around and take him. He pushed me a few feet and spun us around, toward the mirror next to the dresser. "Dani, you're not yourself. Breathe."

"What the hell do you—"

My brows furrowed together at my reflection. My eyes were pure black with a thin ring of white around the edges, my teeth were sharper than Eros's, and there were goddamn horns on my head.

I stopped struggling and placed my trembling hands on the mirror. "Oh, my God," I said softly. Tears welled up in my eyes. What had I become? Killing Javier, wanting to kill Eros. I was a monster.

Eros wrapped his arms around my waist, holding me close to him. "Deep breaths, Dani."

After five minutes of breathing heavily, I watched my eyes fade back to their normal brown color. The horns disappeared and the fangs shortened into regular teeth.

"What is going on?" I asked Eros.

He looked at Lucifer, and Lucifer nodded to him. When his

gaze met mine, he paused for a few moments. "You're half demon, half angel, Dani."

"What?" I asked in disbelief.

"Your mother was an angel and your father was a demon." Eros grabbed my hand with the ring on it and looked down. The band was a garnet red again, still buried into my skin, and the rose-gold *v* pendant, which was fastened near the bottom base of the band, looked identical to Mom's pendant. "This ring was your father's marriage band, and the pendant was from your mother's. Before he died, he asked me to give it to you."

Lucifer stepped forward. "And thanks to me, the band and pendant have been merged again as one."

I gazed between the two men, then focused on Eros. "You... you knew my father?" I asked. Mom never mentioned him and didn't have any pictures of him, so I assumed that she didn't know who he was or just didn't want me to know him.

"My parents... ordered for their murders," he said.

The woman with the red eyes was hired by Eros's family to kill Mom, to take away my entire childhood, to murder the one person who had loved me to the fullest. And what about my dad? I never even met him and I never would. I clenched my fists. "I want to kill them."

"They're already taken care of," Eros said. "I killed the two succubi in my room, had to make it look like I fucked them so my parents wouldn't question me, then persuaded them to talk alone in the throne room so I could kill them." Eros grabbed my hands. "If you don't believe me, you can go check for yourself. But you should know that I would never do that to you. And, if I had to, I would never enjoy it."

I sat on the bed on the verge of tears. From Trevon to visiting Hell with Eros to finding out my whole life was taken away from me by his parents, this was all just too much, too quickly. "Why did they kill my parents?"

"Because they didn't think your father was fit to rule the

Kingdom of Lust since he was committed to one woman who was an angel." He shook his head with so much sorrow in his eyes. "And my mother has royal Envy blood but was a bastard child, so she never had a chance to command her kingdom. She was jealous of your father's position, so much so that she made my father lust for power and agree to kill his commander for her."

My eyes widened. My dad was the Commander of Lust? So... that meant that—

"So, what's the first order of business, Commander?" Lucifer stared at me with a smirk on his lips.

"You brought me here to rule?" I asked in disbelief.

Eros brushed a finger across my bottom lip and smiled. "You're heir to the throne, Keeper of the Ring, Queen of the Kingdom, and now the Commander of Lust. There's no one more fit to rule than you."

Chapter Forty-Four

"**H**arder."

Eros shoved me against the wall, one arm wrapped under my leg, his other hand wrapped around my throat. I dug my fingers into the stone above me, looking for something—anything—to hold myself up. He pulled me closer with every thrust.

My cheeks warmed, and I breathed slowly out of my nose, my head in a fog. "More," I said. I needed more.

I wrapped my legs around Eros's waist. He thrusted faster and drew my nipple into my mouth, his teeth grazing against it. I clenched around him, ready to release myself, but he pulled out. "I didn't say that you could cum yet, did I?"

"Don't stop," I whimpered.

He sat me on our mahogany bed and grasped my chin. "Did I?" he asked. I smirked at him, eyes wide with excitement. I could devour him for days upon days and never get tired of him. He teased my clit with his fingers. "Answer me, Dani, or I'll rub your sensitive little clit all day and not let you cum once."

I rested one of my arms on his shoulder, gazing into his black eyes. The pressure was building in my core, and I could just feel the head of his dick poking at my entrance. I was so damn close.

My lips parted, and he jerked his hand away. I pulled it back. "No, don't stop, please. I'll be good."

"What do you want?" he asked, fingers hovering over my clit. The heat from his fingers radiated off of them, and I ached for more.

"I want you."

He thrusted back into me quite roughly, and I came almost instantly—not being able to hold off anymore. I took a deep breath and sunk into the velvet comforter on our bed. "How long have we been here?"

"Three, maybe four hours." He rolled off of me, breathing heavy. "You're building your stamina nicely."

One week had passed since the night I found out about my true origins. Eros's parents and Javier were gone, and we had been living in the palace. To say, I'd adjusted to the way of life down here would be a lie. It was still freaky to walk into the Lust Room hall and see half-naked people, but Eros said that it'd be second nature someday.

I had been visiting Dr. U every day—even on the weekends. Though I didn't tell her about becoming the Queen of Lust, she knew that something was off that first morning I peeked my head into her office and brought her more Fervor Crisps as a thank you for loving me for years when nobody else had. Unlike usual, she didn't pry for information, just told me that she would be there for me through anything. And, for the first time in a long time, I felt like her and Mom were truly proud of me for everything that I had become.

I turned onto my side and gazed at Eros. "Was this your plan all along?" I asked. I'd been thinking about how I ended up in Hell and why I was really here for a few days now. The official Commander ceremony would happen next month, and I had realized that I didn't know much about my journey to Hell. "Was your plan always to get me to rule the kingdom?"

Eros faced me and placed his hand on my bare hip. "Yes."

"So..." I motioned between us. "Were we part of the plan?"

"No," he said, cheeks turning a light pink. "At first, my goal was to see if you were ready and to flirt with you a bit. But you were too irresistible. I found myself thinking about you more than I planned to. And one day..." He shook his head and smiled. "One day I just knew that I had feelings that were more than lust for you."

I grinned, feeling like a little girl again. "And when was that?"

"The Halloween party."

"Oh, God." I playfully slapped his chest. "That was the worst night you could've fallen for me. I was sobbing and puking and—"

"And wearing those horns. Sexy, powerful, and strong. Such a bad night to fall in love with you, right?"

I curled into his arm, feeling comfortable and happy for once. "Was Lucifer part of this plan?"

"After my parents banished me, Lucifer had a distaste toward them, so he's actually the one who suggested that I find you soon."

"And the threesome?" I inhaled his relaxing cinnamon aroma.

He chuckled. "That was my idea. I figured Lucifer would like you and I wanted you to get comfortable with sex."

"You couldn't prepare me for Lust by yourself?"

Eros grasped my face gently, some strands of his dark hair falling onto his forehead. I pushed them away and smiled. "I could, but you're really strong. You took Javier's life with a single kiss. Nobody in this kingdom can do that. And as you get stronger, you're going to need to feed off of more sexual energy than I can provide you with," he said.

I shook my head. "No, I don't need anyone else but you." I hoped that it wasn't true. "My dad did it with Mom—had one mate, I mean. I can too."

"You are so much stronger than your father, Dani. You don't

understand the power you wield. You will need more than just me, and, when that time comes, I understand that I will need to be okay with that."

But I didn't want anyone else. I wanted him, only him.

"What about my angel abilities? Can't I sort of... stop that feeling with them?"

"I'm not sure. We'll have to wait and see once they manifest, but I don't know if they will down here in Hell." He smiled at me, thumb brushing across my cheek. "But we can worry about that when the time comes. Why don't you go get ready for the party tonight?"

I rolled out of bed, tied a black silk robe around myself, and gazed out of the window. We were on the highest floor of the castle, amongst the feathery white clouds. On a clear day, I could see everything from up here—the white walkways, the trees with soft pink leaves, the Garden of Passion, even the nearest town that was always bustling with demons from all the kingdoms.

Eros walked up behind me and rested his chin on my shoulder. "I actually have a few things to tell you before you go. Trevon was released from The Chains. He seems to be doing okay, but I'm keeping a watch on him. Zane and Maria will be coming over tonight. And... Kasey is still mad at me for killing our parents."

I gnawed on the inside of my cheek. She had been ignoring all of my texts this past week. Mycah didn't say much to me either. When I saw her at Ollie's yesterday morning, I could tell that she wanted to talk to me, but she didn't say a word. I hoped we could resolve this because—although the kingdom seemed much friendlier without their parents—many people like Sathanus, were angry that we killed the King, Queen, and one of the Lords of Lust. And, besides that, I wanted a friend in Hell.

"Also..." Eros smiled against my ear. "Before you get ready, there's an envelope in the throne room for you. Please open it."

"Who is it from?"

"Your father."

"From Dad?" I asked, eyes growing wide. I pulled Eros into a hug, pressed my lips to his, and smiled. "Thank you. Thank you. Thank you." I hurried out of the room, listening to Eros chuckling behind me, and ran down the nearest stone staircase.

The stairs were lit with flaming pink torches and seemed to go on forever. But when I finally made it to the bottom level, I pushed through the doors and navigated the hallway—with the help of some guards—to the throne room.

From the doorway, a large red carpet led directly to a raised red throne. Archways with white candles hanging off of their posts surrounded the room. I stepped in and walked toward the throne, my ring drawing me to it.

A white, tattered envelope laid on the seat. I carefully picked it up, sat down, and opened it. In strong cursive writing, the letter read:

Dear Daughter,

I know I will never get to see you, and that is something that hurts me the most. I wished to watch you command our kingdom with all the supremacy and might I know you will have. But there are people who want our blood and our souls. So, your mother departed to the Heavens to keep you safe. I hope she succeeded.

If you find this message once I'm gone, know that I loved you and your mother—more than I thought a demon could love. I hope you will acquire her gentle heart and forgive those who hurt you. You're the essence of light and dark, good and bad, saint and sinner. Because of that, you will be the strongest of them all.

You must be careful, my Precious Angel. I have seen the strongest men and women sucked into the darkness, never to return. Demons are not afraid to lie, betray, or slay to gain power in Hell. Some will act as friends, others will be your enemies from the start. Always be attentive of who you trust and who you love, for those you love you can't always trust and those you trust you can't always love.

I must warn you of one thing. The beginning of the end is approaching. You will be thrown into chaos when it does. Angels will fall; demons will rise. Hell, as you know it, will cease to be. You will know it is approaching when the Ghoul of Darkness enters the Inferno.

There is a book about the end in my library. Use our family ring to open it. It's for your eyes only. Stay safe.

Love,

Dad, or as your Mother may have called me, Asmodeus the Sorcerer of Temptation

I placed the letter down in my lap and smiled. I was Dani Asmodeus, Commander of Lust.

Continue reading in Demonic Desires.

Also by Emilia Rose

Paranormal Romance

Submitting to the Alpha

Come Here, Kitten

Alpha Maddox

My Werewolf Professor

The Twins

Four Masked Wolves

Monster Lover

Contemporary Romance

Stepbrother

Poison

The Bad Boy

Detention

Excite Me

Mafia Boss

Mafia Toy

Mafia Betrayal

Erotica

Climax: Erotic One-Shot Collection

13 Haunted Nights

About the Author

Emilia Rose is a USA Today best-selling author of steamy romance. Highly inspired by her study abroad trip to Greece in 2019, Emilia loves to include Greek and Roman mythology in her writing.

She graduated from the University of Pittsburgh with a degree in psychology and a minor in creative writing in 2020 and now writes novels as her day job.

With over 18 million combined book views online and a growing presence on reading apps, she hopes to inspire other young novelists with her tales of growth and imagination, so they go on to write the stories that need to be told.

Join Emilia's newsletter for exclusive giveaways, early chapter releases, and more!

Scan the QR code with your
phone to view all of Emilia's books!